THE QUIET SIDE OF PASSION

It is summer in Edinburgh, and Isabel Dalhousie is once again caught between "gossip" and significant rumour. Patricia, the mother of her son Charlie's little friend Basil, is estranged from his father, and she has a somewhat brazen attitude to childcare. Isabel, however, has much more on her mind as editor of the *Review of Applied Ethics*. Along with the work involved for its impending next issue, she needs to get her house in order and tend to the demands of her niece, Cat. But her sharp observation and assured role as confidante soon have Isabel doubting all her recent decisions. What's more, her instinct to help others may have put her in real danger. In her desire to run both a smooth household and working life, has she simply created more chaos?

THE QUIET SIDE OF PASSION

ALEXANDER McCALL SMITH

LARGE
PRINT

First published in Great Britain 2018
by
Little, Brown

First Isis Edition
published 2020
by arrangement with
Little, Brown Book Group

A catalogue record for this book is available
from the British Library.

ISBN 978–1–78541–824–2 (hb)
ISBN 978–1–78541–830–3 (pb)

Published by
F. A. Thorpe (Publishing)
Anstey, Leicestershire

Set by Words & Graphics Ltd.
Anstey, Leicestershire
Printed and bound in Great Britain by
T. J. International Ltd., Padstow, Cornwall

This book is printed on acid-free paper

This book is for Alex and Henry Field

CHAPTER
ONE

"Gossip?" asked Isabel Dalhousie, philosopher, wife, mother, and editor of the *Review of Applied Ethics*. With the first three of these roles she was unreservedly happy; the editorship, though, she would at times gladly have passed on to somebody else — at particularly stressful moments to anybody at all — except that there was nobody to take it on, or at least no one who would do it unpaid, without complaint, and with the enthusiasm and wit that Isabel devoted to it. All of which seemed to suggest that Isabel was the editor of the *Review of Applied Ethics* for life.

She was sitting in the kitchen of her house in Edinburgh, a glass of chilled white wine on the table before her. It was a warm evening, at least by the standards applied in Scotland, where summer is sometimes no more than a promise, an aspiration. On the side of the glass small beads of condensation had appeared, some of which were now becoming tiny rivulets, hesitant at first but growing in confidence. Isabel had a tendency to get lost in her musings, and now the thought came to her that this was the way in which all rivers started: a single drop of water somewhere joined up with another and became something altogether more significant; as with the Ganges, for instance, from whose banks people still bathed in the hope of spiritual gain, indifferent to the coliform load of each drop of that lethal water. Or the Limpopo, the river so alliteratively described by Kipling as great, grey-green, and greasy, all set about with fever trees — though apparently it was not like that at all, she had been told by a friend who had actually seen it. "The Limpopo was somewhat sluggish," her friend had said. "There was no sign of grease, and it was more brown than green." But that was not the issue: what interested her was the observation that a large river starts with a tiny drop. There was a tipping point, it seemed, for everything: fame, fads, political careers — and water.

On the other side of the kitchen, paging through a recipe book, undecided as yet as to what to cook for dinner that night, was her husband, Jamie: bassoonist, father, occasional composer, incidental tennis player, and, in the view of virtually every woman who ever met him, the perfect man. That last encomium was one Isabel herself readily would have bestowed, but only after a third or fourth meeting. When they'd first met, Isabel had been recovering from an uncomfortable divorce and was still wary of her ability to judge men. Some years earlier she had taken up with John Liamor, an Irishman she had met in Cambridge and whom she had then married, to the dismay of her father and just about all of her friends. They had seen what she had not, and over the next few years she learned what it was that she had missed.

There had been another reason why Isabel might have been cautious of Jamie on first meeting: at that time he happened to be the boyfriend of Isabel's niece, Cat, owner of a delicatessen a short walk from Isabel's house. They may have been aunt and niece, but the age gap between Isabel and Cat was small enough for them sometimes to be taken for sisters. But there were limits to such sisterhood as existed between them, as they were very different characters. Both were sociable, but Cat was rather inclined to fall for people — particularly men — before she had any real chance of getting to know them properly. This meant that her boyfriends — of whom there had been a steady succession — tended to be chosen without adequate attention to compatibility. She liked handsome men, and also seemed to cultivate men about whom there was a slight whiff of danger. Isabel was far more cautious in her friendships, and tended to show a certain reticence before she opened up to a new acquaintance. Cat could at times be a bit moody, whereas Isabel usually made an effort to keep bleak feelings to herself. Cat was decisive — a useful quality when running a small business — whereas Isabel was inclined to worry about the pros and cons of any particular action. Isabel reflected on things before she acted; Cat acted and then — sometimes, but not always — reflected on what she had done. Isabel took the view that if one made a mistake, one should be careful not to make it again. Cat's view of any mistakes she made was to regard them as water under the bridge and to move on as cheerfully as possible. Sometimes, of course, that meant she moved on to the next mistake rather than anywhere else.

Cat's life, then, was not an example of the examined life of which philosophers have long written; Isabel's life, by contrast, was a life lived under a moral microscope. In their different ways, both these approaches worked for the two women. Both were happy with their lot; each felt that the other had the wrong approach to things, but tolerated the contrast. Sometimes, though, matters became fraught, and the relationship was tested in an uncomfortable way. That had happened with Jamie, Cat's former boyfriend, and now Isabel's husband.

When Isabel was introduced to Jamie, she imagined that he must be just one more of Cat's unsuitable boyfriends — as unreliable as he was good-looking. She was wrong; Jamie was quite unlike any of Cat's previous men and it was perhaps for this reason that she ended her affair with him after they had been together for little more than a few months. Jamie, it seemed, was not what Cat was looking for. He was simply too safe. Not that Jamie was ever dull — far from it — but if you were somebody like Cat, looking for a man who had just a touch of *wildness* about him, then Jamie was not that. Jamie was decent — "heart-meltingly decent", as one of Isabel's friends had once described him. "And dishy," the same friend had added, "knee-weakeningly dishy."

After Cat had broken up with him, Isabel had continued to see Jamie, whom she had considered a friend. This friendship had in due course become

4

something more, and Isabel and Jamie became lovers, and eventually spouses. Not surprisingly, Cat took this badly — with a complete lack of grace, in fact: no niece expects her cast-offs to be taken on by her aunt, and there ensued a period of chilled relations between the two women. The birth of Isabel's son, Charlie, had made matters even worse, although eventually a thaw set in and Cat accepted the existence of Charlie — huffs can be demanding, even to the huffiest. What was more, Cat needed Isabel's help in running her delicatessen and now Isabel regularly, and generously, provided cover over busy periods or when Cat was short-staffed.

As for Jamie, willingness to cook was one of the qualities that made him the perfect man. He was versatile in his approach, perhaps a bit more adventurous than Isabel, and he had a particular appetite for vintage cookery books, of which he had built up quite a collection. That evening he had extracted a first edition of Julia Childs — signed by Julia herself to one of Isabel's American aunts in Mobile, Alabama, and passed on years earlier as a special birthday present. He was planning a chicken dish, and was taking an inventory of ingredients before he embarked on the recipe.

They were by themselves, enjoying that blissful period of calm so familiar to parents when the children have been put to bed, the scattered toys rounded up and put away, and quiet reigns in the house. Both Charlie and his younger brother Magnus were now asleep, each broadcasting, from their separate monitors, a reassuring sound of breathing, punctuated by occasional snuffles, into the kitchen. Charlie had taken some time to settle, insisting on the re-reading of a book that Isabel had found in the Morningside Library. She rather wished she had left the book there on the library shelf; there was a tiger in this book, and he had no discernible redeeming qualities. He was fortunate, she felt, to avoid the fate of the tigers she remembered from her own childhood reading of a book now suppressed for reasons unconnected with tigers, but that had entailed the transformation of encircling tigers into ghee, Indian butter. As a small girl she had loved that ending, and had imagined that the fate of being turned into butter might be extended to other threatening creatures or even people. In fact, one might even have a "butter list" of such persons, who, even if they saw their names on it, would be unaware of what it entailed. Having an enemies list was too overt, as more than one politician has discovered: the existence of an enemies list could be embarrassing if it fell into the hands of the press — or a fortiori into those of the enemies it listed; a butter list, by contrast, would attract no adverse attention.

Jamie looked up from his recipe book. "Gossip?"

Isabel took a sip of her wine. The glass was cold to the touch; she liked that. "Yes, I was wondering what you thought of gossip."

Jamie smiled; he was used to Isabel's non sequiturs. "That's an odd question, don't you think?"

She shook her head. "Not really. Gossip is a pretty important subject, even if gossip itself is about things that aren't all that significant." She paused, before adding, "If you see what I mean."

He laid aside Julia Childs, marking his place in the book with a small sprig of parsley. "If you're interested in gossip," he said, "have you met that woman who's just started taking her son to Charlie's nursery? The little boy's called Basil. He's got freckles."

Isabel and Jamie shared the task of taking Charlie to nursery school, and they knew most, if not all, of the other parents.

Isabel thought. There had been a freckled child, but she had not taken much notice of him. And the mother? She wasn't sure. "I think I've seen the child. I don't know about her, though. What's her name?"

"Patricia. She's Irish. Rather tall. She wears her hair piled up at the back of her head, like Princess Anne. It wouldn't suit everybody, but it looks good on her. She's a musician, actually. Viola."

"Oh, yes, I think so . . . . Have you worked with her?"

Jamie nodded. "Yes. She stood in for Robbie the other day. The usual thing." Robbie was the viola player in Jamie's regular ensemble. He had a reputation for calling off engagements at the last minute for reasons connected with a complicated, and unfathomable, love life.

"Is that it? Is that the gossip?"

Jamie hesitated. "That boy — Basil — is the son of Basil Phelps."

"Basil Phelps the organist?" Two weeks earlier, they had both gone to hear Phelps play Messiaen at a concert in one of the city's large churches, and had talked to him briefly afterwards. He was a slender man with piercing blue eyes — eyes alight with intelligence.

"Yes. The gossip is that she had an affair with him. They say he didn't want the baby — she did."

Isabel winced. "Awkward."

"Very," said Jamie. "They split up over it. It became acrimonious. She then went and had the baby and called him after his father, although he didn't want anybody to know about it." He paused. "He — Basil Senior — plays the organ at a church over on the other side of town. She took Basil Junior to be baptised there during the Sunday service the other day. Basil Senior wasn't told — and he was on duty playing the organ when the son he's had nothing to do with was brought up to the font and introduced to the congregation."

"Oh no . . ."

"Just imagine the scene. The minister always holds up the child to show to the congregation. So he held up this one and said: 'This child we welcome today is Basil Phelps.'"

Isabel gasped. Public humiliation could be very cruel, but if men refused to shoulder their responsibilities . . .

Jamie agreed. "Why should she be the one to pay all the bills?" said Jamie. "He should know what children cost."

Isabel thought of what lay ahead for the child: how would he feel about a father who refused to acknowledge him? She had read recently of the experience of adopted people using their legal right to discover the identity of their biological parents. It was

8

not uncommon for them to be rebuffed. One woman she heard about had found her mother and been given a half-hour appointment to meet her. "I'm dreadfully busy," the woman had said, which was worse, in a way, than a flat refusal to meet.

Jamie picked up Julia Childs once more. "You started the conversation," he said. "But I'm not sure if I feel entirely comfortable telling you that story. It's gossip, isn't it?" He found his recipe and extracted the sprig of parsley. "In fact, I'm sorry I mentioned it."

Isabel understood. "You feel a bit guilty about it? As if you're taking pleasure in tittle-tattle?"

"I suppose so." He paused. "But you did ask, didn't you?"

She explained herself. "I've been reading about gossip. There's a book about vices that we're going to review. It has a chapter on gossip — how it's a form of social grooming — glue to hold groups together. Gossip also plays a big part in friendships, we're told."

"Some of it might," said Jamie. "Innocent gossip, perhaps. That's all about who's been doing what. Who's going out with whom. That sort of thing." He wondered about the book. "What are the other vices?"

"There's an interesting discussion of snobbery."

"Which everyone agrees is a vice," said Jamie.

"Of course. But, come to think of it, what exactly is snobbery?"

Jamie put down Julia Childs again. It was difficult to plan a recipe at the same time as talking about the sorts of issues that Isabel chose to discuss.

"I suppose it's treating somebody as inferior," he said. "Looking down on people. Or looking down on things, too. Musical snobbery's alive and well."

"So, what do you think?" asked Isabel. "I mean you, personally? You bring up musical snobbery: what do you think of a teenager who knows four guitar chords and calls himself a musician?"

Jamie laughed. "There are plenty of those. Some would-be guitarists know only three."

"And what do you think of them?"

"They're harmless enough," said Jamie.

Isabel pressed the point. "But what about somebody who said of such a person's music, 'It's worthless rubbish'?"

Jamie grinned. "I'd say they had it about right."

"And that's not being snobbish?"

He shook his head. "No, because it *is* worthless rubbish. Speaking the truth is not being snobbish — not at all."

"And what about somebody who's crude and vulgar? Let's say a man who makes derogatory, insulting remarks about women. Would you look down on somebody like that?"

Jamie was not sure about looking down. "I wouldn't actually look down on him — but I'd not think much of him." He frowned. "There is a difference, I think."

"And that's not being snobbish?" asked Isabel.

Jamie felt more confident now. Being philosophical, he decided, was not as hard as it sounded; all that it required was clarity . . . and common sense. "No, not really. After all, we have to disapprove sometimes or we wouldn't be able to distinguish between those who are . . . well, frankly, bad, and those who aren't. We wouldn't be able to distinguish between Attila the Hun, and people like that, and . . . St Francis of Assisi."

Isabel smiled. "Who exactly was Attila the Hun?" she asked.

Jamie looked puzzled. "He was . . . well, he was this . . . well, I suppose he was some sort of Hun — whoever they were. I think he was into rape and pillage."

"In a big way?"

Jamie nodded. "Oh, a very big way. That's why he's become a sort of gold standard for dreadfulness."

"Along with Tamburlaine and Genghis Khan?"

Isabel thought for a moment. She realised that she herself knew very little about Attila. What were his dates? Fourth century? Fifth? Was there anything to be said in his favour? Sometimes tyrants introduced enlightened codes of law or encouraged the arts, or even built enduring buildings. Might Attila complain, "Nobody seems to remember the sonnets I wrote"? She recalled that famous crossword clue — her favourite, in fact — the anagram used by Auden in one of his poems: *He conquers all, a nubile tram. A nubile tram*: absurdity was the quiddity by which an anagram was identified — though one should never judge people by their anagrams, the letters of *Isabel Dalhousie* themselves resolving unflatteringly into *hideous bile alas. A nubile tram* was obviously Tamburlaine, an emperor who, after all, numbered intellectual pursuits amongst his interests — along with wide-scale conquest, of course.

Jamie sighed. "I really must concentrate on dinner — if you want to eat this evening."

"Of course," said Isabel. "*Chicken Tamburlaine.* That sounds quite credible, doesn't it? *Omelette Genghis.*"

"I think I'll stick to Julia," said Jamie.

That night, as she waited to drop off to sleep, Isabel thought about Patricia and the boy with freckles. She saw them alone in a small flat, sparsely furnished, a bit chilly perhaps, waiting for their life to become better. Jamie's words came back to her: *This child we welcome today is Basil Phelps.* Suddenly she wanted to do something for Basil Phelps. But she was not sure what it could be, nor why she felt she had to do it. *Basil Phelps,* she whispered drowsily; and Jamie, asleep before her, stirred slightly in his sleep, his head upon the pillow, his hair slightly curled, as if painted by Raphael.

CHAPTER
TWO

Isabel spent the following morning editing. She had been released from childcare by Grace, whose job had changed since the birth of Magnus. Prior to that, she had still considered herself a housekeeper who occasionally helped out with Charlie. When Magnus arrived, though, she did less and less house cleaning and had correspondingly more to do with the baby. Nothing was said formally, but Isabel had recognised the shift in roles by increasing Grace's salary. This was generous enough; Grace had been employed by Isabel's father and Isabel accepted the duty incumbent on her to look after a family retainer. She did not really need a housekeeper, and would not have chosen to find one had Grace not simply come with the house, so to speak; but Grace was there, and expected to be kept on. Isabel did not argue, and now, with Magnus to cope with, she was relieved to have her. Isabel's job — editing the *Review of Applied Ethics* — was really a full-time one; she needed support in the house. Grace loved children and was only too happy to oblige, but it did mean that the house had become progressively untidier and, in its remoter and less accessible corners, more in need of cleaning. Jamie agreed: a cleaner would need to be employed; willing as he was to do his share of the household tasks, he was too busy with his career — playing the bassoon and teaching it too — to be able to spend much time wielding the vacuum cleaner.

The printer's deadline for the next issue of the *Review of Applied Ethics* was fast approaching and something had gone awry with the footnotes in one of the articles. This could be remedied by comparing the copy-edited version with the author's original — a straightforward enough process normally, but now made more complicated by the fact that the original file appeared to have been corrupted. Electronics made editorial work a great deal easier in some respects, but in others it had introduced new ways for things to go wrong. The old certainties of typescript, of pen and ink, of queries pencilled in along the margins, had been replaced by computer files that usually worked but could be subverted by a tired user pressing the wrong key late at night. Hours of effort might be hidden or even deleted by such a mistake, and not every program had the forgiveness necessary to allow one to undo what had been done.

The forgiveness of machines, thought Isabel, and the phrase triggered an idea. There had been plenty of discussion amongst philosophers of the ethics of robotics — about how we treated robots, and they us. Human-like robots were already with us, and could be abused and mistreated — or loved. But did it matter what people did to them? Could one be cruel to a machine, even one as clever and as life-like as a robot? Or were human — robot relationships an entirely private matter, beyond any moral evaluation? Nasty people would be nasty to their robots, and nice people would be nice to them. Nothing changes.

Isabel's *Review* had already ventured into that territory with several articles. There had been "My lover, my robot", by an Australian professor of machine intelligence, who felt that what went on between a robot and a human behind closed doors was no business of anybody else. That had drawn a response in the shape of a paper entitled "As you are to a robot, so you are to persons", by a firm Kantian from the Free University of Berlin. "Killing a robot of human appearance makes a person a killer in his heart," wrote this author. "Such an act — along with any other act of contempt for the robot — discloses a mindset of contempt for humanity in general. If you can plunge a knife into the breast of what looks and acts like a human, then might you not do the same with a real, living and breathing being? Morally speaking, you are just as vicious in your attitude." But were you? Isabel had disagreed with this — she thought that there was a real distinction, based on actual harm, but she understood the author's point of view and she was glad, after all, that such morally scrupulous people existed. It was the same with fiction: the suffering of people in books was not real suffering, but the tears we might shed for them were real enough, and that said something about the ethics of fiction. An author who subjected a fictional character to cruel treatment, and then showed no sympathy, would soon incur the disapproval of readers.

There had been no discussion yet — in the *Review*, at least — of the issue of how robots might treat us: the reverse side of the coin. A special issue of the *Review* could be dedicated to the question of whether robots would be capable of understanding human limitations, of showing mercy, of bending rules that seemed too harsh for the circumstances. She thought they would not; already there was a big difference between a computer and a clerk. Human clerks forgave, might understand a spelling error, might work out what you meant; computers tended not to do that, and what were robots if not computers with arms and legs? There were no excuses in the robotic world — only algorithms.

It took her several hours to deal with the problem of the corrupted footnotes. By the time she had finished, Grace was at the door asking whether she should collect Charlie from nursery school.

"You look far too busy," said Grace, pointing to the papers on Isabel's desk. "Why don't I go?"

Isabel thanked her, but explained that she had finished and was looking forward to the walk around the corner to the nursery. There was another reason, too; the story Jamie had told her the previous evening had intrigued her as much as it had shocked her and she wanted to take a closer look at Basil Phelps and his mother, Patricia.

She set off early, although the nursery school was only a block away. Parents often arrived ten minutes or so before the end of the school day and would chat to one another before the doors opened and the children streamed out. It was the equivalent of the old parish pump, thought Isabel: people had traditionally exchanged news and views while drawing water for their households. All the business of a village could be transacted at the parish pump: feuds mended, understandings reached, marriages arranged — there was nothing that could not be transacted by neighbours. The parish pump, she reflected, was also the way typhoid and cholera spread.

There were two fathers already there when she arrived. Isabel knew both of them slightly, but did not interrupt their conversation. Instead, she parked herself on a bench the nursery had provided for waiting parents and from there surveyed the small front garden created by the owners of the nursery. The children had decorated this with coloured stones they had painted themselves — these were bright red and yellow against the surrounding greenery.

Her eyes were half closed. The warm weather had continued and the air was languid and unmoving, making it a day for doing exactly what she was doing — sitting on a bench, looking at the world, allowing time to slip through her fingers. From the corner of her eye, she became aware that two other people had arrived at the same time: a woman who was the mother of one of Charlie's particular friends at nursery — a rather discouraged-looking woman whose second child was in the pushchair she brought with her — and Patricia.

Isabel looked up. Patricia had not come into the garden, but was standing just outside the gate. The two fathers standing nearby had nodded a greeting to her but were continuing with their private discussion; one was demonstrating something with his hands — an exaggerated chopping motion, as if he were talking about an obscure martial art.

Isabel rose from the bench and made her way over to join Patricia.

"You're Basil's mother, aren't you?"

Patricia turned round and smiled. "Yes, I am. And you're . . ."

"Charlie's."

"Of course. Basil said something about Charlie the other day. I think they've played together."

Isabel shot a discreet glance at Patricia. She was an attractive woman, rather tall, with the hairstyle that Jamie had mentioned. Isabel recognised her colouring as what she thought of as typically Irish: the pale, almost translucent skin, the green-grey eyes. Isabel found herself thinking of a phrase from Homer's *Odyssey* — Athena, in her many forms, was always described as the grey-eyed goddess. This was Athena. And Homer's sea was the wine-dark sea; the wine dark sea.

Behind them, the doors opened and the children emerged. There were squeals and there was chatter. Isabel saw Charlie holding something that he'd obviously made — a papier mâché object painted, like the stones in the garden, in vivid primary colours. One could never guess what such creations were — in much the same way that one could never guess what some contemporary sculpture represented. ("Nothing," a sculptor might say; "that's the whole point. It's not representational at all.")

She saw the little boy with freckles. He ran towards his mother and wrapped his arms around her legs. Patricia looked up, caught Isabel's eye, and smiled. On impulse, Isabel said, "I live just round the corner — would you like to drop in for a cup of tea? The boys could play."

Charlie was now thrusting his artistic efforts at her, and she did not hear Patricia's reply.

"Sorry," said Isabel. "I was distracted."

"I said thank you — I'd love to." She reached into a pocket of the lightweight jacket she was wearing. "I'll just have to make a quick call."

Isabel had not intended to invite her there and then; it had been an invitation to drop in *some time*, although she had not said that. It was too late now to explain that she had been planning to finish her editing. That would have to wait.

Patricia spoke briefly into her phone. "Something's cropped up," she muttered to the caller. "Phone me later, if you don't mind."

"We could make it some other time," offered Isabel. "Any time, really."

"No, that's fine," said Patricia, reaching for Basil's hand. "Come on, sweetie, you're going to play at Charlie's house."

Basil struggled to escape.

"It'll be fun," said Isabel, leaning down to smile at Basil. "Charlie has lots of toys."

Basil looked at her suspiciously. She noticed how freckled he was — like a scone dotted with light raisins, she thought. A spotted child.

"Come on, Basil darling," said Patricia, taking hold of the child's hand once more. She shot Isabel an apologetic glance.

"Oh, I know all about resistance," said Isabel. "We had a little episode the other day . . ." She glanced to see if Charlie was listening, but he was busy struggling to do up the catch on his lunch box. "We went to the doctor and . . ." She looked again at Charlie. "And we kicked him, I'm afraid. I felt so embarrassed."

Patricia laughed. "Basil bit the dentist. It was at his first check-up, and he sank his teeth into the dentist's fingers. She had to prise his jaws apart to get them out. She was so good about it."

"I suppose that's an occupational risk for dentists," said Isabel. "Charlie occasionally bites. Not often, but now and then he'll give you a little nip."

The children gathered up, they began to walk back towards Isabel's house, barely five minutes away. Isabel noticed that Patricia was looking at the houses as they passed, and she felt a momentary embarrassment. These were well-set Victorian villas, tucked away in gardens, surrounded by trees. Everything about them was expensive, even if there was nothing ostentatious in their appearance. Discretion reigned here; there was no flaunting of wealth, and yet to live here was out of reach of most; a house in Isabel's street would cost as much as several flats put together. She winced at the thought. Her instincts were egalitarian — as the instincts of most Scots were — but the facts of her situation were inescapable: she had more than others — considerably more.

"I've walked down this street before," said Patricia. "I love leafy places like this."

The trees, thought Isabel — the trees at least are free. "I was brought up here," she said, as if in explanation; why, she thought, should one apologise for where life placed you? "It was my parents' house."

She wondered why that should make a difference. If you lived in a house your parents lived in, then you would not have had to buy it. But the house itself represented inherited wealth, and in some eyes, that was somehow tainted.

"You're lucky," said Patricia.

That was precisely it, thought Isabel. Luck. It was luck that her mother — her "sainted American mother" as she called her — had happened to have inherited an interest in the Louisiana Land Company, and that this had filtered down to Isabel. That was pure luck, as was all inheritance, genetic or financial. You were lucky if you had regular features, or a dimple in the right place, or a fine brow. That was just the result of a particular pattern of repeats in a sequence of DNA, an instruction somewhere in that long code that made you what you were. There were only four letters in the code, yet the order in which they followed one another determined everything, or just about everything. There was still a small role for individual effort, but even then you could argue that people would only make an effort to change their fate if their DNA endowed them with the ability to do so.

She looked down at Basil, walking hesitantly beside Charlie, who was eyeing him up as a possible friend.

She saw the freckles. Somewhere in the little boy's DNA there was an instruction — added, perhaps, as an afterthought: oh, and on the skin there will be little blotches of pigment (appealing; ginger), just a fraction of an inch apart — but just on the face and perhaps the shoulders. What accident lay behind such a precise chemical instruction, unless, of course, there lay an intelligence . . . That was another matter — not one to be thought about as she walked down the street with a stranger she had only a few minutes ago inadvertently invited to tea.

CHAPTER
THREE

Grace seized upon the two boys with enthusiasm.

"I'll look after the wee ones," she said, grabbing Charlie's hand. And to Basil she said, "Who are you, young fellow?"

Basil was initially tongue-tied, but on maternal prompting managed to answer, "Basil."

"Good, well come with me, Charlie and Basil. We'll find something to build."

"A fort," shouted Charlie.

Basil looked puzzled for a moment. Then he, too, shouted "Fort!"

"A fort it will be," said Grace.

Isabel smiled. Grace's manner with children was such that they complied. There was only one word for it: compliance, and Isabel, acknowledging it, felt slightly envious — as any parent accustomed to asking numerous times for things to be done would feel.

She led Patricia into the garden room — a room that looked out over the lawn to the high stone wall bounding the back garden. Against this wall Isabel had encouraged fruit trees to grow in candelabra style: apple trees, figs, a couple of pears.

Patricia went to the door, which was ajar, and looked out. "You wouldn't think we were in a city . . ." She left the sentence unfinished. "So much work."

At first Isabel said nothing. But then, "We have help. There's a man who comes for a couple of hours a week. He does three gardens in this street."

She could not take credit for the garden, but she did not want to create the impression that she was attended on all sides by staff. Grace had looked after her father and had simply stayed on; George, the gardener, tended over fifteen gardens in the area and was paid by the hour.

She thought: I don't have to justify myself. I support a lot of causes; I give my money away; I don't indulge myself. I vote for people who support public goods. She stopped. Self-justification was tedious and usually rang hollow.

"You're very lucky," said Patricia. It was the second time she had said this.

"Yes," said Isabel, adding, quite forcefully, "And I know it."

Patricia glanced at her, and Isabel realised that her response had possibly sounded sharp. She changed the subject and asked how Basil was settling in at the nursery.

"He loves it," said Patricia. "He wakes up at six, regular as clockwork, and says, 'Time for nursery.'"

Isabel laughed. "Charlie needs no persuading either."

Patricia sat down while Isabel went off to make tea. After she returned with the tea things, for a few moments there was silence, as if they were both

24

assessing the tenor of the forthcoming conversation. Then Isabel said, "You're by yourself, I've heard."

It was a potentially awkward question, but Patricia seemed happy to answer. "Yes. I'm a single mother."

"I can imagine that it's . . ."

Patricia took over. "Hard? Well, yes, it is — some of the time. Childcare's the big issue, particularly if you're working. What do you do? I'm lucky — I have a cousin who lives in Edinburgh. She doesn't work — her husband's an offshore engineer and he has an odd schedule. They've tried for kids but . . ." She shrugged.

"She must love Basil."

"She can't see enough of him. I just have to lift the phone."

Isabel remarked that this must make life much easier. "I've heard that you're a musician. Jamie — my husband — said he'd —"

"We've worked together occasionally. I stand in for one of the ensemble." She paused. "Basil's father's a musician too. You probably know him — everyone seems to."

Isabel nodded. "Not very well, though."

Patricia was watching her. Her tone, now, was more guarded. "I'm afraid he doesn't see Basil. I tried, but . . ."

"I'm so sorry."

"He does support him, though," continued Patricia. "Financially, that is. I'll give him that."

Isabel was keen to move the conversation on. They talked about the nursery school and the new assistant who had started work there the previous week. They talked about early musical education — Basil was already learning violin according to the Suzuki method. They discussed the age at which the recorder could be started — Patricia suggested that three was not too early: the soprano recorder was small enough for their little fingers, she thought, and they would pick it up quickly enough if they had a good ear. They talked about Ireland, about where Patricia had come from in Dublin, and this somehow led on to the decline of the power of the Catholic Church in Ireland.

"The Church asked for it," said Patricia. "They wanted to keep an iron grip on education. They set out to exclude everybody else, including the Irish state itself. So the state ended up entrusting Ireland's children to organisations that were riddled with distorted, unhappy people. Made unhappy because they themselves were made to suppress their natural instincts."

Isabel shook her head. "How did it happen?"

Patricia did not answer the question. "They locked young women away, you know. Committed them to psychiatric institutions — or places that purported to be psychiatric institutions."

"I've heard of that."

"My mother's sister — my aunt — was one of them, you know. She was effectively locked up for five years because she became pregnant at the age of sixteen. They didn't punish the boys, of course. My aunt never recovered. She was on the verge of tears for the rest of her life."

"But it's a different country now, isn't it?" said Isabel. "All that's over."

"Yes. The Church's power drained away like . . . like snow off a hillside. It just went. Those men in their clerical collars, those bishops, they just folded up when people stood up to them and started to talk about what they'd suffered at the hands of various nuns and brothers."

"All those ruined lives," said Isabel.

"And I must say that I'm pleased to be out of it," Patricia continued. "Sure, I'm fond of the usual things about Ireland, but I'm pleased not to be living there, and instead bringing up Basil in a country that doesn't have such a long history of murderous hatreds."

Isabel looked thoughtful. "Murderous hatreds . . . yes, but didn't we — the British, that is — create so many of those? Look at the way Queen Elizabeth — the original one — treated Ireland. We stole their land. Did our best to crush them. Who can blame the Irish for resenting British colonialism? I don't think I can."

Patricia sighed. "Oh, of course — the past, the past . . . But Ireland's had almost one hundred years of freedom. And what have they done with it? Allowed themselves to be treated as a theocracy for a good part of that. That was de Valera for you. Signed over control of their lives to a religious hierarchy run by embittered men with a lot of hang-ups about practically everything? Allowed gunmen to pursue their agenda while the state turned a blind eye? Then spent European Union money with gusto."

"Oh, I don't know —"

Patricia cut her short. "Well, I do. I feel ashamed of my country. There's the small matter of the Second World War. Where were we then? I learned an odd version at school in Dublin. They explained that we were neutral and did not want to get involved in England's wars. Great. So while the Nazis were overrunning Europe, whose side were we on? Don't ask that question."

"Plenty of Irish people fought . . ."

"Oh yes, as individuals. There were volunteers, all right. And even deserters from the Irish army who went over to help the British. But the Irish state? Who signed the condolence book in the German embassy in Dublin when Hitler died? De Valera himself. Him again. Can you believe it? Condolences. And even after the war, he never once admitted that the Allied cause was just. Maybe he didn't see the photographs of Belsen and places like that." She paused. "The Catholic Church taught us to be hypocrites and boy, were we good at it."

Isabel felt uncomfortable. "Didn't the Irish government apologise a few years back?"

Patricia was dismissive. "Eventually. They pardoned the men who had fled the Irish army to fight with the Allies — most of them were dead anyway. The Minister of Defence made a big speech. He said that our failure to do anything in the face of the Holocaust amounted to moral bankruptcy — I think those were his words. But rather late, I thought."

There was an anger in Patricia's voice that disturbed her. And yet, Isabel wondered, should it? The problem with living in Edinburgh was that it was so rational, so considered. Edinburgh had never been oppressed in the way that other places had been; there was no inheritance of resentment.

"So, you're going to bring Basil up as Scottish?"

Patricia nodded. "Looks like it."

"I suppose he's half Scottish, anyway."

Patricia looked away — just for an instant. Then she turned to face Isabel again. "I'm sorry if I sound strident," she said. "You pressed a particular button there when you started talking about Ireland. I can't help myself — it all wells up, all of it, and I know it can sound as if I see only one side of it."

Isabel was quick to reassure her. "One need not apologise for feeling strongly about something. What did Yeats write in that poem of his? About the best lacking all conviction?"

Patricia made a dismissive gesture. "Oh, Yeats was part of all that flim-flam — that romantic rubbish. I've no time for Yeats."

"None at all?"

She looked a bit sheepish. "Well, very little."

From within the house there came the sound of high-pitched shouting. "They're enjoying themselves," said Isabel.

"I'll have to be going before too long," said Patricia. "My cousin's coming to the house. I have to play in Glasgow tonight and so she's looking after Basil." She looked at her watch. Isabel noticed that it was made of rose gold; it was not inexpensive.

"Basil will be very welcome to come again."

"Thank you," said Patricia. "And perhaps Charlie will come to us."

"I'm sure he'd like that very much," said Isabel.

"We live in Albert Terrace," said Patricia.

Isabel struggled to disguise her surprise. Albert Terrace, which was only ten minutes' walk away, was an address that might be thought to be out of the reach of a struggling single mother.

Isabel thought that Patricia noticed her reaction.

"My parents had a house in Dublin," she explained. "They gave it to me when they went to live in Donegal. You know how expensive Dublin is. I sold it and bought Albert Terrace outright."

"It's very convenient for the nursery," said Isabel, embarrassed.

"There are any number of single mothers worse off than me," said Patricia. She hesitated, and then continued, "I don't need people to pity me."

Isabel struggled. "Oh, I wasn't pitying you. Of course I wasn't."

Patricia rose to leave. "Tomorrow? Would he like to come tomorrow?"

Isabel felt that she was being rushed. The invitation to tea had been accepted with alacrity, and now the return visit was already being proposed. Was this spontaneous hospitality an Irish trait?

"Of course, if you're too busy . . ." said Patricia.

"No, I'm not," said Isabel. She felt vaguely irritated at the thought of being tied down with this invitation. "I'll bring him round. Same time? After nursery?"

"That would be fine."

Grace appeared with the two boys. "They were asking where you were," she said. "But they seem happy enough to go on playing together."

"Tomorrow," said Isabel. It occurred to her that Grace was a convenient solution. "In fact, would you be able to take Charlie to Basil's house, Grace? I've just remembered I have some work to do." It was, strictly speaking, true; she had just remembered the book on vices. She was going to review that herself and the following afternoon would be the time to do it.

It was just the sort of commitment that Grace liked. She was inquisitive by nature, and there was nothing she liked more than seeing the inside of other people's houses.

Isabel turned to Patricia. "Is that all right with you? May Grace come in my stead?"

Patricia nodded. "That will be absolutely fine," she said. But Isabel could detect a note of disappointment, and wondered what lay behind it. Loneliness? Or something else?

CHAPTER
FOUR

Her day did not work out quite as she had hoped. She took Charlie to nursery, as planned, telling him that it would be Grace who would pick him up. The announcement of the play date at Basil's house had been greeted with excitement. Basil, he said, had a train set and they would make a railway station and play Train to Glasgow, a game inspired by a song Jamie had taught him. In this song, a "fortunate boy" named Donald McBrayne was given a ride on the train to Glasgow, a great adventure for him.

Returning to the house, Isabel spent time with Magnus. He was crawling now, and the mobility had seemed to go to his head as he set off in whatever direction his nose was pointing in, determined to escape to the far-flung regions of any room he found himself in. A playpen would have contained him, and made him easier to supervise, but Jamie had been against it. He had read something that persuaded him that playpens were stifling, and that children reared without them were more creative. Isabel was sceptical; those who criticised playpens were probably not mothers at the end of their tether, struggling to look after two or three young children while wrestling with the burden of housework. There were plenty of people prepared to give advice, but how many of them had actually done what they were advising others to do?

Jamie had volunteered to look after Magnus that day, and with Grace taking Charlie to Basil's house after nursery that meant Isabel would be able to get in a more or less full day of work. She was looking forward to clearing the backlog that had built up on her desk; she would do that in the morning, she decided, and then spend the afternoon getting the review of *The Virtues of our Vices* out of the way. By the time Charlie returned from his play session with Basil, she would be able to give him her uninterrupted attention. Motherhood, she felt, ought to come first in the order of the moral claims on her. This was followed, in sequence, by her duty to Jamie, her work with the *Review*, her obligations to those immediately around her . . . She stopped herself. Then it became difficult: how did one balance the claims of friends against the claims of others one did not happen to know?

She suddenly thought of the Cambridge spies — the group of highly placed young men who had become Soviet agents in the 1930s and who, when the net closed in, had abandoned their country rather than betray their friends. Blunt, Burgess, Maclean and the highly accomplished liar, Kim Philby, who had come close to being appointed head of a branch of British intelligence, all professed a greater loyalty, as such people often did: loyalty to the Communist cause, which they ranked above their duty to their own country. And the same was true of more recent examples, minor functionaries or obscure clerks who betrayed state secrets under a claim of moral duty. Patriots were outraged, government officials even more so, and with good reason: clearly no country could allow individuals to regard loyalty as an option one could reject if one disagreed with the policies of the government. And yet where did such a position lead? To "My country, right or wrong" — a form of patriotism that hardly survives moral scrutiny. Officials who defected from North Korea were heroes in Western eyes, as were those Germans who had plotted against Hitler, or those who planned the demise of the Soviet Union from within. Loyalty itself — unquestioning and uncritical — was not, then, invariably a virtue; disloyalty, similarly, had to be assessed in the context of what it was one was being disloyal to. Those who betrayed bad governments were good; those who betrayed good governments were bad. By that token, Isabel thought, the spy who betrayed a liberal democracy had a major hurdle to overcome — probably an insurmountable one — if he sought to justify betrayal. Ultimately liberal democracies, even if imperfect in some respects, were infinitely preferable to dictatorships and tyrannies.

She sighed. Another special issue of the *Review* was taking shape in her mind: *Loyalty and Betrayal — the Moral Issues*. Perhaps she would be able to persuade a retired traitor to write an article explaining how he justified his actions. Blunt, the art historian who spied for the Soviet Union, would have been ideal, had he still been alive, as he could write so elegantly. She

34

possessed a copy of his large book on Poussin, although she had never got beyond the first five pages because she found it so coldly intellectual. He would have declined, of course, because he did not want scrutiny and understood that nothing could justify what he had done. His was a retirement of regret and, towards the end, public humiliation, whereas Philby, re-emerging in Moscow as a full-blown KGB colonel, had been unrepentant. He had written his *apologia pro vita sua* and might have been tickled by the chance of philosophical rumination on his stance. But he was dead too, and so of no help.

She dwelled for a moment on the fact that all these traitors had been men. Was treason a male pursuit — one that women found uncomfortable? Few of the great traitors were women, which made one wonder whether women were more circumspect, or even less inclined to betray their own side. That led to an interesting train of thought — feminist philosophers talked about an ethic of care, which had concomitants of greater attentiveness to the needs of friends and family than might be involved in a more formal male-centred philosophy. This might support the view that women were more loyal than men, which might, or might not, be true. Had anybody actually measured that — as they seemed to have measured just about every other aspect of human nature?

Outside her window, a bird burst into song — a sudden clarion of sweet, pure notes. She looked up, and saw that a thrush had alighted on a bough of the tree nearest her window, a small silver birch; they were rare callers now, for some reason, or were more timid in showing themselves. *In a calm enclosure, with thrushes popular* . . . The line occurred to her unbidden, as did most of her thoughts when she was in this kind of reflective mood. It was Auden, of course, who came to her at these odd moments and illuminated so much; somehow made the ordinary moment more special, more arresting.

Thrushes . . . in Belfast years ago, in the Ulster Museum, she had wandered into a gallery and found herself face to face with Edward McGuire's portrait of the poet Seamus Heaney, seated at his desk, his back to the window; and beyond this window a bush, a laurel, from behind the leaves of which thrushes, more numerous than one might expect, peeked, intelligent-eyed, secretive. *With thrushes popular* . . . The bird seemed to notice her, or at least was alert to some movement within, and cocked its head inquisitively. Again there came a clear call, a couple of piped notes, and Isabel found herself thinking: do some birds sing for the world, and not just for themselves?

The telephone rang, jolting her out of her reverie. At the other end of the line, Isabel heard the voice of Eddie, Cat's employee in her delicatessen in Bruntsfield.

Eddie tended to launch straight into a telephone conversation, ignoring the niceties of the enquiry after the other's health or a remark on the prevailing weather.

"Eddie here," he said abruptly. "She's had to go out. She asked me to ask you whether you could help out here this afternoon. Otherwise, I'm on my own all day."

Eddie always referred to Cat as *she*. Isabel had pointed out that this sounded vaguely derogatory, but he had shrugged and simply said, "It isn't. She *is* she."

Isabel did not answer immediately. Jamie had said he was happy to look after Magnus that afternoon, but if she went to the delicatessen, then her review of *The Virtues of our Vices* would have to be put off, possibly for a week or so. And yet she had never yet refused to help Cat, who only asked her when she really needed her.

"I suppose so," said Isabel. "I mean, yes, of course. What time?"

Eddie explained that if she could be there for a couple of hours in the afternoon, it would a great help. She agreed, but she knew the day was ruined.

Eddie was clearly grateful, although he could not conceal his displeasure with Cat.

"You know, she never gives me any warning," he complained to Isabel as he greeted her in the delicatessen. "She just says, 'Oh, I have to go out,' and then she leaves — just like that. She claims it's business, but I bet it isn't — at least some of the time. She'll be meeting some guy somewhere. You know how she is about men. She's into them in a big way."

He looked at Isabel conspiratorially. This, after all, was a discussion about his boss, his employer, who was also her niece, yet they had talked like this before and Isabel had not objected. Now she smiled. "Come on, Eddie. Don't get carried away. Cat has to see her suppliers." She gestured towards the shelves behind them. "She's probably off at some wholesale bakery somewhere."

Eddie was about to remonstrate further, but a customer had arrived at the counter and he contented himself with a disbelieving glance in Isabel's direction. Isabel started to clean the cheese counter — crumbs had built up at the edges, a melange of blue cheese, Parmesan, strong cheddar; there would be regulations somewhere about this sort of situation, food purity standards being what they were. Only the week before there had been a cheese scare involving raw-milk cheese made on a Scottish farm; passions had been inflamed, with some arguments being voiced that raw-milk cheese should be banned outright. People should be protected against the selling of potentially dangerous foods, they argued, and raw-milk cheese could harbour E. coli. Others objected strongly to what they saw as interference in people's right to eat something that they thought tasted much better and helped protect against allergies. In this view, if people wanted to eat unpasteurised Camembert, then they should be allowed to do so. A few might fall ill if an infected batch of cheese were to be sold, but this risk was worth taking. Or, even if it were not worth it, it was a risk that people should be allowed to assume if they so desired.

Cheese and freedom, thought Isabel. It could be the subject of another special issue of the *Review*. But who would contribute? There would be libertarian philosophers, of course, who would defend the right to eat and drink as one wished, who would talk disparagingly of "cheese fascists". Professor Lettuce came to mind — he was not a libertarian, as far as she knew, but he certainly looked as if he might be a gourmand, with his fleshiness and his large, rather covetous eyes. She imagined him tucking into a plate of Welsh rarebit, a white napkin tucked under his chin, the rarebit being made with an unpasteurised cheese; and Lettuce would be smacking his lips and mumbling, "More of this, if you don't mind!"

It was a delicious thought, and might have been prolonged had another customer not come into the shop and asked for a particular sort of egg-based pasta for which Isabel had to search.

"It's not that tube stuff," said the customer. "You know those short, quite thick tubes . . ."

"*Rigatoni?*"

"If that's what the tube-like stuff is called — no, not that. It's thinner than that — I'd know it if I saw it. And it's not that stuff that twists round and round."

"*Tagliatelle?*"

"That becomes straight, doesn't it? You put it in boiling water and it becomes straight and floppy. It's not that."

Isabel moved from behind the counter to the shelf where the pastas were stored. She thought she knew which sort of pasta the customer wanted, but she could not recall the name. There were so many shapes and varieties, including one called *strozzapreti*, which meant priest-stranglers. She smiled at the memory. Nobody had ever asked for that. *The Geometry of Pasta* — had somebody not written a book with that title, and it really was about the different shapes of

39

pasta. One could not always trust a title to reflect what was in the book, however; *A Short History of Tractors in Ukrainian* was, after all, a novel.

She found the pasta the customer wanted and sold it to her, along with a large jar of tomato-based sauce that claimed on the label to be ideal for every sort of pasta. Even for *strozzapreti*? Isabel wondered.

"Now you have everything you need," Isabel remarked to the customer.

"Yes, I do — thanks to you."

For some reason, Isabel glanced out of the window. She saw Grace with the two boys, Charlie and Basil, one holding each of her hands, walking by slowly. In the other hand, each boy had an unusually large ice cream cone that he was licking — and smearing generously over his face. It was a completely unexpected sight, and the customer, noticing her surprise, laughed. "What a sight!"

"Yes," said Isabel.

"All over the face — and clothes too, I imagine."

Isabel stared at Grace. Charlie was meant to be at Basil's house, and Patricia was meant to be in charge. What were they doing here, covered in ice cream outside the delicatessen? Isabel was unsure what to do. She wanted to go out and ask Grace what had happened, but she was reluctant to do that. Grace was sensitive and might interpret this as a questioning of her ability to look after Charlie. She had been entrusted to take Charlie to Basil's; there was nothing unusual about that — Grace was allowed to take Charlie out if she so desired. Isabel had no cause to complain, then, except that this was not how she had imagined he would be spending his afternoon. And then there was the ice cream — Charlie was allowed ice creams, and other sweet foods, but only in moderation. When he had ice cream at home — and that was a rare treat — he had two small scoops, no more than that. This outsize cone would have had at least four scoops, Isabel thought. Or possibly five.

Grace seemed too preoccupied with the two young boys to register that she was just outside Cat's delicatessen. In normal circumstances, she would at least have glanced in and waved; now she simply continued with her walk. For a moment, Isabel considered going outside to greet her, but she decided against that. Another customer had arrived — a woman who always asked for thinly sliced ham — and she would have to prepare the slicer for the task.

She thought, quite suddenly: What am I doing here? Why am I allowing myself to be cajoled into helping Cat — without pay — when she should be engaging an extra staff member? What am I, editor of the *Review of Applied Ethics* — also unpaid — doing worrying about cutting ham thinly enough to satisfy some demanding customer?

The customer was addressing her. "You know that ham I bought last week? Serrano, I think. Remember it? I don't like to complain, but it wasn't sliced thinly enough."

Isabel looked at her coolly over the counter. "Oh, really? How interesting."

The woman was taken aback. "Yes," she said defensively. "I wouldn't have raised it with you if it weren't the case. It affects the taste of the ham, you know."

Isabel felt the back of her neck getting warmer. "I very much doubt it," she said calmly.

The woman seemed to recoil. "I beg your pardon: what did you say?"

Isabel articulated the words carefully. "I said: I very much doubt it."

"Well!" said the woman. "That's not very polite. Thick ham definitely tastes different from thinly sliced ham."

"That's what I said I doubted," said Isabel. "It's the sort of thing for which there'll be absolutely no evidence."

She was surprising herself. She was normally scrupulously polite to others, and this sudden pugnacious engagement with this woman was quite unexpected. *I'm losing my temper*, she thought. *I was irritated by the sight of Grace with Charlie and I'm taking it out on this poor woman. Stop it. Get control of yourself.*

The woman was glowering at her. "I don't know why you need to be so rude to me," she said.

Isabel looked down at the floor. She would apologise — it was the only thing to do.

"I'm sorry . . ." she began. But then she continued, "I'm sorry that you're so fussy. If you want to cut the ham yourself, please do. You can come around this side of the counter and operate the machine. But watch your fingers."

This brought a gasp. "I want to speak to the owner," said the woman truculently. "Where is she? I want to complain."

Eddie had now heard what was going on and was standing anxiously at Isabel's side.

"She's out on business," he said. "She's not here."

"And I'm her aunt, anyway," said Isabel.

Eddie looked at Isabel in astonishment.

"I can go elsewhere," said the woman. "There are plenty of places to buy ham."

"Well, I'd agree with you on that," said Isabel, wiping her hands on her apron.

"Really!" exploded the woman.

"I'm sorry," said Isabel. And she was sorry now. She had behaved childishly — egregiously so — and she was embarrassed.

The woman turned on her heel to leave the shop. Isabel noticed that Eddie was staring at her in frank disbelief. "What's wrong?" he said.

Isabel shrugged. "I don't know. I suppose I just lost the plot. I don't know why."

Eddie grinned nervously. He was looking at her with something close to admiration. "It was very funny. I've never seen you like that. I wondered if you'd been smoking something. Or drinking."

"I don't smoke anything," said Isabel. She wondered whether Eddie did. She knew that it was common enough, but the world of drugs was a closed book to her — she had no taste for them. Wine was another matter altogether, but she never drank during the day, nor by herself.

Eddie let out a whistle. "You really got rid of that old bag."

"Please don't call her that."

"But that's what she is," said Eddie. "She complained to me about the Parmesan the other day. She more or less accused me of substituting *grana*. She's a real pain. Big time."

Isabel looked out onto the street. The woman was on the other side now, but was glancing back. "I have to go after her," she muttered.

"But she asked for it," said Eddie. "Leave it."

She shook her head. "No, she didn't ask for it. I lost my temper — and none of it was her fault. I can't just leave it."

She remembered as a child one of her teachers had said something about never leaving your anger unapologised for. "What if you're struck by lightning and you haven't said sorry? What then? It'll be too late, you know. You can't say sorry once you've been struck by lightning." It was just the sort of advice that would have a profound impact on a child — and would return at odd moments over the years, always inducing unease and anxiety. On such advice were superstitious rituals founded — childish promptings that required one to utter *sotto voce* some protective nostrum on seeing an ambulance — or, worse still, a hearse — or before climbing into bed.

She struggled out of her apron, handing it peremptorily to Eddie. "I'll be back," she said.

He remonstrated with her. "There's no point . . ."

But she paid no attention, and now she was out on the pavement and then, through a break in the traffic, making her way to the other side of the road.

Isabel soon caught up with the woman. "Please," she said. "Please will you let me explain something?"

The woman looked flustered, but did not try to stop Isabel speaking.

"You see," said Isabel, "you had the misfortune to get me at a rather odd moment . . ."

The woman raised an eyebrow.

"Yes," Isabel continued. "I was thinking about something altogether different. I suddenly had doubts about my job — or this job, in fact, helping my niece. She doesn't pay me, you see — I just help her out when things get busy or when she's away. And suddenly I realised that I was spending time doing this when I could have been spending the same time with my little boys."

She was getting through to the other woman; Isabel could sense that. She, too, was a mother perhaps, and understood.

"If she doesn't pay you," said the woman, "then perhaps . . ."

"Oh, it's not the money. That's not the main consideration. It's time, really. I happened to see my little boy with the woman who helps me — they were walking past and I suddenly felt that I should be there instead of her." She paused. "I don't know if I'm making sense."

The woman hesitated. "It's just that those thick slices . . . You know, I'm the last person to make a fuss about anything — the very last person."

Isabel suppressed a smile. *No, you're not*, she thought. People who said they were the last person to do anything were usually confessing to something of which they were ashamed — to some flaw. Although not always — some people were the last people to claim to be the last people . . . She could not help herself, and she smiled.

A shadow passed over the woman's face. "Did I say something . . . ?"

Isabel was quick to respond. "No, not at all. You're quite right, and I'm going to be very careful about the thickness of ham in the future."

"Paper-thin is best," said the woman. "At least for smoked ham, as I said . . ."

"Yes, absolutely." Isabel paused. "Would you let me do some for you — some really thin slices? They'll be complimentary — a gift."

The woman shook her head. "Oh, I couldn't."

"But why not?" Isabel felt herself getting irritated again. If somebody offers you a gift, it's important to accept, she thought — to accept gratefully. If you reject gifts, then you prevent those offering them from doing something they may really wish to do. Giving gave every bit as much pleasure as receiving — if not more, and denying that pleasure to others could be churlish.

"It's just that . . ." The woman faltered in her explanation. Then she continued, "It's just that I don't want you to feel bad."

Isabel assured her that she no longer felt that way. "I did until I was able to apologise to you," she said. "And then I felt better about myself. I don't normally lose my temper with people, no matter how irritating they are."

The last phrase slipped out; it was greeted with silence.

"Not that I thought you irritating," said Isabel hurriedly.

The woman looked at her. "You need to watch what you say," she muttered.

Isabel blushed. "Oh, I'm so sorry. I really didn't mean that; well, I suppose I did. This business about ham tasting different somehow got under my skin. It wasn't your fault, it was mine. There was no call for me to get hot under the collar."

The woman pursed her lips. "It does taste different," she said.

Isabel smiled at the absurdity of the situation. It was ridiculous to stand on an Edinburgh pavement arguing about something like this with a woman she did not even know, trying to give her ham and being refused, and then persisting with the argument. "I'm sure you're right," said Isabel decisively. "I'm wrong; you're right."

"Good," said the woman. "And now, if you don't mind, I have things to do."

"Of course," said Isabel. "I've been wasting your time — and I really am sorry, you know."

The woman threw her a sceptical glance. "Let's forget all about it," she said.

"Yes," agreed Isabel. "But if you do come into the shop again, please let me cut you some extra-thin ham."

The woman acknowledged the offer with a nod of the head and left. Isabel returned to the delicatessen, where Eddie was waiting behind the counter, grinning broadly.

"What happened there?" he asked.

"I apologised for my rudeness," said Isabel. "I offered her some ham, but she was standing on her dignity, I'm afraid."

Eddie laughed. "Her loss," he said.

Business had slackened off, and the shop was now empty. "You don't have to stay," said Eddie. "I'll cope fine now by myself."

Isabel suggested they have a cup of coffee together before she went home. Eddie made this, and they sat down at one of the tables to drink it together.

"You know what I said about Cat?" Eddie ventured. "About her going off to see some man?"

Isabel nodded. "Yes." Eddie looked thoughtful. "I think I've worked out who it is. I saw her, you see, at a movie the other day. It was at the Dominion Cinema."

Isabel smiled. The Dominion was an old-fashioned cinema in Morningside, famous over the years for its owner's habit of greeting his patrons in the lobby in evening dress. "She always liked the Dominion."

"It was that film about that guy who fell into a time warp. You know the one?"

Isabel shook her head. "I can't say I do." She paused; Eddie was not strong on irony, but she continued nonetheless. "There seem to be an awful lot of time warps around these days. It's quite unsettling, don't you think?"

Eddie was impassive. "I don't think you need to worry too much," he said. "I don't think there are any time warps here in Edinburgh."

Isabel stared at him. Did he really believe in such things? "I wasn't being entirely serious," she said.

"But it *is* serious," responded Eddie. "If you're in the wrong place at the wrong time, you could wake up to find yourself back in . . ." He shrugged. "Back in the seventeenth century. Just like that."

Isabel resisted the temptation to laugh; Eddie was sensitive, and she had learned that he was easily upset. "The seventeenth century? Not very pleasant . . . in Scotland at least."

Eddie agreed. "Sure. No electricity. No internet."

Isabel raised an eyebrow. "No internet indeed. That would be pretty hard to bear."

"Yes. Imagine not being able to find things out. Not being able to connect with people . . ."

Isabel thought for a moment. Eddie was in his early twenties, and the internet was invented . . . when? It must have been before Eddie was born; the internet, then, was as natural to him as the telephone and long-playing records had been to her.

"You'd miss it, wouldn't you, Eddie?"

"Of course I would. It's . . ." He broke off, before continuing, with a frown, "I suppose it's part of my life. It's the first thing I do when I wake up."

"You go online?"

He nodded. "Just to check whether anything's come in."

"Messages?"

He looked surprised. "Yes, of course. Photos. That sort of thing."

Isabel said nothing. There were new addictions, she realised, and some of them were so subtle, so mainstream that those afflicted had no idea they were addicted — until their prop was taken away and separation anxiety set in. So far, she had avoided internet addiction, as had Jamie. Charlie was the one at risk, though, as he was already taking a close interest in computer screens. She hated the thought of what that could do to childhood, to the imaginative world of Winnie the Pooh, of nursery rhymes, of songs that children learned, of the little things that made up the culture of the very young.

"Of course, there would be other unpleasant things about the seventeenth century," she said. "Particularly in Scotland. Religious fervour. Burning of witches and heretics."

Eddie looked worried. "Burning? They burned people?"

Isabel did not reply immediately. There were times when she was as surprised by what Eddie did *not* know as by what he did know. She was not sure what history was taught in schools now, if they bothered to teach it at all. Eddie, she had discovered a few weeks previously, had never heard of Mussolini; nor of Stalin for that matter. And American presidents started, for him, with President Bush — although, as he said, there had been "some guy before him" whom he could not quite remember.

She was not sure where to start. "In those days . . ." she began.

"When?" asked Eddie.

"In the seventeenth century — we were discussing the seventeenth century, I think."

"Oh yes."

"Everybody had to conform. You had to be a Christian. You had to go to church or you'd be chased up by the local presbytery. And if you dared to argue with what the religious authorities said, then you could be accused of heresy and put to the stake."

"An actual stake?"

"Yes, a big post in the ground. And then they'd stack wood round it and set a match to it." She paused. It was not all that long ago, she reflected, and you should never assume that things that had happened would never happen again. When was the last witch burned in Scotland? 1727. She remembered the date because it had been drummed into them at school by a teacher who had a jaundiced view of her fellow Scots. "We have only recently stopped burning people at the stake, girls — only very recently. 1727, I should point out. 1727." But then when was the last public execution in France? 1939.

Eddie had been struck by this talk of the Scottish auto-da-fé. He had seen a flaw. "Did they have matches in those days? Are you sure about that?" Then he thought of something. "Unless they got some matches from a time traveller," he suggested. "That's always possible, I suppose."

Isabel looked at him, then looked away. "It was a dreadful way to die," she said. "It must have been the most agonising end imaginable."

Eddie agreed, but he was still wondering how they started the fire.

"They had tinder boxes," said Isabel. "Now that you've pointed out the lack of matches, I've remembered. They had flints, and you struck a flint against a bit of metal and it gave you a spark."

"Oh, I know that," said Eddie. "That's how muskets worked."

"Precisely."

Eddie frowned. "But why did they burn these people?"

She replied that it had to do with conformity. People, she said, generally wanted other people to believe the things they did, and would punish those who deviated. *And*, she went on to think, *there are still plenty of people like that*. There was still an orthodoxy, and it was quite capable of being oppressive; there were still those who believed that people should be hounded out of their jobs for using the wrong words or not toeing an ideological line. There had been a teacher recently who had found himself in deep water after addressing a group of schoolgirls as "girls" when one of them was in fact a girl who defined herself as a boy; his offence was "misgendering", and the innocence of his mistake had been an irrelevance. There were many such snares placed in the way of the unwary, and the consequence

52

of inattention to the enforced wisdom of the times could be a medieval public shaming.

Eddie became silent. "You'd never imagine these things happened," he said.

Isabel thought about this. If you knew very little history, then there was much that you would find difficulty in imagining. She glanced at her watch; she would need to get back to the house, although she still wanted to find out about Cat's new boyfriend.

"So you saw her at the Dominion?" she prompted.

"Yes," Eddie replied. "She was there with this guy and another girl. I thought that the guy was with the girl, not with Cat, if you see what I mean, and so I didn't think much more about it. But then a few days ago I saw the same girl with another guy — not the same guy at all. They were snogging in a pub. Really snogging. And so I thought: that first guy must have been with Cat, rather than this girl — unless she was snogging some old friend or something — just for old times' sake."

Isabel laughed. "Snogging in a pub. They were probably an item."

Eddie allowed himself a smile. "That's what I thought. And then I saw him again — the first guy. He was sitting in that tattoo parlour down near that dodgy restaurant — the one that poisoned my friend Harry last month. He was really sick, you know. Spectacular. Throwing up all over the place —"

Isabel interrupted him. "I get the picture, Eddie."

"So there was this guy in the tattoo parlour — and he wasn't a customer, he was the owner, I think. It's his place. He's a tattoo artist." Eddie paused, scrutinising Isabel's face for a reaction. "So you see, what I'm saying is: Cat's new man does tattoos."

Isabel opened her mouth to say something, but then closed it. She turned away and looked out of the window. Then she muttered to herself, *chacun à son goût, chacun à son goût, chacun à son goût*. Mantras, she had always felt, could help, and intoning the phrase *chacun à son goût* could be as calming, and as encouraging of tolerance and acceptance, as the repetitive chanting of *om mani padme hum*, the precise meaning of which she had never really found out.

CHAPTER
FIVE

Isabel was well aware that procrastination was a failing of hers, but had always consoled herself with the thought that it was, at least, a failing that she knew all about. There was a difference — and an important one — between those failings we knew we had, and those of which we were unaware. So the fact that she acknowledged her tendency to procrastination made it more likely that she would do something about it — and she did, with the result that she now very rarely allowed matters to ride. Letters she had to answer were dealt with timeously; unpleasant tasks such as unblocking drains when Jamie was not there — he loved that task — were usually performed in good time, and without too much hesitation. *If I don't do this now, I'll never do this*, was what she said to herself in such situations, and this undoubtedly helped. According to a psychologist friend of hers, there were plenty of psychological tricks, nostrums, private invocations, that we could use to make things better; all we needed to do was to learn them.

And yet failings still persisted, like rocks below the surface of the sea. She thought about this. She knew that we might arm ourselves against them, we might do our best to defuse them by facing up to them, we might do the very opposite of what our failings prompted us to do, and we might feel that we had succeeded in overcoming them. But they would still be there, lurking, ready to show themselves and remind us that we were still the same, flawed people we had always been. So the dieter, knowing of a weakness for chocolate éclairs, may control that particular appetite, may never yield to the temptation of buying a chocolate eclair, but will forever be at risk of succumbing to those fatal confections. So, too, might one burdened with an underlying bad temper be calm and controlled in most dealings with others, but will know that in the right — or wrong — set of circumstances that temper could manifest itself in some sudden and vivid explosion. We live with our failings, Isabel thought, denying some, indulging others, knowing all the while that life is a constant battle between the good to which we all aspire and the flawed and venal lurking within us — or, in Plato's view, between the two horses that pull the chariot of our soul: one that wishes to take it upwards, and one that, lumbering and obstinate, would drag it down.

When it came to replying to Professor Robert Lettuce, procrastination had definitely set in. Isabel realised this, and had told herself that she really should not ignore his letter, but it was over two weeks before she eventually picked it up and did something about it. It had lain on her desk, in full view, with its condescending salutation written by hand while the body of the letter was in typescript. *My dear Isabel*

Dalhousie, he had begun, and in this seemingly innocuous opening, Isabel had already found sufficient offence to make the back of her neck feel warm. There was nothing wrong in beginning a letter with *My dear*; it was, in a way, much friendlier than simply writing *Dear*. But Professor Lettuce had not written *My dear Isabel*, he had written *My dear Isabel Dalhousie*, and there was something about that particular form of address that made Isabel's hackles rise. It was condescension, she decided. If Lettuce were treating her as an equal, he would have written *Dear Ms Dalhousie*, or *Dear Dr Dalhousie*, as Isabel had a doctorate, even if she rarely used it. She knew that when he wrote to male colleagues, Lettuce often simply used their surnames; she had seen correspondence between him and Dr Christopher Dove in which Lettuce had begun *Dear Dove*, and had then signed *Lettuce* at the bottom of the page. That, she thought, was a masculine thing, going back to Lettuce's schooldays; she knew he had been sent to an all-boys boarding school, some dim and distant place in Northumberland, and she imagined that in such places first names had not been widely used. Of course, that had changed, but in those draughty days Lettuce would have called all the other boys by their surnames.

It was not just the mode of address that irritated her, however; it was also the content of the letter. Lettuce had begun with some anodyne remarks to the effect that he hoped she was well and that it was a matter of great regret to him that they had not seen much of one another since he had moved to Edinburgh. "My chair involves me in so much administration," he wrote. "Scarcely do I have time for what I am really meant to be doing, and what I most enjoy — teaching students." Isabel had decided that this was meretricious. Lettuce had never enjoyed teaching, as far as she knew; indeed, he had somehow managed to delegate teaching responsibilities to junior staff, or to teaching assistants recruited from the ranks of his postgraduate students. She knew this because she had heard some of those assistants grumbling about it; they would have been happy to do the teaching, they said, if only Professor Lettuce had paid them to do it. When he had been head of philosophy at one of the lesser colleges of the University of London, he presented the teaching to his assistants as "an opportunity for career development" and therefore not something for which the university should be expected to pay. This would not have been countenanced by the university itself, had it known what was going on, but Lettuce had said nothing about it. The assistants themselves, being at the bottom of the academic food chain, had been loath to make a fuss. They knew the consequences awaiting those who, at the beginning of their careers, complained about pay and conditions; understanding that, they chose to remain silent.

Returning to the offending letter, Isabel had read on, only to find her irritation mounting. "But let us not bemoan the contact that somehow has not materialised — *mea culpa*, I confess; *mea maxima culpa* — let us see if we can do something about it!" At this point Isabel had thought: a dinner invitation! She and Jamie were about to be invited to dinner with Robert and Clementine Lettuce in their flat off Palmerston Place; but then, no, that was not the *lactucian* intention. She smiled, momentarily distracted by the word she had invented. As far as she knew there was no adjective to describe the state of being a lettuce. In an idle moment, curiosity had sent her off to the dictionary to see if such a word existed, and she had drawn a blank. So a simple resort to the etymology of the Middle English *letuse*, itself based on the French *laitue* and the Latin *lactuca*, had led to her muttering "lactucian". She liked the sound of it: *lactucian*; it was a useful word, she felt, if one needed to describe the doings of a lettuce, which were minimal, of course; lettuces *grew* — they did little else, other than to propagate themselves. So the essence of *lettucehood*, the things that constituted the state of being a lettuce, was *lactucian*, a word that until now had not been used because nobody, it seemed, needed it. Well now, if they did, it would be there for them.

So there was no lactucian social invitation; instead, there was a suggestion, if not a command — and here she caught her breath at the sheer effrontery, the sheer lactucian effrontery, of the suggestion that *she* should come and see *him* in his office. "So," he wrote, "I would be most grateful if you would come and see me at the university. I'm in the David Hume Tower and you'll see the telephone number at the top of this page. If you call my secretary, Mrs Balvenie, she'll find a time that suits me." He had then signed the whole affront *Professor Robert Lettuce, FRSE, MBE.*

When she first read the letter, it had taken Isabel several minutes to recover. She could scarcely believe Lettuce's presumption; you did not write to somebody and "suggest" that he or she should come to see you. You did not do this unless you were that person's employer, grandparent, probation officer, bank manager (and then only in the case of overdrawn accounts), doctor, or head teacher. Apart from these obvious relationships, there was nobody who could command your attendance like that — apart from the Queen, of course; invitations from the Queen were, through long tradition, commands, but even there the etiquette was that you were first approached to see if you would accept the invitation before it was issued. Lettuce had simply summoned her to come at a time to be arranged. She looked at the wording again. It was there on the page, rank in its offensiveness: *a time that suits me*. Me! Him! The metaphorical taking away of her breath became almost actual.

And then, of course, there was the signing-off. The FRSE that he had attached to his name stood for Fellow of the Royal Society of Edinburgh, Scotland's learned academy, membership of which was an honour given to people of intellectual distinction in science and the arts. It was not entirely surprising that Lettuce had been admitted to that, but what surprised Isabel was that he had used the distinction in an ordinary letter to somebody he knew. That was ostentatious, as was the inclusion of the civilian honour, MBE, something that was awarded for general service to the community or for notable achievement in some field. Professors could

60

well be singled out for an MBE — and Isabel had met a number who had been. There were also those of less exalted status who were awarded the honour for things they had done: long-serving charity workers; valued rural posties — as deliverers of mail were called in Scotland; the coxswains of lifeboats who saved lives in coastal waters, and so on. They all deserved recognition, but none of them, she thought, would sign their letters with "MBE". It was laughable; Lettuce was just impossibly pompous — incorrigibly so, she suspected.

She thought all this, and had decided to ignore the high-handed summons, but then she stopped herself. She had never liked Lettuce, and she had never approved of his machinations, in particular those conducted with his sidekick, Christopher Dove. Lettuce was a plotter, a schemer. Lettuce was interested only in gain and glory for Lettuce — and perhaps the award of the MBE was for self-interest. She smiled at the thought, imagining the citation: *For service to self: Robert Lettuce.*

But then she remembered her conversation with Clementine Lettuce in the Scottish National Gallery on the Mound, when Lettuce's wife had suddenly opened up with the heart-rending story of the loss of their daughter. The young woman had been killed in a car accident on the way to a university open day, and since then, Clementine explained, Robert Lettuce had lived with a broken heart. That had brought Isabel up short, and she had reflected on her lack of charity towards him. He was not the scheming, manipulative professor;

he was a man who had lost that which he most loved in this life. In his sorrow, he was just a person like anybody else; an ordinary, vulnerable person, whose life could be shattered by grief.

The loss of another's life, Isabel reminded herself, was a cause for sympathy, and one effect of sympathy was to prompt us to cherish, if not love, those on whom our sympathy was focused. And that had been its effect in this case: although she and Lettuce had not sought one another out since his move to Edinburgh, her antipathy to him had largely disappeared, and indeed she had not thought much about him. But now this letter had arrived and it had all been stirred up again.

Yet she had to respond to his letter. Even extreme rudeness should not be answered by the same token. She knew that, and she knew that she would go to see Lettuce — even at a time that suited him — and would find out what it was he wanted. She was sure he had invited her for that reason — Lettuce always wanted something — and the only way of finding out what it was would be to go and discover the lactucian agenda.

She made her way across the Meadows shortly before noon. Her appointment with Professor Lettuce was at twelve-twenty — a time that had been proposed by Mrs Balvenie when Isabel had telephoned her. Isabel had been surprised by the twenty minutes; most arrangements were made for more obvious times — for the quarter- or half-hours, or for the simple hour itself. Why would Lettuce not have chosen twelve o'clock, rather than twelve-twenty? Lettuce was trying to intimidate her; he wanted to show that he was someone who could suggest a meeting at twenty past the hour; he was trying to show that his day was so finely calibrated that twenty-past meetings were inevitable.

The Meadows, a large park that separated the South Side of Edinburgh from the Old Town, was thronged with people taking advantage of one of the first warm days of summer. Like most of Scotland, Edinburgh moved from spring into summer with a gradualism that could sometimes be taken for reluctance, as if the weather were frightened to abandon the ambivalence of spring for the certainty of summer. Now the change seemed unequivocal, and groups of young people — students for the most part — had trustingly taken to the grass and the sun, lying scantily clad, sprawled out in the warmth of the sunlight; or clustered in small groups around somebody with a guitar; or playing an informal game of cricket with tennis balls and bundles of clothing as stumps. Somebody not far off was playing music, and it drifted across the grass — *Carmina Burana*, of all things. She stopped for a moment to listen to it, and smiled. *Carmina Burana* was not music for a summer's day; it was no pastoral, but it was certainly music for nineteen- or twenty-year-olds, who felt the passion of youth. *Olim*, sang the anguished tenor; *Olim lacus colueram/olim pulcher exstiteram/ dum cignus ego fueram . . . Once I lived on lakes, once I looked beautiful, when I was a swan.*

It was obviously too much for the person playing it and it was switched off suddenly. Isabel continued with her walk. There was laughter from a group of four young people — two men and two women; somebody chanted the word *olim*, and there was more laughter. Isabel sighed. In a different, more interventionist universe she could have gone over to them and said, "But that's a heart-rending song," but she could not do it, because you did not talk to complete strangers about the music they were playing, and they were also too young to realise that *olim* could be the saddest of words, not something to laugh at. *Olim* was full of regret once you had something to regret, but not before.

She thought about *Carmina Burana* all the way to George Square. A singer friend of hers had told her that he hated singing it. "Nasty, fascist music," he'd said. "Aggressive stuff."

It had made her think of the moral flavour of music. Could music really have a moral quality in itself, or was it given this by the circumstances in which it was played — and by the reasons behind its performance. Music could be pressed into military service: a triumphal march would be good if played by the right side, and wrong if played by those in the wrong. But that was martial music, which was a special case. What about other forms of music? What about rap? There was positive rap, no doubt, but it sometimes seemed to glorify things that were distinctly negative — violence, drug use, the strutting mistreatment of women. The message was spelled out in the words, of course, but did the music itself, the insistent, monotonous rhythms, have anything to do with it?

And the issue became more complex when one linked music to nation; could *Madama Butterfly* or *Aida* have been written by anybody but an Italian? Or the "Song of the Volga Boatmen" be the product of anything but a people who have suffered long under one cudgel or another; that was music best sung by the Red Army Choir if at all possible. *River Volga, you are our mother* . . . It could come from nowhere else. Then there was Wagner. Could the Ring Cycle have been written by a Canadian composer? The Canadians, surely, were too considerate, too polite to write Wagnerian music; not that the Germans were not polite — they generally were, scrupulously so. Wagner, though, had not been a man of typically Canadian modesty. He had been famed for his arrogance — the very opposite of Richard Strauss, who, summing up his own career, described himself, with admirable humility, as a "first-class second-rate composer".

With these thoughts in mind she arrived at the university building that housed members of the department of philosophy. A notice directed visitors to the office of the departmental secretary, Mrs Balvenie, who glanced at her watch as Isabel entered. Twelve-twenty might have been her idea, thought Isabel.

She was told that Professor Lettuce would be ready to see her in a few minutes, once he was off the telephone. Isabel smiled politely. "I wouldn't want to disturb him unduly," she said.

Mrs Balvenie looked appreciative, even if still reserved. "The professor's very busy."

"I can imagine he is," said Isabel.

Mrs Balvenie seemed to relax. "He has so much to do," she said. "And this is a busy time for us. The students are finishing their examinations, you see."

"Marking exam papers is a thankless task," remarked Isabel.

Mrs Balvenie hesitated, as if unsure whether to divulge a piece of important information. Then she said, "Oh, Professor Lettuce doesn't do that. There are others . . ."

"Junior staff?"

"Yes. But he keeps an eye on things."

Isabel took the seat offered her by Mrs Balvenie. "Your name," she ventured. "Balvenie: it's a whisky, isn't it?"

Mrs Balvenie smiled. "And a castle," she said coyly. "Up in Morayshire — near Dufftown."

"Of course. I've heard of it."

"My husband's people are from up there. They're Douglases, you see."

Something chimed in Isabel's memory. The Douglases were a well-known family in Scottish history, known as the Black Douglases. One of them had been murdered by King James II. Another was called Archibald the Grim, and then there was James the Gross . . . They were a troubled — and troubling — family.

"And your name," said Mrs Balvenie suddenly. "Dalhousie. That's an interesting one, isn't it?"

"Not in our case," said Isabel. "We were very ordinary. I don't think we did anything." She paused. "Which may be no bad thing, actually. All the distinguished names in Scotland can be traced back to murderers and brigands of one sort or another." She stopped. "Although not in the case of the Balvenies, of course."

They both laughed. And that was the point at which a door at the side of the room opened and Professor Lettuce appeared.

"Murderers and brigands?" he said. "This is a very interesting conversation." He took a step towards Isabel, hand extended. "My dear Miss Dalhousie."

She took his hand. It was limp — like a lettuce leaf, thought Isabel; an unexpected handshake for a man as well built as Professor Lettuce was. She glanced at him; he had put on weight since she last saw him, and had developed slightly fleshy jowls.

"Do come in," he said, gesturing to the room behind him. Then, to Mrs Balvenie, he said, "Mrs Balvenie, please don't put any telephone calls through for the next ten minutes."

Isabel smarted. Ten minutes; she was worth ten minutes of the great man's time. Ten minutes.

"It's very good of you to see me." She found herself saying this without any note of irony. She did not believe it, but she said it.

Magnanimous, Professor Lettuce waved a hand in the air. "No, it's a real pleasure to see you — and you're so kind to call in."

"I know how busy you are," said Isabel.

"Yes, it's a busy time of the year." They sat down, Lettuce behind his large, paper-strewn desk, and Isabel in the visitor's chair in front of it.

"I hope you don't mind my not offering you a cup of coffee," said Professor Lettuce, "but our kettle's broken." His tone became vaguely petulant. "Mrs Balvenie was going to bring another one in, but she hasn't got round to it yet."

"It's a fraught time of the year," said Isabel. "She must have a lot to do."

Lettuce thought for a moment before replying. "I suppose so. We're so understaffed, you know. I'm under pressure to give up some of her time to colleagues — it's most vexing. A chair should have a secretary — they always did in the past."

Isabel wondered whether her ten minutes were going to be used up in small talk about the staffing problem of the department of philosophy. She refrained from comment, but waited for Lettuce to continue.

Lettuce cleared his throat. "I mustn't keep you too long," he said. "I was looking forward to seeing you because I have a proposition to put to you."

Isabel tried to hide her satisfaction in having guessed correctly that Lettuce wanted something from her. "Oh yes?" she said.

"Yes. I'm instituting a series of lectures — high profile ones — and I wondered whether you might be prepared to be our first speaker."

She frowned. "Public lectures?"

"Oh yes, very much so. The idea would be to come up with lectures of a philosophical nature, but of relevance to the financial and business community. You, of course, are very much involved in applied ethics — and that would be a perfect fit." He waved a hand airily.

"There's all this interest in business ethics, isn't there? I'm sure we could attract a large audience from all the fund managers and bankers we have in this city."

Isabel was cautious. "Possibly. Although I don't think one can count on it."

Lettuce assured her that he would count on nothing. "But I still have reason to believe we would attract a large and influential audience." He paused. "And that, of course, would help us with our own financial plans."

Isabel raised an eyebrow. "Which are?"

"We need funds to enable members of staff to go off to more conferences. A truly successful department of philosophy needs to be seen at the big meetings — the American Philosophical Association conference, for instance, or the World Philosophical Congress. We need to be represented at all these functions."

Isabel nodded. "So you would hope that the financial firms would support all that?"

"Indirectly," said Lettuce. "They would give a donation but it wouldn't necessarily be tied to a specific event. Everything would be very flexible."

Isabel thought for a moment; it was becoming clear to her who would attend these international jamborees. She decided to confirm her suspicions indirectly.

"It will be a great boost for your junior colleagues to get the experience," she said. "Exposure to these international meetings would be wonderful for their careers."

Lettuce hesitated. "Well . . ." He looked out of the window, avoiding her gaze. "Well, I'm not sure whether junior members of staff are the best people to represent the department. In due course they would be, but I think, on balance, it would be better to send senior people."

"So you'd be prepared to go," prompted Isabel.

Lettuce smiled. "It's my responsibility," he said.

Isabel pursed her lips. "I see."

"Good," said Lettuce. "And the reason I thought of asking you is that you have deep roots in this city. Your father, I believe, was well known in Edinburgh and I imagine that some of these financial people will remember him. Is that right?"

"They may," said Isabel.

"Well, there we are," said Lettuce. "Perfect fit. Your name as the first speaker might persuade many of them to attend."

"I'm not so sure," said Isabel. "Many of these people are fully occupied making money — it's what they do. They may not have time for philosophy lectures."

Lettuce made light of the objection. "Oh, I don't know about that," he said. "I'd be prepared to bet we get a fair amount of interest."

Isabel shrugged. "Perhaps. When would you want an answer?"

Lettuce looked puzzled. "To what?"

"To the invitation you've just extended."

Isabel realised that it had not occurred to Lettuce that she might decline; it was yet more lactucian arrogance.

He looked flustered. "Well . . ."

She took control. "I'll think about it," she said firmly. "I'll let you know in due course."

He thanked her.

"What will the lectures be called?" she asked.

For a few moments Lettuce said nothing. She saw him look down at his hands, which were soft and effeminate. They were not the hands of one who had done any manual work about the house, or anywhere else.

Then he said, "Actually, we were thinking of calling them the Robert Lettuce Lectures." He stared at her, as if nervous about her reaction. He added, hurriedly, "That was a colleague's idea, of course. I agreed only because it would give them a strong identification with my chair. There's nothing personal involved."

Isabel felt the laughter welling up within her. With a supreme effort she quelled it. "Very appropriate," she said, her voice trembling on the edge of a giggle.

Lettuce seemed relieved. "I'm glad you think so."

Isabel rose to leave, but Lettuce gestured for her to stay. "There's one further thing," he said. "I wondered if I could prevail on you to read something I've come across." He reached into a folder on his desk and took out a thin sheaf of papers. "This is a quite remarkable paper I happened to discover. I don't know the author, I'm afraid, but I think it's extremely interesting — indeed, I wondered whether it would suit your *Review*."

Lettuce handed the paper to Isabel. She glanced at the title page. "The Duty to Lie". The author's name appeared immediately below the title: Professor Calderwood Kale. *Kale*. The coincidence struck her immediately. Kale was a popular vegetable: Jamie had a particular soft spot for curly kale. Why would Lettuce espouse the cause of a paper written by somebody called Kale?

Isabel looked up. "How do we know that he wrote this?" she asked.

A puzzled frown crossed Lettuce's face. "But why would we imagine that anybody else did?"

"With that title?" said Isabel.

Again Lettuce frowned. "I have no reason to believe it's not the work of the person on the title page. None at all."

Isabel rose to her feet. "Well," she said, "I must let you get on. I'll read this and let you have my views. We're a bit full at the moment, but there may be a slot if Professor Kale doesn't mind waiting."

She said goodbye to Lettuce, and then to Mrs Balvenie. Once outside the room, she took a deep breath. Talking to Professor Lettuce always had this effect on her — she felt stifled, as if the only thing to do was to have a brisk walk in the open, unpolluted air. "The Robert Lettuce Lectures!" she muttered to herself. And then, once again, "The Robert Lettuce Lectures!"

Halfway along the corridor, there was a board on the wall. Isabel stopped and looked at the notices pinned on it. *Please take notices down after they have ceased to have effect*, said a sign at the top. She smiled as she saw the extent to which this advice had gone unheeded, in spite of being signed *Professor R. Lettuce*. She itched to write in *MBE* after his name, but resisted the temptation. An advertisement for a student party, dated the previous March, still invited people "to come and have a seriously good time" and next to it, on a faded piece of paper, was a small note from a postgraduate student looking for a new flat to move into "round about Christmas". Her eye moved on. There was something compelling about the notices that people pinned on boards: they provided a snapshot of the life of a community. So she saw that there was a reading group devoted to Heidegger; she saw that somebody was offering a copy of Plato's *Republic* and Camus's *The Myth of Sisyphus* for three pounds (for both books); she read the plea for somebody who had removed a light brown jacket from one of the tutorial rooms to return it to its owner. "I'm pretty sure I know who you are," said this notice, which ended with the imprecation, "Have you no conscience?" Presumably not, thought Isabel, as the notice was still there — as must be the rumbling suspicion that the rightful owner harboured.

She turned to go, and at that moment a young woman emerged from a door beside the noticeboard. Looking down at the floor, she failed to see Isabel, and the two of them collided. A plate that the young woman had been holding, on which there was a number of freshly buttered scones, fell to the floor, the scones dispersing over a considerable area, several of them butter-side down.

Isabel gasped. "Oh, I am sorry. I didn't . . ."

The young woman looked up. "No. No. It was me. I wasn't watching where I was going." She looked down again, at the scones. Her face fell. "What a mess."

73

Isabel stooped down to retrieve the plate while the young woman scraped the scones off the floor.

"Isn't there a rule," Isabel asked as she straightened back up, "about buttered things falling face down? Doesn't it happen more times than not?"

Attending to the last of the fallen scones, the young woman laughed. "Yes. I've heard that about toast. It obviously applies to scones too." She stood up, tossed the scone into the nearby paper bin, and took the proffered plate from Isabel. "Thank you. That really was my fault."

Isabel looked at her. The young woman, dressed in a casual white linen top and blue trousers, had a certain elegance to her. And she was strikingly beautiful. *Why do we feel we want to talk to beautiful people?* The question came to Isabel's mind unbidden. And the answer followed immediately: *Because so are we attracted to beauty, as moths are to the flame.*

"Are you on the staff here?" Isabel asked. And then, before a reply could be given, she added, "My name's Isabel, by the way."

The young woman dusted the crumbs from her hands. "I'm Claire. And no, I'm one of the PhD people. I do some tutoring, but I'm not permanent staff."

Isabel nodded. "That's what I used to do," she said. "Years ago."

"In philosophy?" asked Claire.

"Yes. Mostly moral philosophy — in fact, entirely moral philosophy. I edit a journal now. I publish it too, I suppose."

Claire's eyes narrowed. "Which journal?"

Isabel told her, and Claire's face broke into a broad smile. "The *Review of Applied Ethics*? I read it. Every issue — sometimes a bit late, of course." She paused. "I never noticed that it was published here in Edinburgh. Shows how observant I am."

Isabel smiled. "Nobody notices that sort of thing. They read the articles — I hope — but pay no attention to the fine print." She hesitated for a few moments before continuing. "Look, is there still a coffee bar down in the basement?"

Claire nodded. "Yes, there is."

"Would you like to join me?"

Claire looked at her watch, and then at the empty plate. "The scones were for the professor."

"For Professor Lettuce?"

Something passed between them; something unspoken. After a few moments, Claire nodded. "Yes. He . . . he likes scones." Then she said, "But why not? Give me a sec to put this plate away."

She went back through the door from which she had emerged. Isabel waited. She was not sure why she had invited Claire to join her for coffee. Did she want to ask her something? Or did she just want to spend more time with this intriguing, beautiful young woman? Some people have qualities that we feel will somehow rub off on us if we spend time with them. Wisdom, aesthetic sense, beauty, youth; we want to be with such people because we would like to *be* them, or at least a bit more like them. Dangerous, thought Isabel. Foolish. Impossible.

Claire came out again, looking apologetic. "Actually, I'd better not. Do you mind? I promised Professor Lettuce I'd see him and I'd better not keep him waiting."

Isabel searched Claire's expression for something — but it was not there. "No, of course not. Perhaps another time."

"Yes," said Claire. "Another time."

Isabel felt embarrassed as she said goodbye. Had Claire misinterpreted her invitation? It was possible; good-looking people must be used to this sort of thing — to unwelcome attention. Had she thought that? She decided that she had not; Claire was due to see Lettuce — that was all there was to it.

She made her way down the stairs and out into George Square. A group of students, fresh from the examination hall, were huddled together, discussing their recent ordeal, and where they might have gone wrong. Isabel remembered doing that, a long time ago now, pre-John Liamor, pre-Jamie, pre-Charlie and Magnus — before everything, really, that made up her current life. She smiled at the memory. They used to discuss the papers and then go home, watch mindless television over numerous cups of coffee, and try to forget about their mistakes.

While she was walking across the Meadows the thought came into her mind: *By what right does Lettuce have his scones buttered for him by a member of his staff?* It was a petty question — and Isabel realised that. Lettuce brought the worst out in her; he was like a red rag to a bull. *I shall not let him do that,* she told herself; I shall not. But she still felt annoyed, and remained annoyed all the way back across the Meadows, until she saw a child flying a kite on the Bruntsfield Links and heard his cries of delight and joy as the breeze took the flimsy paper construction up into the sky; and Isabel put Professor Lettuce and his posturing out of her mind, to share in the pleasure of the wind, and the things that the wind can do.

CHAPTER
SIX

Jamie said, "What lies ahead?"

It was one of their private expressions — the set way of saying things that married couples develop — shibboleths for admission to their private world. Either of them would ask, usually over breakfast, what lay ahead, and the other would say something about the day's plans before enquiring, in return, "What lies ahead for you?"

But it was Charlie who answered this morning. He was eating — or spreading, rather — his boiled egg, and he looked up from this task to say, "I'm going to play with Basil."

Jamie glanced at Isabel and smiled. "That's very exciting, Charlie. Are you looking forward to it?"

To which Charlie replied, "Eggs."

"You're eating an egg," said Isabel. "Boiled egg. Your favourite."

"Kind hens," said Charlie. "They're very kind to give us eggs, aren't they?"

"Yes, Charlie!" said Jamie. "It's very kind of them."

Isabel thought, *Actually, we steal them*, but did not say anything. And Charlie, too, became silent; the eating of the egg was now a task that required too much attention for him to participate further in a conversation that was clearly not going anywhere.

"So," said Jamie, "what lies ahead?"

Isabel sighed. "More of the same. I'm going to have to spend most of the morning working if we're to meet the printer's deadline. They've become very insistent on that, for some reason. I think they've expanded and have taken on too much work."

Jamie was sympathetic. He knew how hard Isabel worked to get each issue of the *Review* ready for printing. For some time he had felt that the job she was doing was just too much for one person, and that she should appoint an assistant.

"And I must spend some time with Magnus," Isabel continued. "I want to spend time with him. He needs me."

Jamie reached out to take her hand. "I know," he said.

"Because I'm a mother first and foremost," said Isabel.

"Yes, you are." He paused. "And you're a very good one."

She stared at the tablecloth. It needed washing, as the detritus of Charlie's meals had been spread wide.

"I sometimes feel that I'm indulging myself," Isabel continued. "I'm not working for money — as most working mums have to do. I'm working because . . . because . . ." She shrugged. Why did she do what she did? Because she had somehow got herself entangled in the *Review* and had been rash enough to buy it when it had come up for sale? That was the way in which so many human complications started; people did things on impulse and then found themselves burdened with unsupportable obligations that were just too much for them.

She looked at Jamie. He understood; she knew that. He played a full part in the parenting of their children — far more than many other men did. He never complained or tried to avoid his share of the work of the household. He tidied up; he cooked; he dealt cheerfully with all the smelly tasks of looking after babies and small children. And he never once had said to her that she should not have a career; nor did he suggest, or even imply, that his own career was more important than hers. Yet, should she take all that for granted? Should she actually ask him whether he felt that she was trying to do too much, in being a mother and the editor — and publisher — of an important academic journal?

She decided to ask.

"Should I give up?"

Jamie frowned. "What? Give up what?"

"Give up trying to run the *Review*. Give up all this worrying about whether everything's going to be ready for the printer. Give up spending hour after hour sorting out what's going to appear, and how it's going to be footnoted, punctuated, whatever. Give up dealing with difficult authors all over the world who expect me to be a mind-reader, nursemaid, ally in their petty squabbles. Give up all of that. The whole lot."

He shook his head — vehemently. But she continued: "Give up thinking that I can be in two places at once and be two things at the same time. Give up pretending that being a mother isn't a full-time job. Give up —"

He stopped her. "It can't be a full-time job. If it were, then —"

"It *is* a full-time job. Look at it. You have to give your full attention to a small child. They demand it."

Jamie sighed. "That's why it's shared, Isabel. And it has to be — otherwise women couldn't have a career. And you wouldn't want that, would you?"

She did not have to answer. He was right, she thought; it was unthinkable that women should go back to how things were before — back to the kitchen, to the domestic sentence under which countless generations of women had been buried before.

"So, we delegate?" she said. "Is that what you're saying — we delegate?"

"I'd call it sharing. But you can talk about delegation if you like. It's the same thing."

She waited for a moment. Then, "But we already share. You do so much." She reflected on how they divided the task of looking after Charlie and Magnus. He did at least half, if not slightly more, she thought; at least. "You do more than your fair share. More than half."

"But I enjoy it."

From the other side of the table he had been holding her hand; now he let go of it and stood up. He came round to stand immediately behind her, his arm around her shoulder. Charlie watched impassively. "Daddy hugs Mummy," he said.

"Absolutely right," said Jamie, grinning. "Daddy hugs Mummy lots and lots."

She reached up and took his hand. "Mummy hugs Daddy back. One hundred times."

"One hundred times," echoed Charlie, and then added, "Eggs again."

"Eat your egg all up," said Jamie. "Then you'll be strong. Eggs make you strong."

"Hens aren't," muttered Charlie.

Isabel gave an involuntary chuckle. "Did I hear correctly?" she asked.

"A very witty child," said Jamie. "Clearly he takes after his mother."

Jamie sat down. "But, seriously, you need to do something, Isabel. We've had this conversation before, you know. We've talked about how you're too busy. You need to do something about it rather than just talk about it. Seriously. You do."

She drew in her breath. Again, he was right. "If I could find somebody suitable," she said. "And even then, the *Review* couldn't afford a full-time salary. It barely keeps afloat — as you know."

"It doesn't have to be full time. Part time would be fine."

"Mornings only?"

Jamie nodded. "Something like that. And this new person, whoever he or she would be, could do things like proof-reading. That takes you ages, doesn't it?"

It did. And she disliked that job intensely because her mind kept wandering as she read. Being a proof-reader and being a philosopher were fundamentally incompatible, she thought. But at the same time, she would need somebody who *could* do philosophy, who would know how to handle the issues around which the *Review* ultimately revolved.

Jamie reached out to retrieve a piece of egg yolk that Charlie had flicked across the table. "Don't waste your food, Charlie," he said, automatically. This was something that parents said day in, day out, like long-playing records stuck in a groove. *Don't waste your food; say please; say thank you; have you washed your hands?* There were years and years of those refrains ahead and then, almost miraculously, at the end there would be a responsible human being who did not waste food, who always said please and thank you, and who did wash his or her hands. It worked; it was the only way.

He turned to Isabel and was about to say something, but she looked as if a solution had occurred to her. He raised an eyebrow inquisitively.

"I met somebody yesterday," she said. "I went to see Professor Lettuce, as I told you."

"Him," said Jamie. There were few people of whom he actively disapproved, but Lettuce was one of them.

"Yes," Isabel continued. "There was a young woman, a teaching assistant in the department. She might . . ." Isabel trailed off. She was thinking. They had parted on slightly unsatisfactory terms, with Claire declining her invitation to coffee, but Isabel did not think that meant very much. She had her appointment with Lettuce and surely it was to her credit that she would not keep him waiting. *Pacta sunt servanda*. Surely this was to her credit, and suggested that if she took the job — which was mere surmise at this stage — she would be reliable.

Jamie brightened. "Do you think she'd be interested?"

Isabel shrugged. "I could ask her. She's doing a PhD, I gather, and she also does some teaching in the department. Professor Lettuce may be paying her, or may not — I don't know — but she won't be earning very much. This might suit her down to the ground."

"Well, there you are," urged Jamie. "Why not just see whether she's keen? You've got nothing to lose." He paused. "And I have another suggestion. Two suggestions, in fact."

She waited.

"Get an au pair," he said. "Get somebody to help around here."

"But we have Grace."

Jamie sighed. "Grace is great — I'd never say that she wasn't. But . . ."

They exchanged glances, and Isabel knew that they were both thinking the same thing. Grace was a law unto herself, and since the arrival of Magnus she had interpreted her role as being mainly to help with the children. This meant that the cleaning of the house was being sadly neglected. Shelves went undusted, windows uncleaned; rings were left on baths and sinks; nothing looked as clean as it used to.

"I doubt if Grace would approve," said Isabel.

"She might, or she might not. Grace is unpredictable. But whose house is it?"

"Ours," said Isabel. "And I suppose that if we want an au pair then we're entitled to get one."

"Good," said Jamie. "Let's contact an agency today — this morning."

Isabel nodded. She would do both; she would telephone Mrs Balvenie and get Claire's contact details. Then, after she had sounded her out, she would get in touch with an au pair agency. She felt decisive. But Jamie had said he had a further suggestion. She asked him what this was.

"The deli," he said. "Look at what's happening there. Cat keeps asking you to help. How many times were you there last week?"

"Three times," replied Isabel. "But she had to go to Glasgow, and then —"

Jamie stopped her. "Oh, there's always a reason. It's going to Glasgow, or stock-taking, or a dental appointment. There's always a reason, but it goes on and on, doesn't it?"

Isabel shrugged. "I don't mind too much. It's different. I meet all sorts of people."

"And she doesn't pay you," Jamie pointed out.

"Perhaps not."

"No, definitely not. You're unpaid labour."

Isabel pointed out that Cat was her niece; one had obligations to one's niece.

"Not to that extent," he said.

"What would you have me do, then? Refuse to help altogether?"

He said that he did not envisage that, but she might set some limits to the frequency of her sessions behind the counter. "Try saying not more than once a week," he suggested.

"I could, I suppose."

"Good. Then that's settled everything, hasn't it? A new life ahead."

"Sort of new," said Isabel.

She rose to her feet, so she was standing beside him. She kissed him, lightly, on the lips, and then started to wipe crumbs off the table.

Jamie turned to attend to Charlie, but then remembered their unfinished conversation about the day ahead. "So, work this morning and spend some time with Magnus," he said. "And the afternoon?"

Isabel looked guilty, and he knew immediately.

"There's a farmers' market in Fife," she said. "Cat wanted to go and speak to some suppliers. Just for a couple of hours."

"You see," said Jamie, trying not to sound triumphant.

"I can't say no," said Isabel.

"No," said Jamie. "You can't."

"I meant: I can't say no this time. Not in these particular circumstances."

Jamie sighed. "But that's the problem, isn't it? There's always some special reason. And you, being as kind as you are, say yes — without exception. Every single time."

He looked at her. It might have been a look of reproach — after all, he had just pointed out what could be a major failing, a weakness — but it was not that at all: if anything, it was a look of admiration, of fondness; thus do we list the faults of those we love — with the light of admiration in our eyes.

Isabel knew this. She lowered her eyes. "Philosophers have a word for this," she said. "I think we've talked about it before. Akrasia — weakness of the will."

He remembered their earlier conversation. He had been intrigued by the notion: that we could do things that we knew were not in our best interests, but do them nonetheless. "There's that complicated discussion," he said, "about whether the thing you really want to do can ever *not* be in your best interests, because of the very fact . . ."

Isabel nodded. "Because of the very fact that you do it. That means it must be what you really, deeply, truly — whatever term you're going to use — what you *really* want. Otherwise you wouldn't do it, would you?"

"I suppose not," replied Jamie. "And that means you really want to help Cat even if you know — deep inside — it's not a good idea."

Isabel wondered what he meant by *deep inside*. Where was this deep inside of which people spoke? Was it the same thing as Freud's id, a deep, insistent force that required taming by the ego and super-ego? It depended, she decided, on what deep-inside feelings one was talking about. She smiled at him. "I'm guilty of akrasia, then," she said.

He leaned forward and kissed her; it was the second kiss in fifteen minutes. "I wouldn't have it otherwise," he said. "In fact, I'm going to compose something. Perhaps in the style of Thomas Morley. A madrigal. About you — and your akrasia."

"Should I be flattered?" she asked. But then immediately answered her own question. "I'd love that."

Jamie was gazing up at the ceiling. Isabel had noticed that he sometimes did this when he was thinking of a musical idea; it was as if inspiration lay at some higher level somewhere. "I think I have it," he muttered. "How about *Isabel, she is one who, unlike me,/Does great good — but akratically?*"

He looked back towards her.

"You flatter me," said Isabel. "I wouldn't say I do great good."

"You do," he said firmly. "Anyway, the words of those seventeenth-century madrigals are often rather lovely, don't you think? Do you know another one by Thomas Morley, 'In Nets of Golden Wires'? That's the title. Isn't it beautiful? In nets of golden wires . . . Can't you see them?"

She could; the image was strong — and beautiful, like the idea of courtly love itself.

"That's about love," Jamie said. "We enmesh the people we love in a nest of golden wires. Or bind them to us."

Jamie remembered another of Morley's songs. This made him grin. "Morley wasn't always that high-minded," he said. "He wrote a real shocker. Or that's what it sounds like to the modern ear."

Isabel asked him what it was but he simply shook his head. "I can give you the title," he said, "but I can't tell you the words. I'm too embarrassed."

She waited.

"It's called 'Will You Buy a Fine Dog?' "

Isabel said that this seemed innocuous enough.

"It's what follows," said Jamie. "Singers can't bring themselves to sing it with a straight face."

Charlie had been silent, immersed in a picture book between the covers of which he had been placing small pieces of boiled egg. Now he looked up and said, "Will you buy a dog?"

"No," said Jamie. "I'm sorry, but we can't have a dog."

Charlie's face fell. "Why?"

"Because we have a fox already," said Jamie quickly, exchanging a glance with Isabel.

It worked. Charlie nodded.

"Not exactly true," mouthed Isabel. "However . . ."

"Brother Fox has us, rather than the other way round," said Jamie. "But anyway, occasionally you have to withhold the truth in order to keep the peace."

Isabel agreed, but only to an extent. She looked at her watch. If she was going to do what she'd planned, she would have to start doing it now.

"I'll cook tonight," said Jamie. "Venison with potatoes dauphinoise?"

Charlie looked up from his picture book. "Dauphinoise!" he exclaimed. "I love dauphinoise!"

Isabel and Jamie both smiled. "Middle-class kid," said Jamie.

"Middle class!" shouted Charlie with all the enthusiasm of a *tricoteuse*, or a scornful revolutionary. "What's middle class?"

"You," mouthed Jamie.

Isabel glanced at him disapprovingly, and then smiled.

She made three phone calls, the first of which was to Mrs Balvenie.

"I know that you can't give out telephone numbers," Isabel began, "but could you ask somebody to phone me?"

There was a short silence at the other end of the line. "Who?"

"When I was in the department the other day," Isabel continued, "I met one of the teaching assistants — Claire. I didn't catch her surname."

"Richardson," said Mrs Balvenie.

"Well, I wanted to get in touch with her, but I don't have her number."

Mrs Balvenie said that she would be happy to get a message to her. Then she asked, "What's it in connection with?"

Isabel did not answer immediately. She felt that what she wanted to speak to Claire about was none of Mrs Balvenie's business. The secretary was merely taking a message and had as little right to know its content as the deliverer of a letter had a right to demand to see what was in the envelope. She almost said, "It's personal," but did not, and chose the easier course. She did not need to make an enemy of Mrs Balvenie, and what difference did it make if the secretary knew?

"It's about a job," she said. "I'm hoping to find somebody to help me with the journal I edit." It was a simple and truthful explanation.

She heard Mrs Balvenie's breathing at the other end of the line.

"Mrs Balvenie? Are you still there?"

"Yes, I'm still here. You said it was about a job."

Isabel felt a growing irritation. "Yes, a job. Could you ask her to call me? I'll give you my number."

Mrs Balvenie's tone changed. Now there was a note of prickliness that seemed to flow down the line. "But Miss Richardson has a job already. She's a teaching assistant for Professor Lettuce." Lettuce's name was pronounced with awe, as if it were the name of some powerful deity; so might an ancient Greek mutter the name of Poseidon before boarding a ship.

"I know," said Isabel. "But that's not full time, is it?"

"It's very demanding," Mrs Balvenie retorted.

Isabel closed her eyes briefly. Again she struggled to keep the irritation out of her voice. She could not imagine that philosophy departments in universities were overly stretched. People worked hard, of course, but they would hardly be busy in the way in which policemen or farmers or neurosurgeons were busy. Yet there was a tendency — and Mrs Balvenie was clearly affected by it — to overstate the pressures of the academic life and to protest them to anybody who might show an interest. Lettuce would do that, she was sure; he was so busy that he had been able to manage only ten minutes for Isabel.

But she saw no point in arguing with Mrs Balvenie. "I'm sure the job's demanding," she said. "But even so, some people like a bit of variety in their working lives.

The job I'd like to offer her would certainly be interesting."

Mrs Balvenie absorbed this, and then came back with a further obstacle. "I'd have to ask Professor Lettuce about this."

Isabel drew in her breath sharply. "But this is nothing to do with him. This is between Ms Richardson and me. Just the two of us." And not you, Isabel thought; not you at all.

Mrs Balvenie was now the defender of the department. "Excuse me, but it does involve Professor Lettuce," she said. "He is the one who decides the teaching rota. He is the one who keeps the department going. What Miss Richardson does with her time is very much his concern, I feel I should point out." She paused. "And another thing: Professor Lettuce very much feels that teaching is at the core of the department's responsibilities and takes it very seriously. He would not like Miss Richardson to diversify her interests."

"Even in her spare time?"

Now a sliver of ice crept into Mrs Balvenie's voice. "Professor Lettuce asks — and gets — a thorough-going commitment to teaching on the part of his assistants. Miss Richardson is no exception to that. He wouldn't want her to take on anything that could eat into the time she devotes to her job. Teaching is Professor Lettuce's first priority."

Isabel's eyes widened. Lettuce was one of those academics whose ultimate ambition, she thought, was to arrange things so that he had no undergraduate teaching at all. "So," she began, "he must do quite a bit of teaching himself."

Mrs Balvenie's reply came quickly. "Not at all. Professor Lettuce would love to teach, but he's far too burdened administratively to do that."

Isabel wanted to laugh. "Of course."

Mrs Balvenie appeared to have relented. "I'll give you her number," she said. "I'm sure she'll sort it out with Professor Lettuce. They might be able to come to some sort of accommodation."

Isabel made a note of the number and the conversation came to an end. Immediately afterwards, she dialled the number she'd been given and left a message on an answering machine. Then came the third telephone call. This was to an au pair agency, Help When You Need It. The woman at the end of the line was calm and professional.

"We shall have no difficulty in arranging somebody for you," she said. "We have many young women who are only too keen to come to Scotland. They're well qualified, but can't find a job in their own countries."

There was a brief discussion about nationalities. "They all have their particular merits," said the woman. "But I have a soft spot for the Italians. Spanish girls — especially those from conservative households . . ." A note of apology crept into her voice. "By which I mean old-fashioned Catholic households, are very reliable and hard-working, but the Italians are . . . well, you know what the Italians are like. They have a certain sparkle."

"You choose," said Isabel. "I have no preference. Nationality is not the issue." Isabel had no prejudices of this nature; she liked the French, she liked the Italians, the Germans, the Spanish, the Dutch . . . In short, she liked people, and could not conceive of a mindset that viewed any large group, any nation, with suspicion or distaste.

The woman seemed surprised. "But it is!" she exclaimed. "National stereotypes are absolutely accurate. That's why they exist."

Isabel laughed. "Get me an au pair," she said. "That's all I ask."

"I have a young woman coming into the office in two hours' time," said the woman. "I'll take a closer look at her and then contact you if I think she's suitable."

"Perfect," said Isabel.

She did not feel so sure when she rang off. It was a major step inviting somebody into your house, and she had heard stories in the past of au pairs who had proved disastrous, including one who'd burned the house down and another who had seduced, and then run off with, the household's seventeen-year-old son. These were exceptional cases, she thought, and the odds against anything going wrong were very high. She had made a decision, and having done so she was looking forward to meeting the young woman upon whom, although she did not yet know it, Isabel was already counting.

CHAPTER
SEVEN

Claire Richardson returned Isabel's call shortly before twelve. The message had been passed on by Mrs Balvenie, she explained, who had said something about a possible part-time job on the *Review*. Yes, she was interested; more than that, she was sure that if a post were to come up she would most definitely want it. Isabel suggested they meet the following day; Claire could come to the house and they would talk about what the job entailed. By the time the conversation ended, Isabel was sure that she would shortly have a new assistant. The beneficial effect of this realisation was instantaneous: the proofs that were stacked up on her desk now seemed innocuous; the unacknowledged review copies of books, piled precipitously on a shelf near the window of her study, were suddenly no longer oppressive. Relief was in sight.

This made it easier for her to shut the study door behind her and spend a good two hours with Magnus, some of this time in the garden, where Magnus liked to crawl on the grass. He seemed to have a clear idea of where he was going, heading for a flowerbed from which Isabel would snatch him just in time to prevent his disappearing into the undergrowth.

Shortly before two, with Magnus now consigned by Grace to his afternoon nap, Isabel left the house and made her way to the deli in Bruntsfield Place. Cat was on the verge of embarking on her trip to Fife, and managed only the briefest of conversations. Eddie was busy with a customer who was having great difficulty in deciding between black and green olives, and had launched into a long tale of a trip to Tuscany during the olive harvest.

Isabel found a freshly laundered apron, tied it about her waist, and began to clean the chopping boards. When Eddie had finished with the olive customer — who had decided on a mixture of black and green olives — he gave Isabel an account of what he thought they needed to do. Cat had started to sell soup, and although most of this was bought in the hour or so before lunch, there were still customers who liked to take it home with them for their evening meal. The soup, which was cooked in two large pots in the kitchen at the back of the deli, needed to be replenished; if Isabel would look after the counter, he could get on with peeling potatoes and cutting leeks for their popular leek and potato broth.

Trade was brisk for half an hour or so, and then tailed off. This was the mid-afternoon lull when things would be so quiet that Isabel would be able to prepare herself a cup of coffee and drink it at one of the tables, perusing that day's copy of the *Scotsman* newspaper. She liked their crossword, and would invariably gravitate to it after she had read the letters page, her favourite section of the paper. The *Scotsman* was currently hosting a correspondence on taxation; the tempers of the readers had clearly been raised by the Scottish government's latest proposals on income tax levels. The rich were to escape largely unscathed, those who were not quite so rich were to be expected to shoulder more of the burden, while those who were struggling to make ends meet would find themselves slightly better off. This annoyed some correspondents, who believed that the rich should be taxed at such a level that they were no longer rich — an understandable position, as long as one accepted that the rich had no real entitlement to their money and their very existence was an unacceptable affront to those who were even slightly below them on the financial scale. But there were those who wrote to the newspaper to point out that if the rich were taxed excessively, then they might leave the country, rich people having a nose for fiscal hostility. "And if they go," one correspondent wrote, "then the taxes they used to pay will no longer be available to the exchequer, and the government will then be worse off than before." To which another had simply replied, "Good riddance — who needs these people anyway?"

Isabel read these letters with amusement. She liked the names of the correspondents — and the addresses they gave at the ends of their letters. There was a Mr George Henderson McLaren, a tireless correspondent, who often wrote to the editor on subjects of a political or economic nature. He lived in a house called *Tigh na Mara*, which meant "House by the Sea" in Gaelic but which was located, the final line of the address revealed, in Pitlochry. This was as far from the sea as it was possible to be in Scotland, and there was no possibility that even the most long-sighted person could get a glimpse of the coast from where Mr George Henderson McLaren lived. Then there was Mr Archibald P. Raeburn, who wrote from 29 Hogget Road, Auchtermuchty. This was a very strange address, Isabel felt: a hogget was a young sheep that had not yet been sheared. Why would a road be named Hogget Road? And then there was the name of the town itself, which had an almost music-hall ring to it — if one wanted to imagine an archly Scottish small town, expressing every cliché of the national identity from shortbread to haggis and kilts, then Auchtermuchty would be a name one might choose. And yet Mr Archibald P. Raeburn was interested in the affairs of the United Nations, and frequently contributed to the *Scotsman*'s letter columns on the issue of world government. Without world government, he suggested, we were doomed, and this belief led him to end each of his letters with the observation that time was running out. Isabel smiled each time she read one of his letters — he was silent on the subject of taxation, as it happened — but even as she smiled at the sheer predictability of his letters, she realised that he was probably right. Time *was* running out in so many respects — for our tenancy of a world that we were despoiling at an unsustainable rate as well as for the survival of our species in the face of nuclear proliferation. Obviously, this was evident from Hogget Road, Auchtermuchty, but not necessarily appreciated in the centres of world power. How frustrating it must be, she thought, for Mr Archibald P. Raeburn to know this and yet to be powerless to do much about it.

She put down her paper and mused for a moment. She wondered what Mr Archibald P. Raeburn looked like. He was likely to be middle-aged, she felt, as few people under forty believe that time is running out. He was probably retired, because people who wrote regular letters to newspapers needed time to compose them. He would also be argumentative, and would hector those who disagreed with him. He would be well known in Auchtermuchty — what is known in Scotland as a *kenspeckle* character — but people would take care to avoid him in the street.

The front door of the deli opened, jolting Isabel out of her daydreaming. A well-built man, somewhere in his late twenties and with a shock of sandy-coloured hair, had come into the deli. He looked about him for a moment and then walked past Isabel towards the door that led to the kitchen.

She rose to her feet. "Excuse me," she said. "Can I help you with anything?"

He turned round and looked at her. She noticed the bone structure first — the high cheekbones — and then she saw that his eyes were an almost tawny colour. And with that she knew immediately.

"Looking for Cat?" she asked.

He hesitated for a moment before he replied. She saw him looking her up and down, in some sort of quick appraisal, and it disconcerted her. Then he said, "Yes. Is she here?"

Isabel rose to her feet. "No," she said. "She's gone over to Fife on business. I don't think she'll be back this afternoon."

She watched him as she spoke. There was something about him that was deeply alluring, an energy that manifested itself in his demeanour. It was animal, she decided: pure animal. And then it dawned on her what this young man looked like: he looked like a lion. It was the hair — that was a mane, just like the mane of a lion — thick, profuse, framing the face like a halo, and precisely the colour of a lion's mane.

He must have noticed her stare, meeting her gaze as he looked back at her, his expression mildly challenging. It was a look, she realised, that people who were used to being stared at — people with some sort of disability or peculiarity of appearance — gave back to those whose eyes they met. This flustered her, and she said, "I'm Cat's aunt, by the way. Isabel."

This brought a smile of recognition, and now she saw his teeth. They were brilliantly white, and even, but once again they made her think of a lion. These were teeth that could bite.

"My name's Leo," he said.

It was only with the greatest effort that Isabel stopped herself from laughing. Leo. It would have been impossible to invent this situation; here was a man who had the mane of a lion, a lion's eyes, and a leonine physiognomy, and he was called Leo.

She raised a hand to her mouth and coughed. It was the only thing to do, the only way of stopping an eruption of laughter.

"May I make you a cup of coffee?" she asked. "It would be nice to have a chat."

Leo nodded. "I can't stay too long," he said. "But yes, that would be great."

She struggled with the accent. Leo was not Scottish, and he did not sound very English either. Australian? No, there were none of the characteristic rhythms of an Antipodean accent.

"If you take a seat," she said, "I'll ask Eddie to look after the counter."

She found Eddie in the small kitchen at the back of the shop. He was stirring a large pot of soup.

"Can you leave that to simmer on its own?" she asked.

Eddie nodded. "I like to stir it well," he said. "Lumps form if you don't."

"Cat's man is here," she whispered. "I'm going to make him a cup of coffee. Could you look after the counter?"

Eddie put aside the spoon he was using to stir the soup. Putting the lid on the pot, he shifted it to the side of the oven-top ring. "I'm coming," he said. "I want to get a good look at this guy."

Isabel returned to the counter where she prepared a fresh cup of coffee — decaffeinated this time — for herself and one for Leo. Then she took these over to the table where Leo had seated himself. Eddie in the meantime had installed himself behind the counter from where he cast the occasional furtive glance in Leo's direction.

Isabel sat down. "Have you and Cat known one another for long?" It was an innocuous question, but no sooner had she uttered it than she thought that it sounded too intrusive; she did not want their conversation to sound too obviously like an aunt's attempt to find out about her niece's suitor. And yet that was exactly what this was, she thought; there was no disguising the fact that she wanted to find out as much as she could about this young man in the space of the twenty minutes or so in which they would be in one another's company. Cat enjoyed keeping her cards close to her chest, and Isabel could never rely on her to provide much information about her private life. Well, here she was in the company of Cat's latest man and able to steer their conversation in whatever direction she chose. She could not miss the opportunity.

Of course she would try to be tactful. She had heard of two aunts — less restrained aunts — who had deeply embarrassed their niece by taking photographs of a boyfriend brought to just such an initial meeting. No sooner had the boy arrived than one of the aunts sprang to her feet and took a photograph of him. She would not be that unsubtle . . .

He did not seem to mind the question. "Two months," he said. "Ever since I came to Edinburgh. We met in the gym."

The reference to the gym was a detail that she would have got around to eliciting, but she was pleased it had come out so quickly. She knew that Cat used a gym from time to time, and of course a gym would be just the right place for her to meet the sort of men she preferred — fit, sporty men with strong physical appeal.

"I must get to the gym one of these days," Isabel said. "I used to go, but somehow I let it slip."

"That happens," said Leo.

Isabel took a sip of her coffee. She was still not sure about the accent. He had talked about coming to Edinburgh, though, and this gave her the opportunity she needed. "Where were you before?" she asked.

"Kenya," he said. "That's where I was born, actually."

"Ah. I thought you might have been Australian. But Kenya . . ."

"Our family is Scottish years back, you see," Leo continued. "Two generations ago, but these things linger. My grandfather went to Kenya in 1950. Just before Mau Mau. I went to school in South Africa — in Cape Town. Then to university in Scotland, in Aberdeen. Estate management and a bit of chemistry on the side."

"An interesting combination."

"I'd always loved chemistry."

She asked what had happened after that. "Back to Kenya," he said. "My father has a ranch up in the Laikipia Plateau — up north. But what really interested him was hunting. He and my grandfather were great hunters. He organised hunting safaris in Tanzania and he wanted me to run the ranch while he concentrated on that."

"Why Tanzania?"

"Because they still allow it. Hunting big game in Kenya was banned years ago."

Good, thought Isabel.

Leo raised his cup of coffee to his lips. He watched Isabel over the white foam of the cappuccino. "You disapprove?" he asked.

She hesitated, but only for a few moments. "Yes, I do. I don't understand the attraction — I simply don't."

He said nothing.

"It's ghastly," she went on. "There was a photograph in the papers recently of some hunter — an American, I think — who had shot a lion in Africa. There was a row because the lion was a special one that had been given a name, and had some sort of transmitter around his neck."

Leo nodded. "I read about that."

"And then you see these pictures of men standing beside their victims, grinning, and the poor animals are lying sprawled out on the ground. Whenever I see things like that it disgusts me. It simply disgusts me. Some beautiful creature — a lion or whatever — has had its life snuffed out by a grinning bully . . ."

Leo nodded again. "Yes," he said simply. "It's horrible. It sickens me too."

She was relieved; she was worried that she had become too strident in her condemnation and would have offended him. Perhaps he sees things from the point of view of the lion, she thought; perhaps he empathises with the lion because he looks so leonine.

"Did your father . . ." She left the question unfinished.

"Did we disagree? Yes, we did. He knew what I thought about hunting, but he wasn't going to give it up. He needed the money, apart from anything else. He took wealthy visitors down to Tanzania and they paid thousands of dollars for every so-called trophy they got."

"It must have been hard for you," said Isabel.

"Sometimes. But most of the time we agreed to disagree. Once I'd finished in Aberdeen I went back to Kenya and ran the ranch for him. We agreed not to talk about the hunting side of things. Some of his clients came and stayed on the ranch before he took them down south. I had to be polite to them. Sometimes it was difficult."

"I can imagine," said Isabel.

"But you have to live and let live in Africa," Leo went on. "If you start taking a high moral tone you pretty quickly hit a brick wall. You'll have no friends and you won't be able to do anything. Everything's corrupt."

Isabel glanced at her watch. There was more to find out, and she had only ten minutes left. "Then you came back to Scotland?" she said.

"Yes. I came back two months ago."

"You'd had enough of running the ranch?"

"In a way," he said. "But it was a bit more complicated than that. The ranch had been invaded by Samburu pastoralists. They're local people up there, and they resented the fact that the land was owned by ranchers who had thousands of acres and who were also white — foreigners in their eyes even if some of them were born there. You can understand it. They've overgrazed their own lands and they see good grass on the other side of the fence. They saw us as interlopers — on the land that had belonged to them in the past."

"So you gave up?"

"I did. My father still has a manager who tries to run the place, but the grazing's been pretty much destroyed."

Isabel waited to see if he had more to say about Kenya, but he seemed to have gone quiet. She looked at his arms — his shirt-sleeves were rolled up, as it was a warm day. There was no sign of a tattoo. She decided to be direct.

"I heard that you were a tattoo artist."

For a few moments Leo looked puzzled. "Me? A tattoo artist?"

She felt a surge of relief. Eddie had been wrong.

But then he said, "Oh, yes. I share a flat with a tattoo artist. He has a studio down the road. He's called Chris. But he's the tattoo artist, not me." He paused. "I sometimes watch the shop for him when he's busy in the back room doing a tattoo. He doesn't like to be disturbed, and so I sit in the front and deal with any new customers. I show them the design books and we discuss what they want. But I don't know how to do tattoos — that's an art, you see."

"Of course."

"Then Chris comes and talks to them when he's finished doing the business in the back."

Isabel smiled. That explained everything. Eddie had fallen into the trap of reaching a conclusion based on deceptive evidence. Not everybody who sat at a desk in a tattoo parlour was a tattooist. Nor, on the same grounds, could one assume that a woman serving behind a delicatessen counter knew nothing about philosophy.

"Do you like tattoos?" asked Isabel.

"Love them," said Leo. He looked at her wryly. "I take it you don't."

Isabel looked away. "And yet you don't seem to have any."

"How do you know?" he asked. "You can't tell just by looking at somebody's arms. You'll find tattoos in surprising places."

"Of course."

Isabel had long since come to the conclusion that any meeting between people, if it was to lead to anything more than a passing relationship, required a certain willingness — right at the outset — to accept the other for what the other was. If, at the beginning, a fundamental difference of opinion appeared, further attempts at friendship, or even acquaintanceship, might flounder. Thus the lion did not begin his relationship with the lamb with a loud — and hungry — roar; nor did the pacifist cosy up to the militarist with a protestation on the folly of war; nor the authoritarian to the libertarian with a paean of praise for strong government. Isabel sensed that she and Leo were from different places — in the metaphorical sense — and that tattoos were probably high on the list of things that divided them; she knew that, and she knew that the conversation should be steered into bland waters, but to leave the subject alone would be a victory for tattoos, and she did not wish to concede. That was the trouble with being a philosopher, she sometimes told herself; you argued points that did not always need to be argued.

Leo was not ready to move on either. "What's wrong with tattoos?" he asked. There was no truculence in his tone, but the challenge was there.

"Why disfigure the human body?" asked Isabel.

"It's not disfigurement," Leo replied. "It's adornment — aesthetic enhancement."

She thought the expression "aesthetic enhancement" seemed alien on the lips of a man who looked like a lion. But then she went on to tell herself, I should not think that: it's condescending; it implies that this man from a world of Kenyan skies and big-game hunters has no *right* to express views on aesthetics.

She tried to sound conciliatory. "I suppose you're right. We adorn ourselves with clothing, jewels, and so on. Perhaps tattoos are just a version of all that."

He said, "Exactly." She noticed that he clipped the *a* so that it became an *i. Exictly.* It was how the white tribes of southern and eastern Africa spoke.

"And yet," Isabel continued, "the point about a tattoo is that it's permanent. You can take your clothes off, but you can't get rid of a tattoo, can you?"

"They can be removed," Leo said. "Didn't you know that?"

"Yes, but at what cost?"

"It's not all that expensive," Leo said. "They use lasers."

That was not the cost that Isabel had in mind. "There's a physical cost, you know. Scarring and so on."

He shrugged. "It's a trade-off. It's like riding a motorbike. Sure, there's a risk that you'll get hurt, but you weigh that against the pleasure."

No, thought Isabel, that was different. Utility against cost was not the issue here — it was change of mind that mattered. "People regret their tattoos," she said. "You get them done when you're twenty and then you find you don't like them when you're forty — or even thirty. That's the real problem. People think their tastes won't change, but they often do."

Leo was listening, but she could tell that he was uncomfortable. She could have left it there, but she persisted. "We all change, you know. What we like, what we believe in — all of that changes. That's why so many people regret their tattoos. They grow up. What you . . ." — she was aware that he knew she was talking about him — ". . . what you like right now may not be what you're going to like when you're forty."

She could tell that she had gone too far; it was the worst of all arguments to use with somebody younger than oneself: *you'll grow up*. People did not like to be told that, she thought, because we all think that what we are now is what we shall be tomorrow. That was clearly false — but we all believed it.

Leo looked at his watch, not surreptitiously, as one does when one is enjoying oneself and does not really want to be elsewhere, but overtly, as if to underline the ending of a meeting. Isabel realised that there was nothing she could do to change the mood that had developed, and that she herself had created. Leo was lost to her, as most of Cat's boyfriends had been lost.

"Of course," she said. And then added lamely, "I'm sorry we seemed to disagree just after we found we both thought the same about hunting."

It was a late coda to a conversation that had been largely in the wrong key, and all that Leo said as he stood up was "Exictly".

Eddie had been watching, and, Isabel suspected, trying to listen too. Now, as Leo closed the deli door behind him, he came over to Isabel's table and sat down opposite her.

"Well!" he said. "Did you see his eyes?"

Isabel nodded. "They're a strange colour, aren't they?"

"And his hair?" Eddie went on.

"He's called Leo," said Isabel. "You know what that means in Latin, Eddie?"

"Leonard?"

Isabel smiled. She wanted to hug Eddie. She wanted to mother him. She wanted to take him home and read to him to make up for all the things that nobody had bothered to teach him in his young life. "It means lion."

Eddie's eyes brightened. "As in the sign of the zodiac?"

"Yes. As in the sign of the zodiac."

"I'm a Pisces," he said. "My birthday is on the eighteenth of March."

Isabel made a wiggling motion with her left hand; the motion of a fish in water. "So, you're a fish."

Eddie laughed. "I had a magazine that told me all about Pisces. It said that we're compassionate."

Isabel nodded. "Which you are."

"It also said that we're no good at business. It said that we're too sensitive to take charge of a business."

Isabel looked away. The problem with astrology was that it was complete nonsense, but it was a nonsense that every so often would, by sheer chance, get it right. It was rather like the apology for the entirely broken clock: twice a day it would tell exactly the right time.

CHAPTER
EIGHT

When Isabel returned to the house that afternoon, Grace told her that Patricia had called to invite Charlie to Albert Terrace the following day. She had suggested that he go there immediately after nursery school and should stay until seven. Grace was invited too; Patricia said that there was plenty for them to talk about. They could take the children for a walk and perhaps drop in for coffee somewhere. Grace said that she would be willing to take him, but there was something that was making her feel uncomfortable. It was an unusual invitation.

"I don't know if I'm imagining it," Grace said. "I just feel that there's something not quite right."

"I'm not surprised you're not sure about it," said Isabel. "Frankly I find Patricia a bit pushy."

Grace frowned. "I know what you mean," she said. "She's one of those people who seems very keen to be your friend." She paused. "That sounds odd, I know — why shouldn't somebody want to be your friend? It's just that there are times when you want things to progress a bit more gradually."

"Natural reticence," said Isabel. "That's what we're talking about. None of us likes to be overwhelmed.

Friendship is a bit of a dance, isn't it? You stand back from one another, look one another over, and then make the first moves. But those moves are usually cautious, aren't they?"

Grace agreed. "I like things to develop slowly. You see somebody a few times and then you decide. You don't jump in with both feet right at the beginning."

"No," said Isabel. "You don't." Then she added, "Or, most people don't. There may be some who do." She paused. There was something else that she wanted to ask. A play date that ended at seven was unusual. Not only was that four whole hours, but seven in the evening was half an hour beyond Charlie's bedtime. Allowing time to get back from Albert Terrace — even if it was just around the corner — would mean that he would probably not be fed, bathed and tucked up in bed much before eight.

Isabel asked Grace how she had replied to the invitation.

"I accepted." Grace's tone was sheepish. "I had to. I didn't know what to say."

"'No' would have done fine," said Isabel.

Grace looked at her reproachfully, and Isabel immediately apologised. "I'm sorry, Grace. I didn't mean it to sound like that."

Grace looked down at the floor. "You often don't think of what you need to say until much later."

"No, you're right. You don't. And I probably would have done the same as you."

Grace kept her eyes on the floor. "There's something about her that makes it hard to stand up to her. I don't know what it is, but there is."

Isabel spoke soothingly. "No, neither do I. But it's there nonetheless. There's something wrong about that woman. Something . . ."

Grace looked up. "Something dishonest?"

"Perhaps," said Isabel. "Perhaps that's it."

Grace remembered something, and smiled at the memory. "I had an uncle — he was married to my mother's sister, my aunt. So, he was no blood relation. He came from the Western Isles — South Uist, in fact."

Isabel had been there years ago, as a student, to stay with a friend whose family owned a cottage on the island. The name was enough to bring that back: the smell of the peat fire, the late light of the summer evenings, the sea lochs that fingered into the land from the green sea; the sheepdog who slept on her bed and woke her in the morning when the first noises drifted through from the kitchen.

"My uncle had a very strong sense of smell," Grace went on. "He was famous up there for being able to smell whisky, they said, from half a mile away. He said that the smell travelled on the wind and he could pick it up from there."

"A considerable talent," said Isabel.

"Yes. But he also said that he could smell lies. He said that you could blindfold him and he would still be able to tell whether somebody was telling the truth just by sniffing at the words as they hung in the air."

For a few moments, Grace remembered him: Uncle Hector, who would stand by his sheep fank on the island and turn his face to the wind. Then he would sniff at the air — that air of the Scottish islands that is laden with the iodine of the seaweed, and the fish landed on the pier, and the salt of all the seas, and he would say *The wind is in the north and I can smell them — somebody is telling awful lies up in Lewis. I can smell it.* And the children would laugh, but would be secretly afraid that he would turn to them and say that their lies — small, childish lies about the unimportant this and that — were on their coats, biblical stains that he could detect and reveal.

"An even more considerable talent," Isabel remarked. "Think of the job opportunities. Insurance investigations, police work, journalism . . ."

"As children we were frightened of him because we worried that any fibs we told would be sniffed out by our uncle."

Isabel laughed. "But did you inherit his talent?"

"No," said Grace. "And yet when it comes to Patricia, I get a whiff of something. I don't know exactly what it is, but it's a whiff of dishonesty. There's something about her that doesn't quite ring true."

"I can't sniff things out," said Isabel. "And yet my nose is telling me the exact same thing here." She looked at Grace, who had forgiven her now — a fact she could deduce by the very same faculty of intuition that told her there was something not quite right about Patricia. There were people, she knew, who trusted their noses, which of course meant their intuition, for guidance on just about everything. This could work, and could be plausibly defended — there was a school of thought in ethics that put our intuitive moral sense right at the heart of any decision as to what was right or wrong — but it also had its opponents, who regarded it as a silly, almost thoughtless dead-end street. If people said "I think this is wrong" just because they *felt* it was wrong, then morality became a matter of subjective individual preference. And that shut down debate quickly enough, thought Isabel. If all we had to think about was our intuitive sense, then she could close down the *Review* because there was no point in discussing any of the issues it explored — that, at least, would lighten her load in life.

But the most devastating argument against ethical intuitionism was that it relied on experience for its justification. Our intuitive beliefs, it said, came from our experience of the world; but what was experience but observation, coupled with some reflection on what we experienced? That reflection was morality; that moment of thought was the foundation stone of everything — of Aristotle, Kant, Hume, of all of them. Intuition was the impulse buy; reflection was the considered purchase.

Grace was staring at her now. Grace knew her so well, and was familiar with these short absences when Isabel seemed to be drifting off in thought. "What are you thinking about, Isabel?"

Isabel thought: I could tell Grace that I was thinking about how intuition comes from experience, and experience involves observation and thought, but she

116

knew that this would simply annoy her housekeeper. Grace was an intelligent woman, but she rapidly became impatient with philosophical speculation; she knew what was right and what was wrong, she had said on more than one occasion, which meant, of course, that Grace was an ethical intuitionist without ever having described herself as such. Isabel smiled, remembering those lines from Molière's *Le Bourgeois gentilhomme*, where Monsieur Jourdain is delighted to discover that he has been speaking prose all his life.

"You're smiling," Grace accused her.

"You're right," said Isabel.

"About what?"

"About there being something not smelling right. That woman wants something. Or is she hiding something?"

Grace shrugged. "Yes, but what?"

"I have no idea," said Isabel.

With the children in bed, Jamie went off to his music room. It was Isabel's turn to cook dinner, and she was preparing that simplest and most satisfying of stand-bys, a fish pie. This she would make in double quantities, with the result that even after she and Jamie had had a helping that night, along with peas — which Isabel believed were the only vegetable that belonged completely and unconditionally to fish pie — there would be enough left over to provide a light lunch the following day, and dinner for both boys.

She had bought strips of monkfish from the fishmonger in Bruntsfield. It had been lying on a slab, ready prepared, alongside a large and reproachful-looking black-skinned fish that was still whole, still glistening with what might have been the water from which it had been plucked. She looked at this fish, which stared back at her with outsized round eyes, and imagined its life, somewhere down in the depths of the North Sea, no doubt content in its dark fastness, until it was suddenly brought up to the light, and to the air that spelled death for fishkind. The thought disturbed her, and she concentrated on the monkfish. That, at least, no longer looked like a living creature, and could be thought of in pie terms.

Now it was further transformed, placed in a dish, covered in potato, doused in white sauce, and was ready to be placed in the oven. She washed her hands, set the table with knives, forks, and water glasses, and then joined Jamie.

"I'm not disturbing you, I hope."

He looked up from the piano. "Not really." That meant yes, but was a polite way of saying it.

She sat down on a stool near the piano. "What are you playing?"

He grinned. "The piano."

"You know what I mean."

"Oh, what music? Well . . . This." He turned back to face the keyboard; a series of ascending arpeggios, easy on the ear, effortless. "But the problem, with that," he said, "is that we run out of room on the keyboard. We get this high . . ." He demonstrated. "And then we can go no further. So we have to come down." The notes descended, like falling water.

118

"Lovely," said Isabel.

"But not architecture," said Jamie. "Whims. Floating clouds. Streams. Not like Bach. Bach is a building, you know — a great edifice."

She agreed. She could envisage the intricate structures of Bach: blocks of stone delicately placed one upon the other, all connected with one another, all holding one another up.

He stopped playing. "Fish pie — I can smell it." He then continued with an emphatic chord. "That's what I think of fish pie. Roll it on."

Isabel opened her mouth to speak. Jamie played another few chords — a fanfare of sorts for what she was about to say.

"Sorry," he said. "I couldn't resist. Go ahead."

She told him what Grace had told her about Patricia's invitation.

Jamie applied the quiet pedal, and the piano was silenced. "Three until *seven?*" he said. "That's ridiculous."

"That's what I thought."

He shook his head. "Kids of that age get fed up with one another's company after half an hour," he said. "Put them together for four hours like that and they'll be crying their eyes out. They'll think they're going to have to spend the rest of their lives together."

"Grace accepted," said Isabel. "I'm not blaming her — it's difficult to turn down an invitation, especially when you have to say yes or no on the spot."

"But why seven?" Jamie mused. "You'd think that . . ." He stopped, and looked up at Isabel. "It's suddenly occurred to me. Yes. That's it."

She waited.

"Patricia is playing with a chamber orchestra at the moment. They're rehearsing in Edinburgh tomorrow — at the Queen's Hall. Tom told me." Tom was a violinist friend with whom Jamie kept in touch via a sporadic and often eccentric email correspondence. He thought for a moment. "Have I got it right? Yes, I'm sure I have. Tomorrow's the fifteenth, isn't it?"

"Yes."

"Then it's definitely tomorrow. And I know she's playing, because Tom said something about their viola player being in hospital with something or other. He mentioned her specifically. He said she was really good."

"You don't think he might have got his dates mixed up?" Isabel asked.

Jamie was adamant. "No. The fifteenth, because he wanted to meet me in the pub after their rehearsal and I couldn't because I'm teaching early evening on the fifteenth. It's in my diary."

They looked at one another, both of them astonished at the conclusion they were drawing.

"Do you really imagine she would do it?" asked Isabel.

"I don't really know her," replied Jamie. "Do you think she would?"

Isabel felt the back of her neck getting warm: witnessing effrontery had that effect on her. "The sheer nerve," she said. "Grace is being used as childcare. Unpaid too — or unpaid by her."

Jamie imagined how it would work. "Grace goes there, and then suddenly Patricia looks at her watch and says, 'Oh my God, I'm due at a rehearsal in twenty minutes.'"

Isabel took it up. "And then she looks at Grace and says, 'Do you mind terribly? They're having such a good time together.'"

"Yes," said Jamie. "And next thing she dashes off to the Queen's Hall with not a care in the world. Those rehearsals end at six-thirty, which would give her time to get back to Albert Terrace by seven at the latest."

They stared at one another wordlessly, sharing their distaste for the deception that they were sure they had just uncovered. Isabel broke the silence. "I'll ask Grace to call off."

"She may not like that."

"I'll ask her nonetheless."

The next morning, when Grace arrived at the house, she listened attentively as Isabel told her of the conclusion that she and Jamie had reached. "I think Patricia's planning to use you as unpaid child cover," she said. "She's going to be rehearsing this afternoon — Jamie is pretty sure of that."

Isabel had not expected what came next. Grace became animated as she recalled what had happened a few days earlier. "That's funny you should say that. I was there with Charlie, at her house, when she suddenly remembered a dental appointment. I said it was fine for her to go off — I could handle both boys. But she was away for almost three hours."

"Dental appointments don't usually take three hours," said Isabel. She thought that this must have been when she saw Grace in Bruntsfield with Charlie and Basil.

"What should I do?"

Isabel thought for a moment before answering. She was angry with Patricia and did not want to continue the new friendship. "We keep our distance. We cancel the play date."

"I can't cancel," said Grace. "I told her I'd be there."

Isabel reassured her that she understood. "No, I can see why you feel this way. I thought I'd ask."

Grace looked anxious. "You don't think I'm being cowardly?"

"I'd never think that of you."

"You don't think I'm frightened of her?"

Isabel threw up her hands. "Of course not!"

"Because I am . . . a bit."

Isabel sighed.

"You think I shouldn't be frightened?" Grace challenged.

Isabel was soothing. "No, definitely not. I just think it's a pity that she should have that effect on people. And I also think that we need to be very careful in how we handle this. We need to disengage, but we need to do that in a way that doesn't lead to a row." She paused before continuing. "You see, I think this woman is one of those people who would bear a grudge. She just might. And as a general rule, I think there's no point in making more enemies in this life than you need to."

"So?" asked Grace.

"So, go this afternoon — as planned. Do the babysitting, if that's what happens. But then, if she tries to make another arrangement, put her off. Say that Charlie needs to go to the doctor, or something like that."

"Lie?"

Isabel smiled. "Every week we get an article submitted on some aspect of truth-telling," she said. She gestured towards her study. "Half of the papers in there are about that. But there *are* cases where you just can't tell the truth and have to tell . . ." she held up a thumb and forefinger, barely apart ". . . to tell a tiny lie. That size."

"I agree," said Grace.

CHAPTER
NINE

Isabel had arranged for Claire Richardson to come to the house for coffee that morning. She would be working, as would Jamie, who was due to teach at the Academy; Charlie would be at nursery and Grace had agreed to take Magnus for a session at a playgroup called Friend Time.

She had been careful not to describe the meeting as an interview, referring to it as a casual chat, an opportunity for Claire to take a look at the position she had mentioned. "Actually," said Isabel, "calling it a position is perhaps a bit grandiose. It's really just a part-time job; a position suggests . . ."

Claire grinned. "A title? An office?" She paused. "A desk and chair?"

Isabel relaxed at this friendly response to her words. They were standing in the entrance hall of Isabel's house, and Claire was still wearing her raincoat; a summer shower had swept in from the west, but had not lasted more than a few minutes. Light patches of moisture extended across the shoulders of the mackintosh, and her hair, thick and blonde, was speckled with minute raindrops.

"You can have all of those," said Isabel, leading Claire through to the kitchen. "Except the office, perhaps. The *Review* is run from right here, in the house, and my study is the office. There isn't a spare one, I'm afraid, but it's a large room and there's a table at the far end that could be yours."

"It's more than I have at the university," said Claire. "I don't even have a seat there, as far as I know — or at least I don't have one that is exclusively mine. Others can use it, if they like."

"You share?"

Claire made a gesture that suggested resignation — or hopelessness. "There's a room set aside for the philosophy post-graduates. It's quite a nice room, as it happens, in Buccleuch Place. We look out at the back over the Meadows. There's a set of tennis courts there that you can see from the window."

"I know them," said Isabel. "When I was at school we sometimes played there."

Claire continued, "We had a Japanese post-graduate student last year who was, I think, desperately homesick. He stood at the window for hours on end watching people playing tennis down below. If there was a good match going on, his head used to turn from side to side — like the heads of people watching games of tennis do — rather like a metronome. This could go on for ten, fifteen minutes, and then the game would become less exciting and he would simply stare out without moving his head."

Isabel was struck by the poignant image. She pictured the Japanese student, unhappy in Scotland because it so clearly was not Japan, watching tennis. She wondered what had brought him to Edinburgh. Where did he live? Did he have friends? Were there other Japanese students at the university — there must be — with whom he could go off and drink tea and speak Japanese and converse in the way that a shared language allows — a conversation of private allusion and unspoken understanding?

"This poor young man," said Isabel. "What did he do?"

"Apart from watch tennis from the postgraduate room?"

"Yes."

Claire thought for a moment. "He was writing a thesis on the Scottish Enlightenment. It was for his own university back in Japan somewhere. He had been sent to Edinburgh for a year, to do further research on that. I think he rather expected to find David Hume and Adam Smith still wandering around; I don't know. He certainly looked disappointed."

Isabel remarked that people often feel they have to go to places in search of what used to be there — and don't always find it. "Pilgrimage, you see. Classicists go to Rome, to Athens — they always have. They're two thousand years late — more if you're going in search of Odysseus."

Claire thought that you would at least see the places the ancients had seen; that was something.

"Yes," said Isabel. "Circe's island, I suppose — or an island rather like it. Horace's farm — or somewhere

where Horace might have had a farm. That sort of thing."

Now, in the kitchen, Isabel gestured for Claire to sit down while she prepared the coffee. "We don't have to stay in here," she said. "We'll go to my study once I've made the coffee."

"I like kitchens," said Claire. "I work in my kitchen — I don't mean work in the cooking sense — peeling potatoes, et cetera — but actual work. Marking student papers and so on. I give them back covered in butter and marmalade. Well, not quite, but they do pick up the occasional stain."

Isabel confessed that the same thing happened with articles for the *Review*. She had spilt a glass of water all over one that had been printed on an ink-jet printer, with disastrous results. "I could have written back to the author saying that his paper was fine as far as it went — but go it did. All the ink ran and I couldn't read it. It was the only copy I had."

Claire's eyes widened. "Embarrassment!" she said.

"Yes. I had to come clean. I had to write to the author and ask him for another copy. I explained what happened. He sent another one immediately — that was before I accepted electronic submissions. He said that he hoped the dog wouldn't eat the new copy."

Claire laughed. "Dogs have done such damage to homework in their time, haven't they? Apocryphally, of course."

"But there must have been some dog, somewhere," Isabel said, "that actually ate some poor child's homework. The index case, as the epidemiologists would have it."

She poured the ground coffee into the cafetière. She was thinking of the Japanese student again. She saw the tennis courts — she had walked past them only last week; she saw the window above — one of the windows looking down from the old tenement block — and he was there at the window, standing slightly back, but touched by the slanting sun, illuminated in his unhappiness. One of the tennis players shouted; they were scruffy — four students, two young men and two young women; the young women wearing sandals, ill-shod for the court; the young men in shorts, their white legs showing that they were Scots, as yet unused to summer; all bad players, except for one of the boys, who was lithe and threw himself around the court with confidence.

She became aware that Claire was looking at her expectantly. "I'm sorry," she said. "I have a tendency to drift off a bit. I was thinking of that Japanese student, and you probably said something to me."

"I said: have you lived in this house for a long time?"

"Just about forever," said Isabel. "It was my childhood home. Then I went away, Cambridge, followed by a short time in the States. I came back not long before I inherited the house from my father. So it's pretty much the only permanent home I've ever known." She looked at Claire. She was oddly disturbed by her beauty. "What about you?"

"I come from Callander," said Claire. "You may know it."

Isabel did. Callander was the archetypical Highland town; the inspiration for any number of paintings of Highland Scotland. "Of course I do. Very pretty."

"That's the word for it: pretty."

"I don't use it in any demeaning way," said Isabel. "It's an attractive town."

"My parents ran a toffee shop," said Claire. As she spoke, she looked up at Isabel, as if to watch her reaction.

Isabel had to smile. Callander was just the place for a toffee shop, of all things; the toffee would be sold in tartan-edged boxes, with pictures of Highland cattle on the front. Summer visitors would buy these boxes in their thousands.

Claire returned the smile. "Yes, a toffee shop. I used to help during the summer months when people came on their way to the Trossachs. They bought toffee from us and then went on to a woollens shop down the street, where they bought tartan scarves and Rob Roy bonnets."

"And then?" asked Isabel.

"I made it to Glasgow," said Claire. "I think my parents had been secretly hoping that I'd marry a farmer's son from up the glen. In fact, I think they had the actual boy in mind, but there was no chemistry, even if I had been prepared to stay. He was called Robert. He used to stare at me in church on Sundays. He sat there and stared."

Isabel could imagine it. Of course the boys would stare. "Were you surprised?" she asked. She had not intended to ask the question; it slipped out, as questions that reveal what we are really thinking tend to do. This one was unfortunate: people who looked like Claire tended to be well aware of their looks and of the effect they had on others; some might be happy to talk about this, but others were embarrassed by the attention. Her unwitting comment would now reveal to which group Claire belonged.

It was as if the question had not been asked. Claire ignored it, continuing instead, "I discovered philosophy in Glasgow. I went there to study German and Spanish — I had done rather well at languages at high school — but I was able to take a minor subject in philosophy. I was bitten. I wanted to know more."

Isabel understood that. She remembered the first philosophy she had read — Plato's *Symposium* at the age of sixteen. That had determined the course of her life.

"So I changed degree courses and ended up doing philosophy. And then went for two years to Leiden, where I held an exchange fellowship. After that, I worked for a year and a bit in an investment firm in Edinburgh. I didn't like it, and applied to do my PhD with Professor Lettuce. I was lucky to get funding, but I did." She shrugged. "And that's me, I suppose."

The coffee was ready, and Isabel poured it. As she got the milk from the fridge, she asked about Lettuce. "You've enjoyed working with him? With Professor Lettuce?"

Claire did not hesitate. "Yes. Very much. He gives me a lot of his time."

130

Isabel looked into her coffee cup. Yes. Of course he would. *Uncharitable thought*, a voice within her said. So she told herself: why should Professor Lettuce not appreciate beauty as much as everyone else? Why should this appreciation not be free of sexual interest, as an appreciation of beauty could be? As in Roger Scruton's book on beauty, itself such a beautiful object that Isabel had once found herself kissing its cover, platonically. *Because that's highly unlikely*, retorted the voice. *Because Lettuce is Lettuce — and he's a man.*

"Now *that's* uncharitable," Isabel muttered internally; or thought she muttered internally.

"I beg your pardon?" asked Claire.

"Oh, nothing," Isabel said hurriedly. And made a silent resolution: do *not* engage in private dialogue. *Do not.*

She handed Claire her cup of coffee. "Shall we take these into my study?" she suggested. "That's where the *Review* happens."

She watched as Claire rose from her chair at the kitchen table. Botticelli, she thought; she might have stepped straight from his studio.

In the corridor, just as he was about to go into the kitchen, they encountered Jamie. The bassoon lesson he had been due to give had been cancelled, and he had come home. Thinking Isabel alone, as he came down the corridor he had started to tell her vociferously about his unreliable pupil.

"That boy Geoffrey Weir," he half shouted. "He's a real pain in the lower section of the bassoon. He cancelled ten minutes beforehand. Ten minutes. Man flu, or in his case boy flu . . ."

He stopped mid-sentence as Isabel and Claire emerged from the kitchen. Isabel introduced them. She was looking at Jamie as he was looking at Claire. She saw his surprise, and noticed as it turned to something else. It was the reaction, she suspected, that must greet Claire on virtually every meeting — nothing more than that, of course, but that very specific, momentary acknowledgement of beauty.

At lunchtime, preparing a meal of puréed carrots for Magnus, Jamie said to Isabel, "Is she going to take the job?"

Isabel turned the question back on him. "What did you think of her? Would you?"

"I hardly met her," said Jamie. "Just those few minutes in the corridor. I hardly had time to judge."

"No, I don't suppose you did," she conceded. "But what did you think, anyway?"

Jamie concentrated on the puréed carrot. "She's a bit of a stunner, isn't she?"

There had been tension; now this disappeared. Isabel laughed. "Yes, she is. I didn't think much about it when I met her the other day, but today . . . she looked different; it was more striking."

Jamie crossed the room to where Magnus, strapped into his high chair, was awaiting his lunch. "Carrots," he said breezily, trying to enthuse his small son. "Totally delicious carrots."

"Of course, her looks are neither here nor there," said Isabel.

"Of course not."

The first spoonful of carrot was presented, sniffed at, and grudgingly admitted.

"We talked quite a bit," Isabel continued. "I explained what the job would entail, and it seems to me that she'll be able to do it very well. She asked all the right questions."

"So that's it then," said Jamie. "I think you should take her on."

Isabel agreed. She was ready to offer the job, she said, but she had wanted to run it past Jamie first. "She'll be working in the house," she said. "You have to feel comfortable about it."

Jamie shrugged. "I've no objection. Although . . ."

He put down the spoon. Magnus had been distracted by his mug and was intent on dribbling it over his plate. Jamie, distracted too, did nothing to stop him. Isabel waited.

"With somebody who looks like that," he said, "there's almost a presumption that it's not going to be simple."

Isabel frowned. "In what way?"

"Well, good-looking people can be . . . how should I put it? Brittle? Selfish? Pleased with themselves? It's because they're used to people looking at them, fawning over them — they become dependent on it. They expect to get their own way. They expect their whims to be indulged."

Isabel thought about this. "Examples?" she said.

Jamie seemed taken aback. "You want me to give you examples?" he asked.

"Well, you've made a bit of a generalisation about good-looking people. Give me some examples." He himself, she thought, was the best counter-example, but he would never recognise that.

Magnus reached for the spoon and banged it on the table.

"I can't," said Jamie. "Not just now. And it was a passing thought. As long as you think she'll fit in, that's fine."

"All right," said Isabel. "Let's take her."

"Fine," said Jamie.

She watched him feeding Magnus. He was gentle with the boys, but there was still a masculinity about the way he handled them. It was different from the way in which a woman would do the same thing; a woman envelops a child, embraces it; a woman holds a child in such a way that reveals she will be holding it for a very long time, for years, in fact; a man holds a child — may hold it with affection and gentleness — in a way that indicates he is going to hand it back. It was one of those odd little differences that people did not see, but that Isabel had always noticed.

She left the kitchen and went to her study. There she typed a message to Claire to tell her that she had given the matter thought and the job was hers, if she wanted it. The terms would be as they had discussed; Claire would be paid at an hourly rate, on the understanding that there would be at least ten hours' work a week, reading proofs, corresponding with authors, and doing a preliminary sift-through of the constant stream of submissions that the *Review* received. She could choose the hours she wished to work, and Isabel would be as flexible as possible in order to fit in with her university commitments. An hour later Claire's reply came through. She was happy with everything Isabel suggested, and would start tomorrow, if that was not too soon.

"No time like the present," Isabel wrote back.

She sought out Jamie, who was entertaining Magnus in the music room.

"I've just offloaded half my burden in life," she announced.

He grinned at her. "Feel lighter?"

"Yes. And there's another thing: the au pair agency has phoned. They have somebody in mind. All I have to do is accept and she'll be ready to start next week."

"And are you going to accept her?"

"I already have," said Isabel.

Jamie raised an eyebrow. "You're not letting the grass grow under your feet, are you?"

"She's twenty-one and she's called Antonia," said Isabel. "She's Italian — from Reggio Emilia. She's studying at the University of Bologna but she's taking a year out. She wants to bring her English up to scratch."

"Good," said Jamie. "If she's Italian, she'll like small children." He bounced Magnus on his knee, and the little boy beamed with pleasure.

"Do you think we could ask Grace to babysit tonight?" asked Isabel.

Jamie looked surprised. "We aren't going out, are we?"

"I'd like to," said Isabel. "I'd like to celebrate. Dinner. Somewhere different. Perhaps at one of those seafood places down in Leith."

Jamie pointed out that Grace would have had a long day of it, with the lengthy play date in Albert Terrace. On the other hand, he could prepare a special meal for her and chill a bottle of the rosé wine she liked. She enjoyed babysitting, he thought.

Grace was doing the ironing upstairs. She would be happy to babysit, she said. And yes, some of that rosé would be very welcome. "Just a glass or two," she said severely. "I don't overindulge, you know."

"Of course you don't," said Isabel.

"Unlike some," added Grace.

Isabel looked puzzled. "Anybody in particular?" she asked.

"Oh, there are plenty of people in this city who drink far too much," said Grace disapprovingly. "And in Scotland as a whole."

Isabel agreed it was a problem. "I wouldn't press the rosé on you," she said.

"Oh no, I wasn't referring to myself," said Grace hurriedly. "And the Scottish government is doing its best to stop people overdoing things, but they have an uphill battle."

"On every front," said Isabel.

"I'll tell you something," said Grace, pressing the iron down firmly on the sleeve of one of Jamie's shirts. "I wouldn't be First Minister for all the tea in China."

Isabel laughed. "You'd make a very fine First Minister, Grace."

Grace looked pleased with the compliment. "I wouldn't do it, though. Not if they begged me."

"Very wise," said Isabel. "I wouldn't either."

Grace began to fold the shirt. "Where are you going for dinner?" she asked.

"There's a place called the Quayside," Isabel replied. "It's down in Leith." Leith was Edinburgh's port — a place of cobbled streets and of whisky warehouses, of grain merchants and chandlers, of frequent mists that rolled in from the North Sea.

"Leith," sniffed Grace. "I can't remember when I was last down there." She paused; the folded shirt was placed neatly on a shelf in the laundry room. "Be careful," she added, and then muttered under her breath, not for Isabel's benefit, but for her own, "Leith."

CHAPTER
TEN

"There's one thing you have to remember when it comes to lobster," said Jamie. "Never over-cook it. Many people do." He glanced over the table at Isabel, almost as if she might be the type to ruin a lobster through over-cooking.

They were examining the menu at the Quayside. Isabel was vacillating; she liked lobster, but sometimes found it a bit too sweet for her taste; she liked mussels, but was not sure how satisfying they would be — *moules marinière* were all very well, but they were soup, she thought, rather than a main course; and then there was sea bass, which could be just perfect, but was offered here with a caper sauce, and Isabel, prejudiced for some forgotten historical reason against capers, did not fancy that.

"They get very stringy if you cook them for too long," Jamie continued. "You find out the weight, and then you cook them according to that. It doesn't take long."

Isabel nodded. She was looking at an item further down the menu — a seafood platter for two people. The provenance of the food was set out in detail: the scallops, from the Sound of Mull, were hand-dived; the prawns came from the Isle of Skye, where they had presumably been happy enough; the smoked fish from Pittenweem, in the Kingdom of Fife.

Jamie had more to say on the subject of lobsters. "They don't have a central nervous system," he continued, "and so some people say they don't feel pain. I don't believe that. I think they must, because every creature needs a way of recognising danger. Otherwise they wouldn't survive."

"I'm sure they feel pain," said Isabel. "If they're cooked alive, they'll feel pain."

The discussion was deterring her from choosing lobster.

"That's why you should freeze them first," said Jamie. "If you put them in the freezer, that numbs them. It's more humane than putting them into the pot while they're at room temperature. Once frozen, they're unconscious. I hate the thought of that, but I know they deal with lobsters humanely here."

Isabel laid the menu aside. She had flirted with vegetarianism when she was younger, and it still held a strong appeal. But she had never taken the step of committing herself to it, and now it all seemed too complicated to her, as any rethinking of a fundamental position tends to be.

"I'm going to have sea bass," she said. "I'll ask them to do it without the caper sauce."

"Just with butter," said Jamie. "I don't see what's wrong with butter. There's no need to add anything else."

The waitress was hovering, and Jamie picked up the wine list.

"New Zealand?"

Isabel smiled. "Of course. Although, as this is a special occasion, I might go a little bit off-piste. Is there a Chablis?"

"There is." He signalled to the waitress and pointed to a wine on the list. "And half a dozen oysters too. Each."

"Delicious," said the waitress, noting the choice on her pad.

"Sinful," whispered Isabel. Oysters, like any self-indulgence, made her feel guilty; it was part of being Scottish, she thought — a tendency to disapprove of the sybaritic.

The waitress left, and Isabel said, "Have you ever known a waiter to express disgust at your choice? They say things like 'Delicious', as she just did, or 'Good choice', but you never hear them say anything critical."

"Not their job," said Jamie. "Waiters want you to feel good. Which is quite right, don't you think? They want you to enjoy yourself and come back."

"And yet that involves their having to say things they don't believe."

Jamie shrugged. "What job doesn't involve that?" He laughed. "Being pope?"

"I think it's clear enough that the Pope believes in what he says."

Jamie looked doubtful. "Most of the time, yes. But don't you think it possible that some popes have had their doubts? There must have been moments when they wondered whether there really was a God. They must have."

"Perhaps."

Jamie sat back in his chair. "Do you think the Pope goes out for dinner? To a restaurant, I mean. Do you think he sometimes says, 'I'm going to go out tonight and treat myself to a steak,' or whatever it is that popes like. Do you think he can do that?"

Isabel thought it unlikely. "He'd be pestered if he went to a restaurant. People would spot him and bring babies in for him to bless and kiss. His food would get cold." She thought of something else. "Or they might come and try to confess their sins. Imagine trying to work your way through a plate of spaghetti carbonara and somebody from a neighbouring table is trying to tell you about how he's been having lustful thoughts, or whatever it is he feels the need to confess."

Jamie's eyes lit up; he loved Isabel in fantasy mode. "So he sits there in the Vatican every evening, all by himself."

"I imagine he has plenty of people fussing round him," said Isabel. "And there are cardinals to talk to if he wants conversation." She pointed out that the current pope lived in a Vatican guesthouse. He must take his meals with other people staying there at the time; an admirable, democratic thing to do.

"And the Queen?" asked Jamie. "I suppose she's never been able to go out to a restaurant."

"Sometimes, I think," said Isabel. "But it can't be easy for her."

Jamie had an idea. "Perhaps very grand people get around the difficulty of going out by having people go out *for* them. Perhaps they say, 'Please will you go out and have a meal on my behalf?' Something like that."

Isabel laughed. "You may joke about that, but I read about an Indian maharajah who was so rich, and so grand, that he had somebody whose job it was to wear his jewellery for him. He had so much of it, you see. So the maharajah would appear, all bedecked in jewels, and then, walking a few paces behind him, would be the lackey wearing all the stuff that the maharajah couldn't pin on himself."

Isabel reached for a piece of bread. There was a bowl of olive oil, and she would dip it in that — a small treat, but a delectable one. Her hand moved, and then stopped. The door out onto the street had opened, and a man and a woman were coming in. The woman was Patricia.

They did not catch each other's eye. Isabel and Jamie were seated in an alcove, and there were several tables between them and the door. Patricia was looking in the opposite direction as she entered, but Isabel had a clear view of her. She saw her hand her coat to the waiter who had opened the door, and she saw her touch her hair, which had been dishevelled by the wind outside. Then she saw the man, who turned briefly in her direction. At first she noticed the jacket he was wearing, which was one of those raffish striped blazers that people wore to regattas; then she looked at his face.

Patricia and her friend were shown to their table. There was no direct view of this from where Isabel and

Jamie were, but once the other couple was seated, there was a mirror in a neuk on the other side of the room affording a view of their table. Patricia had her back to the mirror, but the man was visible enough.

"What?" asked Jamie.

Isabel leaned forward. She broke the bread roll and dipped a piece into the olive oil. "Patricia," she said, her voice lowered, although in the hubbub of the restaurant there was no need. "Over there. Look in that mirror."

Jamie looked. "That's her?"

"Yes," said Isabel. "Back view."

"She's had a busy day, then," said Jamie. "Rehearsal, then dinner. Just as well she had Grace to help her."

"Look at the man," whispered Isabel.

"You don't need to whisper."

"Just look at him."

Jamie stared at the image in the mirror. "Smart blazer," he said.

"Look at his face," said Isabel.

Jamie threw another glance at the mirror. "Freckles," he said. "Lots of them."

Isabel dipped another piece of bread into the olive oil. "You have your phone with you, I assume."

Jamie felt his pocket. "Yes, it's there. Why?"

"Could you take a photograph of the mirror? Pretend you're looking at emails. Nobody will notice."

Jamie frowned. "Isabel, what are you up to?"

A droplet of olive oil had fallen from the bread onto her chin. She dabbed at it with her napkin. "He's the image of Basil. You know, Charlie's friend — Patricia's son."

"So?"

"Please, just take the picture."

Jamie complied reluctantly. As he finished, the waitress appeared with the bottle of Chablis and the oysters. The wine poured, Isabel raised her glass. "To my new, stress-free life."

Jamie touched her glass with his. "Your new life will be stress-free as long as you don't get involved in things that don't concern you."

It was a familiar refrain in their marriage. Isabel helped people; it was what she did. Jamie knew that. He knew, too, that she found it difficult, if not impossible, to say no to a request from anybody who needed her help. He had urged her time and time again to be careful; the world was full of need and there was a limit to what one person could do. Isabel agreed; she knew that in theory we only had to do so much, and that it was reasonable for us to keep enough time and energy for our own projects. But that was the theory; in practice, it was much more difficult and her attempts to disengage from the world had all failed.

He tried again. "Don't get involved in Patricia's affairs," he said. "I thought you'd agreed that with Grace. You said that the two of you were going to keep her at arm's length from now on." He paused. "You did say that, you know. You told me yourself."

She listened, but did not respond directly. Instead, she said, "What if that man is Basil's father?" The possibility had just occurred to her. It struck her as outrageous, and yet . . .

144

Jamie sighed. "It's none of our business who Basil's father is."

But it is, thought Isabel, it simply is. The things that happen to people we know *are* our business. John Donne had said that; *every man is a piece of the continent* . . . the unfamiliar, seventeenth-century analogies were as true now as they had been when Donne uttered them. Isabel's voice took on the urgency of an appeal. "Just think . . . what if Basil Phelps, the organist Basil, is being made to pay for young Basil's upkeep in the mistaken belief he's the father?"

"That would be unfortunate," said Jamie. "But I suppose that sort of thing happens."

Isabel struggled to keep her voice even. "I know Basil Phelps," she said. "And so do you. We can't ignore this."

In her mind, that was enough to create the obligation to do something. And Jamie, after a moment's thought, came to the reluctant conclusion that she could be right. Basil Phelps was a much-appreciated member of Edinburgh's musical community. He was a mild man, who gave a lot of his time to various charitable causes. He played the organ free for young couples who were getting married on a budget. Last year he had undertaken a much-publicised organ marathon — six hours at the keyboard — for the city's homelessness appeal. He was widely liked.

"All right," said Jamie. "But what now?"

Isabel became calmer. "We enjoy our meal. But we'll have to think about it later."

145

Jamie wondered just what that meant. "You're going to go and talk to Basil Senior? You're going to tell him, 'We saw your ex-lover with a man who had freckles just like young Basil. We saw him in a restaurant and we have a photo to prove it'?"

Isabel had no plan, but made light of it. "Not necessarily," she said.

Jamie, who did not want to spoil the meal with an argument about involvement, decided to change the subject. The waitress was now ready to take their order. There was a crab salad starter that they both liked the sound of, and then there was the sea bass for Isabel and, after the briefest final indecision, the lobster for Jamie.

"Terrific choice," said the waitress.

They both kept off the subject of Patricia for the rest of the meal. Isabel stole an occasional glance at the mirror, but it had little to reveal, other than the sight of a man and a woman seated at a table in the warm light of the restaurant. They found they had much to talk about, including the new au pair, whom they had yet to meet. Isabel was planning her duties. She could take Charlie to nursery school, which would free both of them at a time of the morning that tended to be hectic anyway. There were various housekeeping tasks that she could take over from Grace — the ironing of Jamie's shirts, for instance, was a chore that Isabel thought Grace might willingly hand over.

"It might be a way of winning Grace round," Jamie suggested.

"If she needs to be won round," said Isabel. "You never know with Grace; she might take to Antonia."

Jamie had a strategy in mind. "The best way of getting Grace to endorse something," he said, "is to imply that it was her idea in the first place. That works, you know. Remember that business about my shirts being folded rather than left on the hanger?"

Isabel did remember it. It had been the cause of one of Grace's huffs; a period of painful silences as the shirts, pointedly and punctiliously folded, were left on the bed in silent accusation.

"I spoke to her about it," said Jamie. "I told her what a great system it was that she had introduced and how well it was working."

Isabel smiled at the memory. "She can't resist you. You walk on water as far as she's concerned."

Jamie was embarrassed. "Nonsense."

They returned to the subject of Antonia. Would she be expecting to cook for herself? Would she have to entertain her friends in her bedroom, or could she bring them into the kitchen? Could she use the living room whenever she wanted, or was that to be their private space?

Isabel felt that they should treat her as a member of their household — in the same way they would treat a long-term guest. "You can't tell your guests which parts of the house they can use," she said. "That would be rude, don't you think?"

"But most guests don't stay for a year."

"No, true. But . . ."

"I think we should feel our way through it," she continued eventually. "Let's see how it works out."

They reached the coffee stage, and it was while the waitress was serving it that Isabel noticed that Patricia and her companion were readying to leave. She signalled to Jamie with a movement of her head, and then, turning to the waitress, she said that they needed their bill and would have to go. Jamie was surprised, but Isabel was firm.

"I just want to see where they go," she said.

He rolled his eyes. "They'll probably get into a taxi. What's to see about that?"

"Just let me satisfy my curiosity," said Isabel. "Please."

Jamie gave in. He had sometimes said, jokingly for the most part, that Isabel saw herself as some sort of sleuth; now, it would seem she was proposing to follow somebody. She had never been that overt before. He decided to smile and join in. He was never going to change the way she was, and if she had got it into her head to follow somebody through the streets of Leith, then he would be unlikely to be able to dissuade her.

The waitress was quick with the bill, and Isabel had her card at the ready. Their finances were conjoint — a true marriage of funds — and it did not matter who paid. That most of the money was Isabel's had never been an issue; Jamie spent very little, anyway, and had to be encouraged by her to make what purchases he did.

"I take it everything was all right," said the waitress.

"More than all right," said Isabel. "But we really do need to be on our way."

She glanced in the direction of the door. The man had ushered Patricia out and was now halfway through the door himself. Isabel had left a coat with the waitress, who now retrieved it for her.

"Wait just a moment," Isabel whispered to Jamie. "Let them get out into the street."

Jamie grinned. "I feel vaguely ridiculous," he said. "Scottish *noir*?"

"Be natural," said Isabel, taking her coat from the waitress.

"And how exactly do you do that?" asked Jamie.

Isabel was not paying attention to what he was saying.

Jamie was suddenly taken with the absurdity of the situation. "Do you really think we should be doing this?" he muttered. "We're two grown-ups proposing to follow two other grown-ups out of a restaurant . . . and what for?"

Isabel continued regardless. "Right," she said. "We can go out now."

He followed her. One of the restaurant staff opened the front door for them; outside, even at ten-thirty at night, this far north there was still light in the sky although the streetlights, yellow and fuzzy, had flickered into life. The Quayside was on the water, and directly on the other side of the road was a small white-painted ship, now converted into a floating restaurant tied up at the quay. A man stood on the deck, slouching, caught in a beam of light from the ship's interior, smoking a cigarette. He raised a hand to Jamie and Isabel — a casual, unsolicited greeting — before stubbing out his cigarette, turning on his heel, and retreating down the ship's companionway.

Isabel looked about her. There were a few cars parked on the street, but no people.

"There you are," said Jamie. "They've jumped into a taxi. I thought they would. We can go home now."

Isabel looked down the street. When taxis came to the restaurant, they hovered outside the front door; that meant they could be seen from within. There had been no taxi since she had first noticed Patricia leaving; she was sure of that.

"I think they walked," she said. "They must have gone along there." The end of the street was only a short distance away. There it joined the road that crossed a bridge over the canal basin, leading, in one direction, to Granton and the Firth of Forth, and in the other, to the heart of Leith.

"Come on, Isabel," said Jamie. "Time to go home."

But she was not going to give up. "Let's just take a look up there," she said. "I'm sure we'll see them."

Jamie followed her reluctantly. "I don't know what you imagine we'll see," he said.

"Since they're on foot, I suspect he lives around here," she said. She could see that Jamie was not convinced, but she continued, "I'd like to know where they went."

"And then?"

"We could find out who he is. Anyway, come on."

He followed her reluctantly. "We could just ask the restaurant people," he said. "We could just say, 'Who were that couple?'"

"Restaurants don't give out that sort of information."

Jamie objected; sometimes Isabel gave rulings on matters on which she really should not pronounce. "How do you know?"

"I just know. Come on."

When they reached the junction, they looked up and down the wider street; there were a few cars — nothing much at this hour — but no people in sight.

"Strange," said Isabel.

"I told you: they must have taken a taxi."

Isabel insisted. "I don't think they did."

"Well, they can't have vanished into thin air."

Isabel hesitated. She decided that Patricia and her companion must have turned off this street onto one of the smaller streets that branched off on either side. But which way would they have gone — to the left, or to the right and over the bridge?

She turned to face Jamie. "I'm going to go off to the left," she said. "Can you go and take a look on the right. Over there — over the bridge."

Jamie bit his lip. "What's the point?" His voice was filled with resignation. "If I find them, then what? Walk behind them? With a straight face?"

Isabel remained calm. "Just see where they go," she said. "Then we'll meet back here."

She left it at that, and set off along the road to her left. She did not turn round to see whether Jamie was heading off in the other direction, but he was. He looked over his shoulder once he reached the bridge, and saw that Isabel had reached a corner and was about to disappear. He felt a momentary doubt, asking himself whether he should be meekly accepting being sent off on what was surely going to be an utterly pointless mission, or should be backtracking to join Isabel. Leith had a reputation for toughness — it was, after all, a port, and ports were not places you went wandering about late at night. He stopped, and turned. The street behind him was once again deserted. There was no sign of Isabel.

CHAPTER
ELEVEN

She hesitated. There was nobody about, and she was beginning to think that Jamie had been right in suggesting that Patricia and the freckled man had summoned a passing taxi. Unless they had been walking very fast, surely she would have seen them by now — assuming, of course, that they had come in this direction rather than make their way over the bridge.

She looked down the small side road. It was very much a byway — one of those unexceptional residential streets that cover wide swathes of Edinburgh and Leith with rows of nineteenth-century tenements. The centre of the city might be composed of elegant Georgian squares and crescents, but this was where most people actually lived — in these solid, stone buildings, with their shared doorways leading to four, sometimes five, storeys of flats. Here and there, from the façades of these dour buildings, light escaped from curtained windows; or music; or the sound of television in its persistent babble. A woman came out, dressed in a housecoat, her hands full of household detritus. She glanced at Isabel, no more than a glance, and then made her way to the communal rubbish bins before going back inside, slamming the stair door behind her, as if to make a statement.

The evening light had now almost faded away completely. The street was lit by streetlamps, but not very well, and there were pools of darkness along the pavement. Isabel began to walk down the street; she would go just as far as the next junction, she decided, and then, if she saw nothing, she would return. Her footsteps sounded on the stone, echoing against the walls of the tenements.

The flats at ground level had no gardens, but faced directly onto the street. A passer-by, then, walked directly past the front windows, and if there were no blinds or curtains, was able to see right into the living rooms. Isabel did this now, passing a window through which somebody's well-lit sitting room was on display. It was not a large room — these flats were very modest — and it was sparsely furnished. There was an easy chair, a sofa, and a table. There were several plates on the table and a jug of water. A television in a corner flickered its drama to a non-existent audience; nobody was there to watch. On the wall was a picture of a stag on a mountainside — a cliché of nineteenth-century Scottish art. Feeling guilty over the intrusion, she looked away and continued to walk.

A man got out of a parked car. He looked in Isabel's direction, and she stopped. He approached her.

He spoke before he reached her: "Hello, dear."

She stood quite still. This could be a polite evening greeting, or it could be something else altogether. Her mouth and lips felt dry as she struggled to respond. Eventually she managed. "Nice evening."

She started to walk again. The man stepped in front of her. Now there was no doubt in her mind that this was serious. She looked over her shoulder; the street was still deserted, apart from herself and this man from the parked car.

"You out for a walk?" the man said.

She looked at him. He was in his forties somewhere; dressed in jeans and a zipped-up windcheater. His voice was local.

"Going home," she muttered. It was the first thing that came into her mind, but if he thought that she lived near here, she reasoned, then it might put him off. One of these doors could be hers; behind one of these windows might be her family, her people.

The man was staring at her. "You sound very posh," he said. "Not from round here, I think." He leered at her. "Expensive, I'd say."

She moved to one side, hoping to dodge him, but he shifted, standing obstinately in her way. He reached out suddenly and gripped her arm. She felt the power of his grip through her clothing; there was shock in the unwanted contact, the assault.

"Don't be so stand-offish with me," he growled. "You people think you can pick and choose, don't you? You think you're too good for the average punter."

There was a slow-motion horror to her plight, but Isabel found that she was thinking clearly. She could scream; she could try to defend herself, kicking at whatever target presented itself; she could struggle to free herself and then run back towards the junction with the bigger road, along which cars would pass sooner or later. But then she thought that each of these entailed some risk; this man could easily overpower her, could clamp his hand across her mouth and silence her.

She thought quickly of strategies: de-escalation would give her time; humour him; play along, and await your moment.

She put on a coquettish voice. "No," she said. "I don't think that. And I'm no more expensive than the other girls." She surprised herself; at first she had no idea where the voice came from, but then she realised: it was the voice of Celia Macdonald, with whom she had been at school. Celia had been famous for her ability to flirt; boys loved it because she was so overt and undemanding; girls laughed at her, imitating her — just as Isabel was now — but seething with jealousy underneath. Celia Macdonald, whom she had not seen for how many years, who married an airline pilot at the first possible opportunity and who went down to live in England, in a small suburban house near Heathrow Airport, now came to her rescue.

He let go of her arm. "That's more like it," he said.

"My place is back there," she said. "Just around the corner. You can leave your car here — it's not far."

He was looking at her keenly. "No funny business," he said.

She forced a giggle; Celia once again. "Funny business? Not me."

"Okay," he said. "We can go there."

156

They started to walk. He was close to her, but did not touch her, and she wondered what his intentions were. Was he thinking of this as an abduction, or was it simply the way he handled transactions with the women who plied their trade in the darker corners of Leith? Isabel knew that this took place — everybody did, as there were regular articles about it in the *Evening News* — but thought it was confined to one or two notorious spots; she had not seen the name of this street, but she did not think it was one of them.

They passed a builder's skip, half filled with old plumbing and discarded wooden planks from a nearby renovation; somebody had added an ancient pram, its wheels buckled and its hood torn, and a slew of tins and bottles. Her eye fell on a length of twisted lead piping, wrenched from ancient plumbing; she could grab that and use it as a weapon, but he was between her and the skip and it would not work. De-escalation, she reminded herself.

"I've got some beer in the flat if you fancy it," she said. The offer came from Celia Macdonald, who made the word *beer* sound suggestive, such was her skill.

"Cannae drink," said the man. "Under the doctor."

It was a curious, old-fashioned expression, one that was rarely heard these days. When you were being treated for something, you were "under the doctor".

She turned to him. "Under the doctor? You all right?"

"My stomach," he said.

Celia Macdonald could be sympathetic. "That's a pity."

"Aye, well it means no drink for three months."

Isabel laughed. "Big party after that?"

She could see that he was smiling. He was more relaxed now, and she saw her opportunity. He had stopped because the lace on one of his shoes had come undone and he was bending down to tie it. She leaped forward, breaking into a run, throwing herself headlong down the street in the direction of the busier road. She screamed as she did so; a long, inarticulate siren of a scream.

He was quickly back up on his feet. He lunged after her and caught her easily, before she had managed to cover more than a few yards. Isabel felt terror overwhelm her as his hands fell upon her, grasping her arms, pinning them back painfully. She screamed again, and kicked wildly at his shins. He let out a roar of rage.

A door opened a short distance from where they were standing. It was the woman she had seen earlier — the woman in the housecoat. She took the scene in quickly, and came running towards them.

The man relinquished his grip.

"What's going on?" shouted the woman. "You — you all right, hen?"

The man took a step backwards.

"No," said Isabel. "This man . . ."

She gestured towards the man.

"A domestic disagreement," said the man. He took another step back and then turned on his heel and made his way back to his car.

Isabel was trembling. The woman put her arm around her. "Do you want me to call the polis?" She used the local pronunciation of *police*. Poh-lis.

Isabel shook her head. "No, but would you mind just walking me round the corner? My husband's back there."

The woman was peering at her. "Are you sure you're all right?"

Isabel wondered why she had turned down the suggestion that they call the police. She had spoken without thought, but now it occurred to her that the man was dangerous and she had a duty to call the police.

"The police . . ." she began. She felt confused. She had to tell the police about this, but she felt foolish. She should not have been there in the first place and she did not know what she would say to them. But that was not the point, she told herself; I am the victim here. *I am the victim.*

"Yes?"

The man's car now drew out from the kerb and shot past them.

"Too late," said Isabel. "He's away." Again, she said this without thinking.

"I'll shut my door," said the woman. "Then I'll come with you."

They walked slowly. Isabel felt her heart pounding within her. It was hard to believe that this had happened, right out in the open; was this what it felt like to be assaulted?

The woman said, "Sorry to ask, but what were you doing? Are you on the game?"

Isabel gasped. "No. No. I was . . . I was looking for somebody who lives round here — I think. Somebody whose name I don't know. A friend of a friend."

The woman looked interested. "Oh yes?"

"A man who's about forty, I should think — very freckled face. Freckles all over."

The woman responded immediately. "Archie? Archie McGuigan?"

"He has a very freckly face," said Isabel. "You can't miss him."

"No," said the woman, "you couldn't miss Archie. He lives just back there." She pointed to the far end of the street.

"That must be him," said Isabel. "Do you know him?"

"To say hello to," said the woman. "People know one another down here — it's that sort of place." She paused, and looked at Isabel enquiringly. "What do you want with Archie?"

"I wanted to ask him about my friend. But not now. Some other time."

The woman seemed to lose interest. "I haven't seen him for a little while. People come and go."

"They do." Isabel was beginning to recover from the shock of her recent experience. Fright had been replaced with anger over what had happened to her, but now that anger was yielding to a feeling of quiet satisfaction. She had found out what she wanted to find out. Her impulse to follow the couple had paid off: she now knew the name of the man with freckles and also knew, roughly, where he lived.

They rounded the corner, and she saw, only a short distance away, the approaching figure of Jamie. The woman noticed Isabel's reaction. "Your man?"

"Yes, my man."

Jamie was before them. He looked at the woman and then at Isabel, seeking explanation.

Isabel touched the woman's forearm. "This very kind person helped me."

Jamie turned to the woman and inclined his head.

"Some low-life," said the woman. "Some sleaze-bag."

Jamie turned back to Isabel. He looked alarmed.

"There was a man," said Isabel. "He tried to pick me up."

"We get them," said the woman. "We tell the polis time and time again that they're coming down here in their cars, prowling around. And what do the polis do? Nothing. Nothing. They say they have more important things to do, but I ask myself: what's more important than protecting womenfolk and bairns?"

Jamie said, "I agree." He reached out to shake her hand. "Thank you for what you did."

"Well," said the woman, fixing Isabel with a warning stare, "you take care now." She paused. "Where do youse stay, by the way?" The local plural — *youse* — was comforting.

"The South Side," said Jamie.

"Morningside?"

Isabel said that Morningside was close enough.

The woman chuckled. "You know what they say about Morningside? It's no Leith, is it? Remember that, hen."

The friendly Scottish term of address *hen* set the seal on the encounter. This was one woman helping another; this was ordinary decency asserting itself. And this still happened — in spite of everything that made the world less personal, less caring, this was still happening. There were still people who looked after one another, called one another *hen*, and walked you round the corner until you were safe once again.

Jamie was insistent.

"You have to," he said. "We must go there right now."

"But what if they ask what I was doing . . ." She trailed off. There was a lot that she wanted to say, but she could not find the words.

He took her hand, but with his other hand he had extracted his mobile phone from his pocket and was beginning to dial the taxi number. "I'm going to ask them to pick us up from outside the restaurant," he said. "We'll go straight to the police. There's a station that covers Leith — the taxi driver will know."

She did not argue, and was silent in the taxi on the short journey. Inside the police station a policewoman appeared and led Isabel off to an interview room. Jamie was asked to wait behind.

"Just tell me in your own words," said the policewoman.

Isabel said, "I was walking along the street."

The policewoman waited.

"I don't know the name of it," said Isabel. "It was round the corner from the restaurant we were in, you see."

The policewoman was patient. She asked for the name of the restaurant and drew a small diagram for herself on a pad of paper in front of her. She named a street. "And that's where you were assaulted?"

"Yes. A man got out of his car and approached me. He thought that I was soliciting."

The policewoman made notes. "And this was not the case?"

"No. It was not."

The policewoman looked apologetic. "Sorry — I had to ask that, you see." She hesitated before continuing, "What were you doing there?"

Isabel looked down at the table. "I was following somebody."

The policewoman stared at her. "You were *following* somebody?"

"Yes. There was a couple in the restaurant. I knew her and she was with this man. I wanted to see where they went."

There was silence. Then the policewoman said, "Why?"

"Because I thought she might be having an affair with him." She told herself that this was true.

The policewoman raised an eyebrow. "Private reasons, then?"

"Yes, private reasons."

There was a further silence. Isabel wondered whether this was where the interview would end. And she would not blame the policewoman if she closed her notebook at this stage and concluded that this was a mental health issue. But that did not happen; rather, the policewoman sighed and asked her to continue. So Isabel told her what had happened and mentioned that there was a witness, if they needed to find one. She could not remember the precise address of the woman in the housecoat, but it was, she thought, the fourth door along from the end of the street. They would find her easily enough if they wanted to.

At the end of Isabel's account, the policewoman sat back in her chair. "I'm very sorry you had this experience," she said. "It happens, I'm sorry to say. There are some men who seem to specialise in intimidating women in these circumstances. You encountered one of these, I'm afraid."

Isabel was relieved that the interview appeared to be coming to an end. She had done her civic duty and reported the incident. All she wanted now was to go home.

"There's one more thing," said the policewoman. "It would be helpful for us if you could take a look at some photographs. Can you do that?"

Isabel agreed, and the policewoman returned with an album that she placed on the table in front of Isabel. "Just the first three pages," she said. "There aren't many photographs."

Isabel looked at the faces staring out at her. She turned the first page, and then rapidly moved on to the second and third.

"Is he there?" asked the policewoman.

"No."

"You seemed to recognise somebody. You reacted to the first page."

Isabel shook her head. She wanted to leave now.

The policewoman was clearly disappointed. "Are you sure he's not there? Don't hesitate to tell me — even if you're less than one hundred per cent certain."

Isabel shook her head again. "No, he's not there."

Jamie called another taxi. They started the journey in silence. Then Jamie said, "That wasn't too bad, I hope."

"No," said Isabel. "She was very supportive."

She looked at her hands.

"And?" said Jamie. "Still upset?"

She turned to him. "She showed me photographs," she said. "They have a book."

"Of suspects?"

"Yes."

"But he wasn't in it?"

"No," said Isabel. "But Patricia's friend was — the man with the freckles. He was."

CHAPTER
TWELVE

Claire arrived for her first half-day of work when Isabel was walking Charlie to nursery school and while Jamie was introducing Magnus to the top two octaves of the piano keyboard. Jamie suspected that Magnus was more musical than Charlie, as he appeared to be able to discriminate between the pitch of different notes. Charlie liked volume, and found no greater pleasure than beating any drum-shaped object as hard as he could; Magnus, by contrast, seemed to listen, and would beam with pleasure at the sounding of the higher notes of any instrument. He was not interested in the bassoon, except in its very highest register, at which he would smile, but only briefly.

"We have one son who will clearly become a percussionist," Jamie pronounced. "And one who is destined for higher things — in the pitch sense, of course."

This was a musical joke, a reference to the sense of hierarchy sometimes found amongst musicians, in which the strings might look down on wind of any variety, and woodwind in turn had a sense of innate superiority to brass players — a "beery lot", as one of Jamie's friends described them. "A beery lot, always off to the pub the moment a rehearsal is over." And if brass players had to look down on anybody, then all that was left was the percussion who, if suitably provoked by a conductor, were capable of making enough noise to drown everybody else out.

Jamie balanced Magnus on his knee with one hand while, with the other, he picked out a series of high chords. Magnus squealed with delight, and reached forward to pound the keys with his fists.

"Not quite right," said Jamie. "Almost, but not quite."

The impromptu music lesson was interrupted by the doorbell, and by the arrival of Claire.

"I know it's early," she said. "But I couldn't wait."

Jamie explained that Isabel would be a few minutes yet, but he would be happy to make Claire a cup of coffee while she waited. She accepted, and he led her into the kitchen.

"What's it like — being a musician?"

She asked the question without preliminaries, and he answered in a similar vein.

"Hard work," he said. "Full of anxiety and disappointment. You have questions that never seem to go away: will I get enough work? Am I good enough? What happens if my lip goes, or I hurt my fingers, or . . . well, there are a hundred different questions you tend to ask yourself in the sleepless hours."

"And yet people do it," said Claire. "You do. Others do. People make a living."

"By juggling things," said Jamie. "Including babies."

He moved across the room to where Claire was standing and offered her Magnus. "I can't make coffee while I'm holding him. And if I put him down he'll crawl off down the corridor at high speed. Do you mind?"

She took the child gingerly, uncertain as to his reaction to her. But Magnus simply stared, his eyes wide, his mouth set in a curious expression of wonderment.

"He likes you," said Jamie. "Look. Star-struck."

Magnus was silent in his admiration. As Claire moved her head, his eyes followed, with the intense, uninhibited stare of the young child. Jamie poured coffee grounds into the cafetière and switched on the kettle. From the hall the sound drifted in of the front door opening.

"I think that's Grace," he said. "Did you meet her when you were here the other day?"

Claire shook her head. "Isabel mentioned that there was somebody . . ."

"A housekeeper," said Jamie. "She looked after the house when Isabel's father lived here. Isabel kept her on — and she's a great help with him." He nodded in the direction of Magnus, who was still visibly entranced with Claire.

Grace came into the kitchen, taking off a light raincoat. "Summer," she said. "Or so they tell us. It's raining. And that stupid bus was late." She stopped as she saw Claire. She looked at Jamie for an introduction.

"We told you about Claire," said Jamie. "She's going to be helping Isabel with the *Review*."

Grace looked at Claire with much the same directness as Magnus did. Beyond a mumbled greeting on introduction, she said nothing: the remarks about rain and the bus had not been intended for strangers.

"I wish I could play an instrument," said Claire. "I never learned as a child. I was offered the chance of piano lessons, but I wouldn't do them."

"The one instrument you can't really learn as an adult," said Jamie. "Or, at least, not properly. The brain pathways just aren't there when you're an adult — and you can't lay them down."

This prompted Grace to contribute. "I don't know about that. I read about somebody who went to bed one night not knowing how to play a note on the piano, but who woke up the next morning and could play the piano perfectly."

Jamie burst out laughing. "No," he said. "Impossible."

"Surely not," echoed Claire.

Grace's eyes had not left Claire; now they narrowed, and she tensed. "There are many things that we think are impossible, but that happen," she said. "All the time. These things happen."

Claire glanced at Jamie, and unfortunately the glance was intercepted by Grace. The glance was subtitled *We're above this sort of belief*, and it was correctly deciphered by Grace, whose lips set in a firm line of disapproval.

Jamie sensed the sudden drop in temperature. "Not everything has an easy explanation," he said. "There are those strange cases of people suddenly talking with a foreign accent. Sounding Swedish, or whatever."

"Precisely," said Grace. "They wake up and find they're speaking Swedish. Those are proved cases — nobody denies them."

"I'm not sure if they actually speak Swedish," said Jamie. "They may sound Swedish, but that's not the same as speaking Swedish. Anybody can *sound* Swedish. You elongate the vowels and add a bit of melody."

"No, they use actual Swedish words," insisted Grace. "Swedish people can understand what they're saying."

Jamie looked doubtful. "I'm not sure about that."

"Well, I am," said Grace. "And lots of other people are too." She looked defiantly at Claire.

Jamie tried to defuse the situation. "Grace is very interested in spiritualism," he explained. "You go to those lectures, don't you, Grace — down at that place off the Queensferry Road . . ."

"The Psychic College," said Grace. "They have the lectures at the Psychic College."

Claire looked at Grace quizzically. "The Psychic College?"

"Yes," said Grace. "I'm surprised you've not heard of it."

Jamie moved across the room to relieve Claire of Magnus. "They have some very interesting events there," he said. "Séances . . ."

"Sittings," Grace corrected him.

"They communicate with the other side," Jamie continued.

Grace gave Jamie a discouraging look. "It's not as simple as you say, Jamie," she said. "I know you don't believe in anything, but you don't have all the answers, you know. What about telepathy? Everyone knows that telepathy exists. How would you explain that?"

"How do you know I don't believe in anything?" Jamie challenged. The exchange between them was friendly, but it was having an effect on Claire, who was unsure where to look.

"I just do," said Grace. "But there are more things in heaven and earth than are dreamed of in your philosophy . . ."

". . . Horatio," supplied Jamie, and then laughed. "True. And in yours, too, Grace — sauce for the goose being, as they say, sauce for the gander. Could you pour the coffee? How do you like yours, Claire?"

Grace looked at Claire for an answer. Her look was discouraging, as if to imply that the expression of any preference, for milk or sugar or for black, would be an irritation.

"Can't you tell telepathically?" Claire replied.

It was an attempt at humour, but it fell resoundingly flat. Jamie stood stock-still. He looked at Grace, and saw that her reaction was as he feared. There were one or two areas about which Grace was inordinately sensitive: parapsychology was one of them.

"Telepathy doesn't work that way," Grace said coldly. "And it's not something that we take lightly."

Jamie groaned inwardly. "Isabel will be back any moment," he said, with forced cheerfulness. "Any moment now."

Jamie had to teach that morning at the Academy, but was planning to return to the house for lunch. There was a concert that evening in the Queen's Hall, and he was playing a rarely performed bassoon concerto with Mr McFall's Chamber, an adventurous chamber orchestra that explored musical byways. They enjoyed experimenting with tango, and there was a new piece on the programme that evening, *The Bassoon in Buenos Aires*, that would test Jamie's technical virtuosity. He needed a few hours to go over the more difficult passages, and had set aside the afternoon for that. He had made sure he would be free: Isabel had agreed to fetch Charlie from nursery and to entertain him thereafter; and Grace was planning to take Magnus to tea with her cousin in Newington. He would have several uninterrupted hours to familiarise himself with his part in the evening's programme.

Shortly before he left the Academy, Jamie telephoned Isabel to suggest that rather than have lunch in the house, they should meet in la Barantine, a small French bakery and coffee shop in Bruntsfield, just over the road from Cat's deli. It was a popular place, its tables often filled with enthusiasts for their strawberry tarts and macaroons, but there were more savoury offerings too, served, as had become fashionable, on small slate slabs doubling up as plates. Customers were addressed in French, and they usually responded gamely in schoolday French, dredged up from the recesses of memory, or, on occasion, in memorable franglais, that curious European pidgin that seemed, miraculously, to be as intelligible to French as to English speakers, and equally amusing to both. *Sur l'autre main* (on the other

172

hand), as one recent customer had said, *je might avoir un green salad avec un peu de soft fromage* . . .

Isabel readily agreed.

"Is she still there?" asked Jamie over the phone. "Can you talk?"

"Claire? No, she's left."

He asked her whether it had gone well, and she replied that it had. "We got through a lot of work. Cleared quite a bit of the backlog — or at least made an impression on it. I'll tell you about it over lunch."

Isabel arrived at la Barantine first and was pleased to find a table free. There were ten tables crammed into the café's limited space, with the result that people at neighbouring tables were shoulder to shoulder. It was not a place for the exchange of confidences or for a discreet lovers' tryst, but for lunch between friends where the gossip was about nothing important, it was ideal. Today it was mostly women, although there was a solitary man at one of the tables near the window, immersed in the copy of the *Scotsman* newspaper that the café placed, along with *The Times*, in a reading rack on the window ledge.

Isabel noticed the effect of Jamie's entrance. At the table next to hers, two women of about her own age paused in their conversation and exchanged glances. On the other side of the restaurant, a middle-aged woman, halfway through the delicate operation of eating a macaroon, put the crumbling confection down on her plate while she stared — none too discreetly. Isabel was used to this; Jamie turned heads — he had always done so, and, most significantly, was quite unaware of the fact. It did not displease her, although she did not enjoy the envy that she sometimes saw in the eyes of other women when they realised that this extraordinarily good-looking young man was with her — not just having lunch with her, but *with her.*

"That boy," said Jamie, as he sat down opposite Isabel.

"Geoffrey something?"

"Geoffrey Weir. He's hopeless at the bassoon, and has a dreadful, clapped-out old instrument that makes it one hundred times worse. I've told him to get it repaired, but he said that the repairer had just condemned it. Said it wasn't worth fixing."

Isabel knew what bassoons cost. It was no easy task for a parent to provide even a low-cost student model. But this should not be a consideration in this case, said Jamie. "His parents could easily afford something better," he said. "His father has plenty of cash — he developed some sort of lawnmower that everyone buys, apparently. Provided they have a lawn, of course." He paused as he glanced at the menu, and then continued, "I spoke to him about it at the school concert. I said, 'Your son's playing would improve greatly with a better instrument.' And you know what he said? 'You can't make a silk purse out of a sow's ear.' Imagine that. That's what he actually said."

Isabel smiled. "Not the normal thing for a parent to say. Parents usually take a pretty optimistic view of their children's talents."

"Not in this case," said Jamie. "Weir père, as we call him . . ." he gave a wry grin ". . . said that his son's

174

playing made him feel nauseous, and that it was only because of maternal encouragement that Geoffrey continued with music lessons. Then he asked me how much a new bassoon would cost. So I told him, and he made a face and said it just wasn't worth it in his son's case." He sighed. "At least the school has plenty of other students who are good. There's a girl called Florence Douglas who plays superbly. She's fantastic. She could get into the Conservatoire in Glasgow if she tried."

The woman who had been eating the macaroon was still gazing at Jamie. Isabel caught her eye and smiled, causing a rapid, embarrassed return to the few crumbs of macaroon still on the plate.

"I'm sometimes tempted to give up teaching," Jamie mused. "Life would be much simpler if I didn't have to worry how those kids were doing — whether they were practising enough, whether they were ready for their music exams, and so on. It would be nice to forget about all that."

Isabel looked at him sympathetically. "If you wanted to," she said, "you could. You don't need the money."

Something crossed Jamie's face. An expression of regret? A wistfulness?

"I need to earn my living," he said quietly.

She was quick to correct herself. "Of course you do. I'm not saying you don't." But she knew, as did Jamie, that this was a fiction. Jamie did not have to earn his living because Isabel had more than enough for both of them. This was a matter of pride, though — of self-respect — and she would not have it otherwise.

"You could spend more time playing, rather than teaching," she suggested. "Session work pays well, doesn't it? Or you could form your own consort — you've thought about that, haven't you?"

He nodded. "Sometimes." The trouble with that, though, was that it would require capital to start a new chamber orchestra or consort. Musicians had to be paid; venues had to be hired; recordings were an expensive business, with all their sound engineers and mixers. Nothing was cheap, and he did not want to ask Isabel to back this financially. Jamie was largely indifferent to money, but had a strong sense of when he did not want to ask Isabel to pay for something.

"Oh well," he said. "I'm happy to carry on as I am. I'll survive the likes of Geoffrey Weir."

Isabel had already ordered; now Jamie did the same. Then he folded his hands and looked across the table at Isabel. "The agenda," he said. "Item one."

She looked at him quizzically. "Is there an agenda?"

"Yes," Jamie replied. "I know it and you know it: what happened yesterday."

"I was going to tell you about Claire's first day at work," said Isabel.

"There'll be time for that in due course. We didn't have the chance to discuss anything when we came back last night, but we can hardly ignore it. You had a real shock, you know."

She had not wanted to make a fuss over that. "At the time it was a bit upsetting," she said. "But no harm done."

He stared at her incredulously. "But something like that's dreadful. You can't just shrug it off."

She explained to him that she was not shrugging anything off. There was a difference, she said, between dwelling on something in an unhealthy way and keeping it in perspective. "If I look at this objectively, it's not all that bad. I was accosted by a very unpleasant man. He probably gets a thrill out of frightening women. We don't know exactly what he had in mind, but he was a pathetic creature, an insecure bully. He can't be allowed to get away with it — I agree — but there's no reason why I should allow somebody like him to give me nightmares."

"No, but —"

She cut him off. "I know that we're encouraged these days to make much of victimhood, but I believe in bouncing back. And I don't think we should allow people to make us miserable — that gives the victory to them."

"No, I see, but —"

"So I'm not going to allow that man to wreck anything for me. I've got better things to think about. I went to the police; I've done all that I can to help them stop him, but in my view that's it. The incident's over."

Jamie was silent. He was not used to such a robust view being expressed. But he thought: yes, I can see it. There is no reason to feel fragile if you aren't in fact fragile. Nursing yourself into fragility could simply compound the consequences of an unfortunate experience.

"Do you see what I mean?" asked Isabel.

"Yes," he said. "I do. But, leaving all that aside, there are other things to think about. And don't tell me you're going to forget those too."

Their lunch arrived: an open sandwich for Isabel, and a mozzarella salad for Jamie. As Isabel removed the capers from the sandwich, Jamie poured a drizzle of olive oil over his mozzarella. Then Isabel looked up to meet Jamie's gaze. "You think I've been thinking," she said.

Jamie smiled. "You think I think. And I think you think. But yes, I do think you have. And I'm pretty sure I'm right. All this is classic territory for you — it really is."

She raised an eyebrow. "Uncertainty?"

He nodded. "A dilemma. These moral dilemmas have your name all over them. You seem to seek them out — or they find you. I'm not quite sure how it works, but the end result is the same: you're in a quandary."

Isabel moved a caper to the side of her plate. In her view, capers were fundamentally inedible — they simply shouldn't be on a plate. She knew that people disagreed with her — that there were people who loved capers, who thought they were a good addition to any dish, but had it ever occurred to them that they might be *wrong*? Capers were flowers, when it came to it, and in Isabel's view flowers were not there to be eaten.

Jamie was looking at her intensely. "What are you thinking about?" he asked. "You're off on one of your private tangents, you know."

178

"I was thinking about capers," said Isabel. "I'm sorry, I know you were giving me a lecture, but I couldn't help thinking about how capers are flower-buds and how we don't like to eat flowers."

"Speak for yourself," said Jamie, reaching for one of the abandoned capers and popping it into his mouth. "And I wasn't giving you a lecture — I was merely raising something that had to be raised." He paused, and reached for another caper. "I like these. They have a lovely olive-like taste. A sort of zing. And anyway, why shouldn't we eat flowers? We eat just about everything else, don't we?"

"It's aesthetic," said Isabel.

"Oh, come on! People eat pheasants. Beautiful birds. People eat them."

He took a third caper. As he did so, the eyes of the macaroon-eating woman followed the movement of his hand with a certain fascination.

"You're being observed," Isabel whispered. "You're being observed eating flowers."

Jamie glanced across the restaurant. "Oh well," he said. "Let's get back to where we were. What are you going to do?"

Isabel sighed. "I have no idea. And you're right — I'm in a real quandary."

Jamie suggested that she define the quandary, and perhaps an answer would emerge. "Describing a problem can sort it, you know."

"Perhaps," Isabel conceded. "Perhaps it will."

He encouraged her. "So, go ahead. What's the problem?"

Isabel sighed again. "The issue is this: I have unwittingly found out that . . ."

Jamie stopped her. "Not unwittingly, surely. You said we should follow them — remember? That was a deliberate choice on your part."

"But I didn't choose to see them together in the first place," countered Isabel.

"You're splitting hairs," said Jamie.

She defended herself. Splitting hairs — as Jamie put it — was really what philosophy was all about. If hairs were there, then they should be split, because most situations were far more complex than one imagined at first sight, and it was only through splitting hairs that you could understand all the ramifications. So if Jamie said she was splitting hairs, she would treat that as a compliment rather than a criticism.

He apologised. "All right, you stumbled into the situation."

She liked that. "Yes, stumbling into it is exactly what happened. I have found myself in a position where I know — or suspect, rather — that somebody is being misled and taken advantage of. What do I do?"

Jamie looked thoughtful. "You said *suspect*. You just *suspect* something. You don't know, do you?"

She agreed that she did not know. But surely, she thought, there were circumstances in which suspected knowledge could be as good a reason for acting as confirmed knowledge. She put that to Jamie, but he was doubtful. "No," he said. "You should be very careful about doing something just because you have your suspicions. What if you're wrong?"

"You may be wrong even if you *think* you know something for certain. You could still be wrong."

He did not argue the point, but instead asked her what she could possibly do.

She thought for a few moments before replying. "On balance, I feel I have to do something. And I suppose the only thing to do is to speak to Basil Phelps. I have to tell him of my suspicions."

Jamie winced. "That's not going to be easy."

Isabel acknowledged this. "No, it won't be easy. But I can't sit on my hands and do nothing."

Jamie thought of something else. "And what about the freckled man? What about his photograph being in that police album?"

"One thing at a time," said Isabel. "That's nothing to do with me."

"Well, that's a relief," said Jamie.

Isabel gestured to their plates. "We have to eat something," she said. "This is meant to be lunch."

Afterwards, when they were back in the house, he took her hand as they stood in the entrance hall. He said, "I'm sorry that I went on at you over lunch."

She made light of it. "But you didn't. The objections you raised were perfectly reasonable."

"You do know," he went on, "that I always approve of everything you do — everything."

She laughed. "I wouldn't recommend that."

He held her more closely. She closed her eyes. It was a miracle, in her view — a miracle that she had this man, this vision of physical perfection, this gentle, beautiful soul.

"All I ask of you is that you be careful," Jamie continued. "I'm not going to be able to stop you from doing the things you do — but I do ask you to be careful in the way you do them."

"I shall," she whispered.

She resorted to whispering because the house seemed unusually quiet and she felt as if there was someone listening. This was impossible, of course, but there were times that she felt that what we said — and did — even in the most private of circumstances, was audible or apparent to somebody, somewhere; some watching presence, some guardian, like the omnipresent *lares* and *penates*, household gods that the Romans believed in. They heard everything, but, being Roman gods, were not inclined to be judgemental; comfortable gods, who liked a bit of attention — the occasional sacrifice or offering — but who otherwise let people go about their business without too much agonising over what was right or wrong.

She looked up at Jamie, and then kissed him.

He returned the kiss, more passionately.

"Are we alone?" he asked.

She said, "Yes."

CHAPTER
THIRTEEN

Suddenly the house seemed to be filling up. Antonia, the new au pair, arrived the following morning, struggling with four over-stuffed suitcases, freshly off a flight from Milan. Grace let her into the house as Isabel was at the time attending to Magnus, who had diarrhoea. Grace had been told of the Italian girl, and had been tight-lipped at the news.

"It's entirely up to you," she said when Isabel announced that there was to be an au pair. "Personally, I see no reason, but then this isn't my house."

"It's just that there seems to be so much to do," said Isabel. "What with the two boys and Jamie having to dash off to concerts and so on, and . . ." She looked at Grace. The case may have been convincing in her own eyes, but was clearly not persuading her housekeeper.

"As I said," Grace intoned, "it's not for me to decide. If you want a teenager hanging about the house, then that's your prerogative."

Isabel corrected her. "Antonia is not a teenager. She's twenty-one, I think."

"And Italian," added Grace. She gave Isabel a reproachful look, as if the choosing of a foreign au pair was somehow disloyal.

Isabel could not let that pass. "Yes," she said. "And that, in my view, is a big plus. I've always liked the Italians. They're warm people; they make wonderful friends."

"I'm sure they do," sniffed Grace. "But whether one *needs* an Italian in the house is another matter, I would have thought."

Now, standing in the hall, Grace was greeted with the sight of Antonia and her copious luggage. She looked at her suspiciously, noting, with disapproval, the bright-eyed vitality, the slightly olive skin tone, the lush beauty of the shoulder-length auburn hair.

"Yes?"

It was hardly a warm welcome, and the young woman at the front door was momentarily taken aback.

"This is Mrs Dalhousie's house?" The English was precise, and well articulated.

Grace pursed her lips before replying. "Ms Dalhousie," she said.

Antonia looked flustered. "Dalhousie?" she asked.

Grace nodded, reluctantly. "You'd better come in."

Unassisted by Grace, Antonia first brought in two of her suitcases before turning back for the others.

"You have a lot of luggage," observed Grace. "Do you need it all?"

Antonia smiled nervously. "My father says I take too many things," she said. "He says that you should only have one suitcase."

"He's right," said Grace. She turned away. "I'll tell them you're here."

184

Antonia was standing in the hall, looking about her, when Jamie came downstairs. He shook hands with her and picked up two of her suitcases.

"I'll take these upstairs for you," he said. "We'll put them in your room and then I'll bring the rest up afterwards." He smiled at her. "You're very welcome, by the way."

They went upstairs, passing the open door of the bathroom where Isabel was dealing with Magnus.

"Antonia's arrived," Jamie called out. "I'm just showing her to her room."

Isabel appeared at the bathroom door. She was wearing a pair of blue rubber gloves.

"I'm sorry not to have been there to greet you," Isabel said. "I was changing one of the boys . . ." She inclined her head towards the bathroom behind her. "An emergency, you see."

The effect of this on Antonia was immediate. "Emergency?" she said. "Emergency?"

"Oh, the usual sort of thing," said Isabel. "Nothing untoward."

But Antonia had already stepped forward and was looking past Isabel into the bathroom. "Oh dear," she said. "I can help."

Isabel laughed. "My goodness, no. You've just arrived."

But Antonia insisted. Almost pushing her way past Isabel she went into the bathroom, where Magnus was lying on a changing mat. The consequences of his stomach upset were still visible, and prolific.

"I can do this," said Antonia. "I insist."

Isabel glanced at Jamie, who was grinning. She peeled off her gloves and offered them to Antonia. "You really shouldn't," she said. "I was coping fine."

"Poor little boy," said Antonia. "This is not a good way for a little boy to start the day."

"No," said Isabel. "I suppose it isn't."

"But I am here to help," continued Antonia.

Grace had now appeared from downstairs and from the landing was watching what was going on. She looked disapproving.

"Antonia has swung into action," Isabel remarked.

Grace said nothing.

"I'm going to take her suitcases up to her room," said Jamie. He and Isabel exchanged looks of satisfaction. They were both as impressed with Antonia as Grace appeared hostile.

"Isn't it kind of her?" asked Isabel.

"Very," muttered Grace.

Antonia was left in her room to unpack; Grace had taken charge of Magnus, whisking him off on a walk to feed the ducks in the canal, ignoring, as Isabel later pointed out to Jamie, the fact that taking a toddler with diarrhoea for a long walk was not the best idea; while Jamie found himself in the kitchen, where Isabel was helping herself to a postponed breakfast.

"Well?" he said. "First impressions?"

Isabel buttered a piece of toast. "Amazing," she said. "How many Scottish girls would do that? Go right in at the deep end?"

"Who knows? But not many, I suspect."

"And she was completely unfazed by it. You can imagine what it was like: poor little Magnus had had what is euphemistically referred to as an accident — a train crash, in this case — and she didn't bat an eyelid. She had him cleaned up and in a new set of clothing in two seconds."

"She must be keen to impress," said Jamie.

"Or she's genuinely helpful. And she was an instant hit with Magnus. He was looking up at her and virtually cooing with pleasure."

Jamie referred to Grace's sourness. "Not everybody was . . ."

He did not need to finish. Isabel groaned. "Grace."

"Yes."

"She'll come round."

Half an hour later, through the open door of her study Isabel heard Antonia coming downstairs. With Charlie at nursery and Magnus with Grace — and likely to remain with her, Isabel suspected, as a gesture of ownership — she was not sure if there was anything for the au pair to do, at least in respect of childcare. She decided to suggest that Antonia take some time to explore the city, and she could start work in the house the following day. But when she put this to the young Italian, the proposal was quickly rejected.

"I can go into the town later, perhaps this afternoon. For now, I must start my work."

Isabel did not argue. Antonia's earlier attention to Magnus had been a foretaste of her enthusiasm — and

Isabel found it endearing. "You could start cleaning the house, if you like."

Antonia's eyes lit up. "That is what I would like to do. You can show me, please."

Isabel nodded. "And one thing: do you want me to correct your English as you speak? Not that you're making many mistakes, but since you're here, really, to improve your English it could be helpful."

"But of course. That is what I want to do. I want to meet people and speak English to them."

Isabel smiled at the thought. It sounded so much like a mission statement of the sort that firms made up for themselves. *Meeting the needs of consumers* — that sort of thing. *Empowering people in their search for authenticity* — she had seen that one printed on a newspaper advertisement proclaiming the merits of a Scottish knitwear firm. She had wondered where authenticity came into it. Could one become more authentic by wearing a cashmere sweater? Or was the reference to the search for authentic cashmere, as opposed to artificial substitutes? She had felt that a more honest, less pretentious mission statement might have been *Empowering people in their search for sweaters*. And even then, *empowering* was a bit much; what was wrong with the word *helping*? Or would it have been better altogether for the knitwear firm simply to state *We sell sweaters*? Perhaps *We sell woollen things* would have been even friendlier. That at least was direct. That did not involve the circumlocution, the slightly pious tone of the typical mission statement. So

188

an au pair might well have the mission statement *I want to meet people and speak English*.

"All right," said Isabel. "You might say: 'Could you show me what to do?' That sounds a bit more natural than 'You can show me'. Not that 'You can show me' is incorrect, but it's just a question of what sounds more natural." She paused. She was not sure whether Antonia was ready for that sort of subtlety; her English seemed really rather good, and it was probably not helpful to be burdening her with such nuanced observations at this stage. And anyway, it might be better for her to concentrate on idiomatic, everyday English, of the sort that people actually spoke. Antonia's contemporaries would not have said "Could you show me?"; they would have said . . . Isabel thought for a moment. What would they have said? "Okay, show me." Or they might even have simply said "Cool", which sufficed to show acceptance in any circumstances, of virtually anything. "Cool. I'm cool with that." Or "Sounds good", which appeared to be replacing "Yes".

"Awesome," muttered Isabel.

"Awesome?" asked Antonia. "Is that what I should say? Awesome?"

Isabel shook her head. "No. I was just thinking aloud. I was thinking that people say *awesome* far too much. Everything's awesome. It's not a word that has any meaning any more. It used to mean something, but no longer." She shook her head again. This was her chance to do something — even a very little thing — to protect the integrity of the English language. If she

189

189

could persuade one person — just one person — to avoid the use of the word *awesome*, then she would have struck a blow against the menacing tide of meaninglessness and debasement that threatened the language.

"So I mustn't say *awesome?*"

"That's right. You mustn't say *awesome* — ever. You must never use that word."

"Is it rude?"

Isabel laughed. "No, it's not rude. It's just used too much — and in the wrong place."

"So it's not like . . ." And here Antonia used an obscene term — in its adjectival form.

Isabel laughed again. "No, it's not like that. That doesn't mean anything at all. That's a swear word. People use it for all sorts of things for no real reason at all. You don't use that word."

"But they do," said Antonia. "I have seen many films where they use that word all the time. I saw a Scottish film where everybody spoke like that."

Isabel wondered how to explain. "There are different sorts of people in Scotland — just as, I imagine, there are different sorts of people in Italy. Some people use that language all the time because . . . well, because that's what they do."

"Vulgar people?"

Isabel hesitated. "We don't use the word *vulgar* very much. It's not polite to talk about other people as vulgar."

"Even if they are?" asked Antonia.

190

"Even if they are . . ." Isabel paused. "I think it might be better if you listened to the people you meet — people of your own age group. Speak like them."

"Even if they're vulgar?"

Isabel nodded. "Even then. But that word you mentioned — it would be best not to say that, especially in this house. I wouldn't want the children to pick it up."

"We have many vulgar expressions in Italian," said Antonia, her tone matter-of-fact. "I could tell you some of them, if you like. Some of them are very funny."

"I'm sure they are," said Isabel.

"Although you're not meant to use them," continued Antonia. "And there's a special way of doing that. You can swear without using vulgar words. You use the word *cavolo* instead — that means cabbage. But everybody knows that you don't mean cabbage, you mean something else. It's very useful."

"Awesome," said Isabel. "Perhaps *awesome* is like *cabbage*." They both laughed. "But let me show you where the vacuum cleaner is. We also call that a hoover, by the way."

"Hoover," repeated Antonia. "That's very sexy."

Isabel looked at her. "Sexy?"

"It's a very sexy word. Hoover." Antonia elongated the vowels.

"Possibly," said Isabel. "I'll show you the cupboard. You can start upstairs. Those rooms haven't been hoovered for weeks."

"That lady?" said Antonia. "That lady I met? Is that her normal work?"

"It was," said Isabel. "But now she has a lot of work to do with the two boys."

"I would like to help her with the boys," offered Antonia. "Then she could get back to working with the hoover."

Isabel was aghast.

"Have I said something wrong?" asked Antonia.

Isabel imagined the scene. "No," she reassured her. "I'm sure you will be able to help with the boys sometimes, but perhaps not too often when Grace is here." She looked at Antonia to see if the message had been understood.

It had. "She likes that job?" asked Antonia. "She doesn't want anybody else?"

"She likes it," said Isabel. She decided that frankness was the best policy here. "And no, I think that she might not like it if somebody took it away from her."

Antonia thought about this. "But there are two boys," she said. "There's the other one, isn't there?"

"Charlie. Yes, there are two, and there'll be plenty for you to do when Grace isn't here."

"I must be tactful? Is that the correct word?"

"Absolutely the right word," said Isabel.

"But she won't mind if I use the hoover?"

Isabel assured her that the use of the hoover would give no offence.

Antonia looked impatient. "Then I must start hoovering," she said.

Isabel showed her to the cupboard where the household devices were stored. The cupboard had a dusty and neglected feel to it, and could itself have done with a major clean.

"Very dirty," said Antonia.

"It's possibly a tiny bit rude to call somebody's house dirty," Isabel said gently. "English is a funny language that way."

The gentle reproach seemed to have little effect. "But there is a lot of cleaning to be done."

Isabel looked apologetic. "Yes, that's why we asked you to come. This house needs help. There's a lot for you to do." She did not want to expect too much from Antonia, and so she said, "Then, this evening, you should go and take a look at the town. There's a lot that goes on in Edinburgh. It's a lively place."

"I shall go out tonight," said Antonia. "But first I have a lot of work to do."

Claire arrived for work a few minutes later, bringing with her a large box file of submitted papers. She had worked quickly, attaching a brief, preliminary report on each of them. This was what Isabel called the "first sweep", in which the completely impossible papers — those from enthusiastic and often obsessive amateurs — were weeded out. When she had first become involved with the *Review*, Isabel had been astonished at the extent to which people failed to understand the nature of the journal and insisted on submitting completely unsuitable material. Over the years she had received articles on fishing, the habits of polar bears, confessional memoirs, and, from one author in particular, a high school teacher in Sri Lanka, papers on mathematical theory. As a matter of principle, she wrote back to every author who submitted anything; if they took the trouble to send things to her, then she would acknowledge their effort, no matter how misguided they were. The teacher in Sri Lanka was a special case: he had received an initial letter in which she had explained that the *Review* was a journal of philosophy and not of mathematics, pure or applied. "I am just not in a position to comment on your paper," Isabel wrote. "We are a philosophical publication, you will understand, and therefore we cannot judge the merits of your paper. I would suggest that you submit it to a mathematical journal, and I do hope that you find a suitable home for it in this way."

This had brought back the response, "Esteemed Sir, I shall endeavour to simplify the introduction to my paper so that you can understand it more readily. It is a well-known habit of mine to be obscure in circumstances where clarity and simplicity are called for. Once I have done that, I shall send the paper back to you for your much-appreciated consideration."

Then there was the man in Toronto who wrote papers on vegetarianism, a subject that at least fell within the scope of the *Review*, in so far as vegetarianism was a moral issue. These papers, though, were light on theory and heavy on recipes. Once again, Isabel was polite in her response: "I must say," she wrote, "that I found your recipe for pasta with mushrooms, spinach and feta most mouth-watering. It's a pity that we cannot publish it in the *Review of Applied Ethics* as we are a philosophical, rather than a culinary, journal." This had not discouraged the author, who wrote back to say that should she eventually publish his article — "I am in no hurry," he wrote — then would it be possible to have some of the quantities in cup measurements, for the benefit of North American readers, rather than just in pounds and ounces, or grams? This exchange had been followed, a few months later, by the submission of a further article from the same source, ostensibly on the ethics of disclosing the source of food in menus, but, for the most part, concerned with tables of the carbohydrate content of the various forms of vegetable.

There were no such articles in the batch that Claire had taken off to read. These were all papers by established philosophers, and written according to the proper formula for an academic paper. There were eight submissions and Claire had selected two for further consideration. One was on the taking down of statues; the other was on parental responsibility for the misdeeds of their children. These two papers, she thought, should be passed on to the editorial board for further reports; the other papers could be rejected at this stage.

Isabel glanced at Claire's reports. "What line does the statue paper take?" she asked. "Leave them or take them down?"

"It's a woman from a university in Florida," Claire said. "She mostly talks about Confederate statues — General Grant and so on. There's some discussion of Rhodes — not a lot — and a bit about the naming of the Codrington Library in Oxford. Apparently,

Codrington was a slave owner. And there was a row at the University of Michigan over the naming of a building honouring a man who was a full-blown eugenicist."

Isabel listened as Claire explained. "She thinks that you can't correct everything, but you can erect competing monuments, or put some sort of footnote on the existing one."

"Telling the other side of the story?"

"Yes."

Isabel looked doubtful. "That won't work," she said. "It's not enough of a victory for the people who want the memory expunged altogether. You couldn't have a statue of Hitler in Berlin with a footnote at the bottom saying that he was also responsible for millions of deaths."

"No," said Claire, "you couldn't."

"Because that sort of approach misunderstands what a statue actually says."

"Which is?" asked Claire.

"That the person portrayed is worth remembering."

Claire thought for a moment. "Worth remembering in a positive way?"

"Yes. That's implicit."

"But does keeping a statue — allowing it to stand — necessarily say the same thing?"

Isabel agreed that there was a difference. "No, I suppose it doesn't. Letting a statue stand where it has always stood says that at a particular time — maybe a long time ago — somebody was admired sufficiently for

196

a statue to be erected. It doesn't say anything about what people feel *now*."

No, thought Claire. No. "You don't think it does?" she said. "Doesn't the statue's continued presence imply that there's still some approval for what that person stood for?" She paused. "It's like keeping a photograph of a former lover. If you have a photograph like that on your table, then surely that means you still have some affection for him. A lover you don't like any longer tends to go on the fire — or in the bin."

"I'm going to have to read the paper," said Isabel, removing it from the pile. "And what about the parental responsibility paper?"

"It says that we should make parents pay for the damage their children cause. The idea is that this is the only way you're going to get them to discipline their unruly offspring."

Isabel looked doubtful. "Unruly offspring often have unruly parents — not the sort of people to pay much attention."

"Not always."

"No, not always, but . . ." Isabel felt uncomfortable with the whole idea. Parenthood was a challenging matter and there were many who failed through no fault of their own. "Is it well argued?" she asked.

Claire thought it was, and the paper survived to the next stage.

"And the others?" asked Isabel.

Claire shook her head. "Nothing," she said.

"I'll take a quick look at them later," Isabel said. The streamlined selection process would work well, she thought, saving her the hours she would otherwise have spent wading through submissions. Already she felt liberated from at least part of her editorial load; if this continued, her life would certainly be easier. *I might even be able to spend time thinking*, she told herself, which was what, as a philosopher, she was meant to do.

After mid-morning coffee, Isabel decided to take a break. Magnus was still with Grace and Jamie was teaching. Judging from the sound of the vacuum cleaner, Antonia was still busy upstairs, and Claire could be left with the proofs of one of the sections of the next issue. Everyone, it seemed, was profitably engaged in what they should be doing, and this gave her a curious sense of freedom. *I can walk into Bruntsfield if I wish*, she thought. *I can pick up some fish for this evening from the fishmonger* — a nice piece of halibut, which always pleases Jamie. *I can spend time chatting to the woman behind the counter about fish; she loves to talk about what is coming in and where it was caught; she lives for fish.* Isabel savoured the words: *she lives for fish*; what an epitaph that would be, she thought — a simple inscription on the stone: *She lived for fish*. How many lives can be summed up that simply? Most of them, she thought. It could be a thing we lived for, or it could be a person. Many of us go through this life living for somebody else — that other person being our be-all and end-all. *She lived for her husband*, or *He lived for his wife*. That would be an accurate summary in many cases of what a life had been; and there was a simple dignity to such an epitaph. Or, *He lived for vintage cars*. She had a friend

198

to whom that might apply; he loved old Bugattis, thought them every bit as beautiful as the ceiling of the Sistine Chapel. *He lived for art. She lived for ballet. He lived for unhealthy food* . . . That, of course, would be one of those epitaphs that contained within itself a judgement on a life — which an epitaph can do, of course, although it should always be gentle. *He lived for unhealthy food, but who can blame him?* might be more charitable.

And, she told herself, I can buy some battered fish fingers for Charlie, for whom they are the biggest treat, even if the woman in the fishmonger thinks that fish fingers are an admission of creative defeat, a sort of vague insult to fish. I can do *ordinary* things that most people take for granted but that I can so rarely do.

It was a brisk ten-minute walk from the house to the fishmonger, but Isabel took her time, savouring the warm air of summer and the scents from the gardens she passed: a mown lawn here, a chopped hedge — vaguely lemony — there; the odd whiff of something drifting from an open kitchen window. As she approached the end of Merchiston Crescent she saw coming towards her the figure of a man she recognised — a man whose name she had once known, as he had been pointed out to her by somebody, but had now forgotten; he lived somewhere in one of the roads off the crescent and had once played chess for Scotland. Local legend had it that he had lost his temper in an important match in Iceland and had upset the board in a gesture of disgust. Now he lived by himself on the ground floor of a converted Victorian house and was said to have no visitors apart from a son, who was the leader of a motorcycle gang in Glasgow. There had been a wife, people said, but she had long since left him.

As they approached one another on the pavement, Isabel deliberately sought to make eye contact. She smiled, and even when his eyes slid away, shy of the contact, she greeted him. His name came back, suddenly and unexpectedly: he was a Mr McGregor, of the same name as the irascible gardener in Beatrix Potter's *Peter Rabbit*; or the man who wrote that book about the history of the world in one hundred objects from the collections of the British Museum; or the Scottish folk hero, Rob Roy Macgregor. So many and varied MacGregors, thought Isabel inconsequentially — of both spellings, Mc or Mac — and her mind had suddenly brought them up before her; the frightened rabbit running for his life from the crusty gardener, fearing incorporation within a rabbit pie; the articulate museum director talking of a sixteenth-century Benin plaque from Nigeria or the ship's chronometer from HMS *Beagle*; the red-haired and ruthless Highlander, Rob Roy, said to have had arms so long he could tie his gaiters without stooping, a consummate cattle thief and scourge of the nobility. All these MacGregors . . .

"Hello, Mr MacGregor."

He started at her greeting, but did not say anything. His eyes briefly met hers, though, and then he inclined his head slightly in acknowledgement; there was nothing more. He continued on his way.

200

For a moment she debated within herself about what to do. She could turn round and say something more to him while he was still within earshot. But what would that be? What could she say to this isolated, unhappy man? Forget about Iceland? Forget about chess, which will only upset you because you will never find any peace from all its moves and stratagems? Forget about the wife who left you, and find somebody new who will appreciate and at least try to make you happy?

In the fishmonger she said to the woman behind the counter, "I would like a piece of halibut."

"For how many?" asked the woman.

"Just for me and my husband. Some fish fingers for the boys."

The woman reached for a large piece of firm white fish. "This is delicious," she said. "We had a piece last night — me and Jimmy. He said it was the best halibut he's tasted in a good long while."

Isabel was only half listening.

"And the monkfish is good," said the woman.

"Yes," said Isabel. "A bit of that too. Not too much, since we have the halibut." She paused, and then continued, "Ellie, do you know that MacGregor man? You see him about here a lot. He lives somewhere off Merchiston Crescent."

The woman was wrapping the fish. "Yes, I know him. Odd fish."

Isabel laughed involuntarily, and Ellie glanced up.

"But he is," said Ellie. "You know they say that he was one of the best chess players in the world."

"I've heard that."

"And you know what he likes?" Ellie said. "I shouldn't tell you this, of course, but since you mentioned him — sardines. He likes fresh sardines. He says he does them in lemon juice — like they do in Portugal."

"Do you think the sardines make him happy?"

Ellie frowned. "I think they do. He buys them every week. I keep them for him. I try to get really good ones for him from the fish market."

"It's a nice thing you do."

Ellie looked puzzled. "No, I'm just doing my job."

"But I think it's kind of you. I suspect that man doesn't encounter much kindness in his average day. He's very lonely, don't you think?"

Isabel took the neatly wrapped parcels of fish and put them in her shopping bag. As she paid the bill and turned to leave, she found herself facing Patricia, who had just walked into the shop.

Patricia's face broke into a smile. "Twice in one week," she said. "Twice in one week in fishy circumstances."

Isabel was flustered. "I'm sorry . . . fishy circumstances?"

Patricia was looking at her with a certain coolness. Her expression was not hostile, but neither was it friendly. "The Quayside. That seafood place." She waited a moment before continuing. "We were both there the other night."

Isabel was aware of the fact that she was not saying anything in response and that Patricia was staring at her in a disconcerting manner, as if enjoying her discomfort. The possibilities went through her mind: she and Jamie had been spotted in the restaurant;

202

Patricia had been aware of her interest and had noticed her looking at her in the mirror; afterwards, she had not gone up the street outside at all but had been standing somewhere in the shadows, unseen, and had watched the two of them in their inept attempt to follow her and her companion.

At last she managed, "The Quayside?"

"Yes," said Patricia. "You were there with Jamie. So was I."

Isabel noticed: she said *I*. Why not *we*?

Now the issue was clear: she could deny that she had seen Patricia, and rely on a lie to save her embarrassment, or she could tell the truth. She thought of Immanuel Kant. He spoiled the comfort of lies for so many people — or at least for those who had read some philosophy; Kant would never have lied. Never. And he was right, of course, although there were circumstances, as surely everybody would accept, where it was permissible to lie — to save a friend, for instance, when a murderer intent on killing him asks you his whereabouts. Not only could you lie in such a case, but you might have a moral duty to do so. Kant was wrong to suggest that one would have to tell the truth even in such a case; he was simply wrong. *Or Kant himself was lying when he wrote that in the case of the enquiring murderer it would be wrong to lie. He was lying because he did not believe what he said.* Had anybody ever suggested that?

Isabel struggled. This was very far from the case of the enquiring murderer. She would have to tell the truth.

"Yes," she said, as evenly as she could manage, "I saw you there."

She left it at that. She had told the truth, without saying anything about thinking that Patricia hadn't seen her.

"Did you enjoy the meal?" asked Patricia.

Isabel nodded. "We did. Jamie suggested that place; I didn't really know it." She was aware that in her anxiety she was squeezing the parcel of fish. The halibut would be flaky and damaged; she must stop. "And you? Enjoyed it?"

Patricia was confident. "Yes, we did."

Isabel started to leave. "Good. Well, I must get back to the house. We have a visitor . . ." That was Claire — or Antonia; that, at least, was true, although perhaps to describe either of them as a visitor was misleading.

But Patricia had more to say. "It was my birthday treat from my brother."

Isabel stood quite still. She was aware that in the background the woman behind the counter was telling another customer about their kipper fillets. They were less salty than many others, she said; kipper could be over-salted. "You can soak them in water before cooking them," she said. "It lowers the salt level. People are concerned about salt these days . . ."

"Your birthday?" Isabel stuttered. She meant to say *your brother*, but it came out as *your birthday*.

"That's right. My brother spoils me."

Did he just pay for it, Isabel asked herself, or was he there? She clutched at the possibility that the brother lived somewhere else altogether — in Ireland, probably

— and might have sent the money for his sister to go out to dinner on her birthday. Patricia had then invited her lover to join her for dinner, which meant that the freckled man was not the brother, but a joint beneficiary of the brother's largesse. But no, that was unlikely. A far more probable explanation was that the freckled man was the brother, and he had been taking Patricia out for dinner; freckles must run in the family, just like red hair, or aquiline noses, or a tendency to certain illnesses. If he looked like young Basil, then that was hardly surprising — like uncle, like nephew. She should have thought of that. There was no reason to think that every man having dinner with a woman was necessarily her lover; brothers went out to dinner with sisters, cousins did, friends did. Dinner was not just for lovers.

Isabel now said, "So that was your brother you were with."

Patricia nodded. "Yes. My brother."

Isabel looked her watch. "I really must . . ."

"Of course you must." And then, "I haven't seen you at nursery for a while. Just Jamie — or Grace."

"I have a job," said Isabel. "Things can get busy."

"Of course."

Isabel said goodbye and walked out. She felt flushed. She was angry with herself for making such a simple and obvious error. Once again she had jumped to conclusions, and had been completely wrong. Fortunately, she had said nothing to Patricia; fortunately, she had not accused her of effectively stealing from Basil Phelps. Fortunately, she had not put her nascent plan into action. Fortunately.

CHAPTER
FOURTEEN

By the time she arrived home from the fishmonger, Isabel had largely recovered from the shock of Patricia's casual disclosure. Shock, in fact, had been replaced with feelings of relief over the fact that she had not acted on her unfounded suspicions. This relief was touched, though, with guilt: Jamie had spoken to her about the difference between knowledge and a hunch. He had often raised this with her — gently, of course, as he never confronted her. She had listened to him, but not *listened*, and there was an important difference between the two sorts of listening. In one, while you heard what was said, while you paid attention to the words, you knew in advance that the words would not sway you, or at least you would not allow them the chance to do so. That was a very common form of listening — for some people, Isabel thought, it was the only form of listening they did. Then there was the other form of listening, in which you heard the words, you weighed them, and you reached a view on the basis of what you had heard. That was listening in the real sense of the word — and that was what she had not done when Jamie had warned her about not acting on the basis of suppositions rather than proven facts. He was right, and she had been wrong.

He was not yet back from his morning of teaching at the Academy, but Grace had returned from her outing with Magnus, who had recovered, she said, from his upset stomach and was busy demolishing a doughnut in the kitchen. Isabel did not entirely approve of doughnuts, although she loved their taste, their oiliness, their unashamed carbohydrateness. Magnus did too, although he did not have the words to express any of those sentiments, referring to doughnuts by the private word "*not*", usually uttered with a heartfelt, close-to-irresistible sigh of longing.

"He can't have doughnuts all the time," Isabel had said. "If he does, he'll swell up like a Michelin baby."

Grace had been defensive. "I hardly ever give them to him," she said. "And you don't want him to disappear. Young children need bulking up."

"Well, let's just be careful. The occasional doughnut is fine, but let's keep them as a special treat."

"That's what I already do," said Grace.

But here was Magnus, mid-doughnut, the tracings of sugar smeared across his face and fragments of doughnut on the table of his high chair.

"There's somebody in your study," announced Grace — eager, perhaps, to deflect attention from the *in flagrante* consumption of the doughnut.

"That's Claire," said Isabel.

"No, it's not. She's there, yes, but I meant somebody else. There's a man. I heard his voice."

Isabel was intrigued. "You're sure?"

"Yes. A man. She was talking to him when I walked past the door."

Isabel tried not to smile. She knew that Grace's curiosity was always aroused when it came to visitors.

"And another thing," Grace now added. "There was a big din upstairs. Clattering and banging."

"Clattering and banging?"

"Yes, like an elephant. That girl . . ."

"Antonia," said Isabel quickly. "She's called Antonia."

"Yes, her. She's very noisy."

Isabel pointed out that Antonia appeared very keen, and was possibly merely being a bit too enthusiastic in her vacuuming. She almost added that vigour might be required there, as there had not been too much dusting or polishing in the house in recent months; but she did not say that, as the reproach would have caused offence.

"She'll have to stop when I take Magnus up for his rest," Grace warned. "He'll never sleep through all that."

"Londoners slept through the Blitz," said Isabel airily. "We can't tiptoe around children. They have to get used to the world, which is a noisy place."

Grace stared at her. "They're noisy people, the Italians," she said. "I went to Naples once, you know — years ago. The noise! I couldn't stand it. I couldn't sleep at night because all those Italians were running around, blowing the horns of their cars, shouting at one another about heaven knows what. You should have heard the din."

208

Isabel was determined not to let Grace have the last word on Italians. "They enjoy themselves," she said. "They're lively. I find that attractive."

"Scottish people enjoy themselves too," Grace countered. "But they don't make so much noise when they do. That's the difference, I think." She looked at Isabel in a way that suggested that the point, such as it was, had been won, and there would be no further discussion of the volume at which Italians lived their lives.

Isabel could not help but conjure up a picture of a group of Scots sitting quietly in a circle, enjoying themselves, knitting perhaps, or reading improving literature, or possibly just silently reflecting on what a good time they were having. She imagined the conversation. "Nice weather we're having." "Oh yes, but we'll pay for it later, we'll pay for it." Such was the reach of Knox and his reformers; such was the legacy, while all around the Catholic cultures danced and sang, raised high their idols and their plaster saints, unworried by Calvinism, and seemed, in general, to have a rather more enjoyable time. Of course there was the small question of the Inquisition, and the Jesuits, and the dead hand of ancient cardinals . . .

The picture faded, as she remembered the man in the study. She was curious. Had anybody been expected? She did not think so; her editorial role was a lonely one; all her dealings with the editorial board or the printers were conducted on the telephone or by email. She very rarely saw anybody, least of all one of the authors she published. Then it occurred to her that this was precisely who it might be; one of her philosophers, visiting Edinburgh in advance of the Festival, perhaps, might have taken it into his head to pay a visit. It might even be the mathematics teacher from Sri Lanka — unlikely — or the man from Salt Lake City who submitted an article about the ethics of polygamy (he was in favour of it). How would Claire cope with that? The Sri Lankan would be charming, as they so often were, and the man from Salt Lake City would be very well mannered, in the way in which people from that part of America usually were. He would be mildly spoken and well turned out — having more than one wife would help in that respect, Isabel thought, as they would take good care of his clothes, if they were old-fashioned wives. And they would be, she thought, if they accepted polygamy — and if, too, he were a polygamist, which was unlikely, as the relevant authorities in Salt Lake City played down that aspect of their history. And yet, there was at least one man in Utah who was prepared to justify polygamy and speak in its favour. She had written back, tactfully, declining the paper and, in passing, observing that polygamous systems were invariably discriminatory, allowing men to have more than one wife, but not permitting women to have more than one husband. She had not expected a response, but there had been one, in which he pointed out that the explanation for this was that few women would actually want more than one husband. "All the experts agree on that," he had said. "There is no doubt about it — lack of demand." Then he had written: "May I ask you something: would you like to have two husbands? Would it be fun, do you think?" She had not prolonged the correspondence.

Isabel made her way out of the kitchen and into the hall. Pausing briefly outside the door of her study, she listened for voices within. There was silence. She hesitated. What if the male visitor reported by Grace was a boyfriend — the sort described by Tennessee Williams as a *gentleman caller*? Should she knock before entering, just in case? That could be tactful, but then again it was highly artificial: one did not knock before entering one's own study, and to do so could be interpreted as distrustful, as if it implied that Claire could be up to no good — reading Isabel's private correspondence or going through the drawers of her desk.

Isabel decided that she would open the door without knocking, but would do so slowly, as if preoccupied with some other task while pushing it open. As she did this, she heard a faint noise inside the study — a step, a shifting of chairs?

She went in. Professor Lettuce was sitting in the armchair midway between Isabel's desk and the table at which Claire worked. Claire was on her feet, half beside the table, half behind it.

Lettuce rose to his feet, grinning. "So here you are at last," he said. He turned in Claire's direction. "Claire has looked after me very well. She said you wouldn't be long."

Isabel crossed the room to her desk. "How nice to see you, Professor Lettuce." She hoped that her voice sounded normal, but she feared that it did not. She was beginning to feel something stir within her — strong resentment that Lettuce should be in her study when she was not there. She glanced at Claire to see if there was any trace of apology. She saw none, but then why should she? She could not assume that Claire shared her antipathy to Professor Lettuce — quite the opposite, in fact: she buttered his scones for him; she spoke of him reverentially. Lettuce was, after all, her patron — the man who could make or break her academic career.

"I was in the vicinity," said Lettuce breezily. "I thought I might drop in and see how Claire was settling in."

"I think she's settled in very well," said Isabel. Looking at Claire again, she went on, "You look happy enough, Claire."

"Hah!" interjected Lettuce. "A happy ship. That's so important, I think."

Isabel sat down behind her desk. "I'm grateful to you for allowing her to take the job," she said.

Lettuce was clearly happy to be given the credit for Claire's employment. "Not at all," he said. "Delighted to help."

"Claire's been showing me some of the recent submissions," Lettuce continued.

Again Isabel glanced at Claire, who looked away. Silence ensued until Lettuce broke it.

"I know I'm no longer on the editorial board," he said. "I miss that, you know. But there we are. Seeing all this . . ." he gestured to the surroundings of the office ". . . seeing all this reminds me of how enjoyable

212

editorial work is." He folded his hands on his lap and looked directly at Isabel, his weak eyes, green in colour, like two . . . tiny lettuce hearts, thought Isabel; just like that.

"It has its moments," said Isabel.

"It certainly does," agreed Lettuce. "When I was editing the *Manchester Journal of Philosophy* I used to experience the most extraordinary elation once I put a new issue to bed. A sense of completion, I suppose." He was looking at Claire as he spoke, and Isabel saw something pass between them. It was unmistakable.

Isabel nodded mutely. She had been going over in her mind what had really brought Lettuce to her door, and the glance between them confirmed her suspicions: he was having an affair with Claire. It was so obvious now: Claire was not just his loyal acolyte — she was his lover. She turned to Claire, looking at her almost as if to say, *How could you?* Not only was Lettuce thoroughly disgusting, but there was a Mrs Lettuce somewhere in the background; Isabel had met her in the Scottish National Gallery. That poor woman — to be married to a lettuce, and to an unfaithful lettuce into the bargain, was not a fate one would wish on anyone.

Lettuce sat back in his chair. "I wonder if you've given further thought to my proposal of a public lecture?"

Isabel looked away. Not only had she not thought about Lettuce's vainglorious plan — the Robert Lettuce Lectures — but she did not want to think about it. And now, in an act she would later, on reflection, regret, she asked, "And how's your wife, Professor Lettuce?"

She held Lettuce's gaze as she asked the question. At first he was impassive, his expression a set mask of self-satisfaction, but then, almost imperceptibly, he flinched. Isabel turned briefly to Claire; she had moved back behind her table and was sitting there, trying, and failing, to look indifferent. But at the mention of Lettuce's wife she could not help it — she glanced nervously across the room at Lettuce.

"How kind of you to ask," said Lettuce, recovering his composure. "She has settled well into Edinburgh. She has been working very hard in her garden."

"*Il faut cultiver notre jardin,*" muttered Isabel.

"Hah!" exclaimed Lettuce. "Voltaire is right about so many things."

"Please give her my regards," said Isabel. And then added, "I hope she isn't too lonely." She said this almost without thinking, but was aware of her cruelty as she spoke. It was like stepping on a worm, she thought; and felt immediate regret at her pettiness.

Lettuce looked up sharply. "Why should she be lonely?" he asked. There was a peevish note in his voice, and she saw him look anxiously towards Claire, just as Claire, a few seconds ago, had sent a glance in his direction.

"You must be away a lot," said Isabel quickly, trying to explain herself. "And most of her friends must be down south, surely."

"We have made many friends since we came to Edinburgh," said Lettuce.

"Of course."

Lettuce was now looking at his watch. "I had better be on my way," he said. He rose to his feet. The dent to his confidence brought by Isabel's remarks seemed to have been short-lived. His manner was breezy now. "One thing, though — I was talking to Claire about the job she's doing here and I suggested — and I'm happy to say she agreed — that I might pop in from time to time and help her with it. I assume you have no objection." He paused. "All hands on deck, so to speak." He smiled magnanimously. "*Pro bono*, of course."

Isabel said nothing. Lettuce looked at her. "Oh, another thing," he said. "That paper I passed on to you. I see it over there." He pointed to a place on a shelf where Isabel had put it, along with a number of other submissions.

Isabel had not thought about the paper, but now it came back to her: "The Duty to Lie", by Professor Kale.

"I think we should publish it," said Lettuce. "It's very interesting. Claire can copy-edit it if you like."

Isabel seethed at his effrontery. We should publish it . . . We . . . She drew in her breath. "No," she said. "I don't think so. Not of sufficient interest. Sorry."

Lettuce glared at her. "But surely . . ."

Isabel was now more or less certain. Kale was a relative of Lettuce. That could be the only explanation.

"Your day?" asked Isabel, standing before the stove that evening, watching a scattering of shitake mushrooms sizzle in the frying pan. She added, "Should I be doing these mushrooms in butter? I'm using olive oil, and I don't think it's the same."

Jamie rose from his chair and looked over her shoulder. "They look nice," he said. "You're putting them in an omelette?"

Isabel nodded. "I thought I would. I was going to do us omelettes since it was lamb last night and we shouldn't eat too much red meat, should we?"

"Not according to the government," said Jamie. "The Department of Health, or whatever they call themselves, published new guidelines a few days ago. It was all over the papers. They said eat more fish and vegetables."

"The United Nations said the same thing, didn't it?"

Jamie corrected her. "That was bacon and processed meats. Very bad for us. The WHO said that, I think."

"It seems odd to be advised on bacon by the United Nations," Isabel mused. "Or on fish by the government. I suppose it's reasonable enough, it's just that one might imagine they would be preoccupied with other things."

Jamie smiled, and put an arm around Isabel's waist. "Those mushrooms tend to be quite tough, you know. They can be stringy."

Isabel gave the mushrooms a poke with a wooden spoon. "I'm giving them a lot of time in the pan. It should soften them." She repeated her question about butter.

"I think so," said Jamie. "But don't worry — they'll be fine. And the government also says we should use more olive oil, although they're discreet about that.

216

They don't come out and say it in so many words — olive oil is considered elitist, you see, and no government wants to be seen as elitist. It's like saying 'Let them eat cake'."

"No government wants a Marie Antoinette moment."

"No, it does not."

"So what do they say?" asked Isabel.

"They say 'Use more vegetable oils'. That's code for extra virgin, cold-pressed olive oil, if you're middle class and like shopping in delis; or sunflower oil, produced in France by the tanker-full, if you frequent the cut-price supermarkets. Tact on their part."

Isabel repeated her question about Jamie's day.

"Uneventful," he said. "Teaching in the Academy all morning." He stopped to think. "Actually, there was a major development. Seriously good news."

She waited. He leaned forward and examined the mushrooms more closely. "They're taking their time, aren't they?"

"Your good news?"

He gave her waist another squeeze. "Geoffrey Weir."

"He's disappeared? Arrested for crimes against musicality?"

"No, not quite — although that could have happened. He's given up. Packed in the bassoon. Declared defeat. Bassoon 1, Geoffrey Weir, 0."

"Poor boy," said Isabel. "You didn't put him off, did you?"

Jamie defended himself. "No, definitely not. I tried and tried. I did my best."

"But it wasn't to be?"

"Exactly." Jamie reached forward to extract a fragment of mushroom from the pan. He blew on this to cool it before popping it into his mouth. "Meaty," he said. "As advertised."

"What did he say?" asked Isabel.

"He said that he thought it might be better if he tried something else. He said that it wasn't his fault — it was his instrument. And there's a bit of truth in that. It was useless."

"Oh well."

"That was the good news," said Jamie. "Then there was the bad news. Apparently, Geoffrey wanted to sell his bassoon and use the money to buy a new laptop. But he said that his father vetoed this. He wants to keep the bassoon because Geoffrey has a younger brother. He's only ten, this brother, and — this is the bad news — he's expressed an interest in learning the bassoon."

Isabel laughed. "He'll be coming your way?"

"Probably."

"Not all Weirs are the same," said Isabel. "The sins of the brother shouldn't be visited upon the brother, so to speak."

Jamie agreed this was so. "I've seen the little Weir, and he doesn't look as bad as his big brother. He has rather odd, sticking-out ears, which are endearing. Geoffrey fancies himself and has very disconcerting plucked eyebrows. Should boys pluck their eyebrows?"

"Not traditional boys," answered Isabel. "But apart from all that, what else happened?"

Jamie told her about a rehearsal he had attended in the late afternoon. A consort with whom he played from time to time was playing a James MacMillan programme at St Giles' Cathedral. "An utter treat," he said. "Not like work at all. Then I came home. That was my day." He paused. "And yours? Where's whatshername?"

"Antonia."

"Yes, her. I take it she's out."

Isabel explained that Antonia had stayed in the house until two in the afternoon and had then announced that she wanted to see something of the city. Isabel had encouraged her, and had given her a bus map. "I asked her whether she would be in for dinner, and she said no. She told me that she would be back some time this evening. She has her key and everything."

"And what else?" asked Jamie.

Isabel put down the wooden spoon. The mushrooms were taking far too long. "I think we're going to have a cheese omelette instead," she said.

Jamie laughed. "I don't really like shitake mushrooms," he said. "I didn't want to tell you."

"You should have. We shouldn't keep secrets from one another."

Jamie grinned. "That's the only secret I've ever kept from you."

She kissed him. "And mine . . ." She kissed him again. "Mine is: I don't really like potatoes dauphinoise."

It was meant as a joke, but Jamie's face fell. "My potatoes . . ."

"No," she said hurriedly. "I love them. I love potatoes dauphinoise."

He said, feigning hurt, "You shouldn't joke about potatoes."

"I won't. I promise."

He retrieved a block of cave-aged cheddar from the fridge. "I'll take over the omelettes. You sit down, have a glass of wine, and tell me about your day."

He found the cheese grater. "Do you remember something you said about omelettes?"

She did not. "I don't recall saying much about omelettes," she said. "Not that I don't have my views . . ."

He reminded her: "You were talking about naming dishes after tyrants. I think you said something about *Omelette Ghengis*."

Isabel remembered, but only vaguely. "Is that what you're going to make?"

Jamie nodded. "Smoked paprika is called for," he said. "As well as cheese. It should be goat's cheese, as Ghengis's people kept lots of goats, I think. Or ewes, perhaps. You could use ewe's milk. And while I'm creating this, you can tell me about your own day."

Isabel sighed. "Lettuce," she said.

"Not with *Omelettes Ghengis*. We're having fennel."

"No, Professor Lettuce."

"Ah."

She told him about how Lettuce had appeared that morning, and how he had — preposterously, she felt — suggested that he should drop in from time to time to help Claire. She mentioned her suspicion that Lettuce was having an affair with Claire.

Jamie was incredulous about both aspects of this: the affair and Lettuce's presumption. "What a cheek!" he exploded. "I take it you said no."

Isabel looked at him apologetically.

"You did, didn't you?" Jamie pressed.

"Not exactly," she confessed. "I was at a loss for words, I'm afraid. And he didn't give me the time to say anything, really. He just made the suggestion and then breezed out."

Jamie shook his head in disbelief. "How can he?"

"Well, he did."

"Write to him," he said. "Write and tell him that he's not welcome." He paused; a better idea had occurred. "Speak to Claire about it. That would be easier from your point of view, and she probably encouraged him. She can put him off."

Isabel was thinking of something else. "I didn't treat him very well, I'm afraid."

Jamie frowned. "You?"

"I scored a cheap point," she said. "I talked about his wife in Claire's presence. I knew it would embarrass him."

Jamie made light of this. "You don't need to beat yourself up over that. He deserves everything he gets."

She did not think this was so. "It was petty of me."

He looked at her fondly. Isabel's conscience was a marvellous thing, he felt; it was sharper, more insistent, and more finely calibrated than an expensive scientific instrument. But it was also frustrating, causing her to stumble over the most inconsequential of matters — things that neither he, nor anybody else he knew, would pay much attention to. So she had offended Lettuce by drawing attention to the fact that he was a married man having an affair — but what could Lettuce expect? No, she did not need to reproach herself, but of course she would, and he knew there was not much he could do to dissuade her.

Jamie repeated his suggestion that Isabel should speak to Claire and get her to tell Lettuce that what he was proposing was unacceptable. "You really must do that," he insisted. "You have to nip it in the bud."

Isabel did not argue, and the subject was put to one side. As they ate the *Omelettes Ghengis* they talked about other matters. Then, after Jamie had done the washing-up, they read and watched a short, pointless television programme. At ten o'clock they went to bed. Jamie said, "She hasn't come back yet." Isabel replied, "She's twenty-one. Did you go to bed at ten o'clock when you were twenty-one?"

"It depends," said Jamie, and smiled.

At eleven-thirty, Isabel was woken by the sound of footsteps on the stairs. For a few moments she was confused, in a state somewhere between sleep and wakefulness, but then she was wide awake and realised that this was Antonia returning. She lay still, eyes fixed on the ceiling, staring up at faint tracings of light from the moonlit night outside. Jamie was sound asleep, his right arm across his chest, his breathing just detectable, a sound like a whisper. She felt one of his feet gently touching hers under the bedclothes, a point of warmth.

Both Charlie and Magnus were sound sleepers but she wished she had mentioned to Antonia that she should be careful about making too much noise when she came in. Sometimes Magnus woke up if they talked too loudly or the telephone rang, and he could be slow to get back to sleep. And if he woke, then Charlie invariably woke up too and demanded a glass of milk or something inappropriate — an olive, perhaps.

The house had three floors. Their bedrooms, as well as the bedrooms occupied by the boys, were below the attic floor, reached by a small back stairway, where Antonia's room was located. Her bedroom, in fact, was directly above Isabel and Jamie's room, with the result that now she heard the sound of Antonia's door opening and footsteps crossing the floor. There was a thump, as if something had been dropped on the floor above — a shoe, perhaps — and then, quite unmistakably, the sound of conversation. There were two voices, and one was male.

Isabel drew in her breath. Antonia had come back with a man.

She sat up in bed and strained to listen. Yes, it was a male voice, and then there was laughter. There was another thump. That was another shoe.

She turned to Jamie and placed a hand on his shoulder. He moved, as if to brush her hand away, but then he opened his eyes.

"What is it?"

Isabel replied in a whisper. "Antonia's back."

Jamie grunted.

"She has somebody with her."

Jamie rubbed at his eyes. When he spoke, his voice was thick with sleep. "Who?"

"A boy."

Jamie turned on his side to face Isabel. Now there was the sound of more laughter from above.

"We should have thought of this," said Jamie, his voice lowered — if they could hear Antonia and her friend, then they might hear Isabel and Jamie just as well. "We should have given her the room at the back."

"She didn't ask," whispered Isabel. "I'm not sure that I like this."

"Her bringing somebody back?"

"Yes. It's our house. If you're a guest in somebody's house you don't bring people back without asking. And besides . . ."

"Yes?" asked Jamie. "Besides?"

"She's a quick worker," said Isabel. "She's been here one day and she's picked somebody up in a club somewhere." She paused. "Am I being old-fashioned?"

Jamie made a non-committal noise.

"I suspect I am," said Isabel. "But I just don't feel comfortable about this."

"I'm not sure if you can dictate to au pairs," muttered Jamie. "Can you tell them how to behave when it comes to this sort of thing? Their sex lives are their own business, don't you think?"

Isabel lay back in bed. "Yes," she said. "But surely we've got the right to know who's coming into our house and spending the night. He could be anyone — absolutely anyone."

"True," conceded Jamie, his voice becoming sleepy again. "Speak to her tomorrow, although heaven knows . . ."

"Heaven knows what?"

Jamie did not reply. He had drifted off to sleep again, leaving Isabel to lie awake with her thoughts. Upstairs there was silence. Isabel closed her eyes. In the darkness, small problems can loom large, and Isabel now felt that in some strange way her house, her space, was being taken over by other people — by Claire, by Professor Lettuce, by Antonia, and by a strange young man whose identity she had no idea of, who was now starting to laugh again just feet above her head, separated only by a ceiling of old pine joists, laths, and the horsehair that the Victorians put into plaster.

CHAPTER
FIFTEEN

At breakfast the next morning nothing was said to Antonia about the events of the previous night. There was no sign of the man and Isabel assumed that the opening and closing doors that she had heard, rather vaguely, shortly after six was the sound of his departure. Antonia herself was bright-eyed and energetic. She had boiled an egg for Charlie and had patiently fed Magnus his baby muesli; now she was tackling the washing-up and asking Isabel what she could do for her that morning.

"There's a whole lot of ironing," said Isabel. "I know it's a thankless task, but it would be very helpful if you could make a start on it." She paused. "And yesterday?" It would have been a bit too pointed to say "last night". "Yesterday? How did things go?"

"I went into the city," Antonia replied. "I saw a lot. The Castle. The Royal Mile. The Scottish National Gallery."

Isabel expressed admiration. "Busy." *Quick worker,* she thought, and then stopped herself.

"Then I had something to eat in a pizza restaurant," continued Antonia. "I thought it very funny — to come all the way from Italy, and then to eat in an Italian restaurant."

"Comfort food," said Isabel. "What you're used to can be very comforting when you're far from home."

"Except we don't eat pizza in my house," said Antonia. "That's a southern dish. We don't eat southern food."

"And then?" asked Isabel, trying not to sound nosy. "What did you do after dinner?"

"I met some friends."

Isabel waited for Antonia to say more, but she did not.

"New friends?" Isabel ventured. "Or people you already knew?"

"Oh, new. I met them in a pub where they play folk music. Sandy something . . ."

"Sandy Bell's," said Isabel. "It's very famous."

"I met them there. They are students at the university."

Isabel took a deep breath. This was the time to say what she had to say.

"I should have discussed this with you yesterday," she began. "But we need to talk about it now. If you want to bring people here — your friends — then that's fine with us."

Antonia nodded. "Thank you."

"But not to stay, of course," Isabel went on hurriedly.

Antonia did not blink. "Of course not."

"Just to visit," said Isabel, thinking *I sound as if I'm speaking to Charlie.*

227

Again, Antonia nodded. "I would not bring anybody back here without asking you."

Isabel looked away. Then she said, "Good," and left the room. Her overwhelming feeling was one of disappointment. She had liked Antonia on their initial meeting, but now the lie that had just been told to her ruined that. How could she trust somebody who was ready to lie with so little hesitation? She couldn't, she told herself. She couldn't trust her now.

Or was it what was sometimes called an *understandable lie* — one of those mistruths we tell when we are unprepared to explain ourselves properly, or when we are caught out unawares. Such misstatements may be aspirational, as when we say what we would *like* to be the case, but which we have not *quite* managed to achieve. Isabel did not condone them, but she understood why they were uttered, and had in the past been as guilty as anybody else of resorting to them. The test of whether a lie was simple: could one add *I'm sure* to the statement? Did you leave the door unlocked/ leave the light on/forget to turn the tap off? *I'm sure it wasn't me* — which can be translated as *It was possibly/probably me, but I really didn't mean to, I won't do it in the future, and you've done it yourself so you're in no position to point the finger* . . .

Thinking about understandable lies made her feel rather more positive towards Antonia. The Italian girl was young; she was in a foreign country; they had not discussed the terms of their arrangement with her — at least in relation to the use of the house. Her bringing the boy back might have been quite innocent — young people thought nothing of sharing a room with their friends of the opposite sex and it might be quite wrong to assume that there was a sexual dimension to this. And even if there were — and Isabel smiled at the memory of one of her Mobile aunts drawing her aside and saying, *Isabel, honey, sex is happening all the time, you know* — *it's going on all the time!* — then did that really make any difference?

Thinking it through helped, and by the time she sat down at her desk to begin the day's work, she felt much easier about the whole situation. She had a feeling now that this was a day in which a great deal would be achieved. But then Cat telephoned.

"I know this is really, really short notice, but could you possibly . . ."

Isabel sighed.

Cat was sensitive. "Was that a sigh?"

"No," lied Isabel. "When do you want me?"

Cat said that by really short notice she meant extremely short notice. "Is there any chance of your coming up here within the next half-hour? Eddie's going to be late in — he has to go to the doctor about . . . about something, and he won't be in until at least ten."

"All right. I'll —" She broke off. It was so obvious.

"Isabel? Is that all right?"

"I'm going to bring somebody with me," said Isabel. "I'll be there."

Antonia accepted immediately. "Would I like to do some work in a deli? Of course I would. Now? I'm ready — I can do the ironing later. There's plenty of time. Can I wear what I'm wearing? This is wonderful."

Isabel felt herself won over by the young woman's sheer ebullience. Last night was forgotten; she liked company, that's all, and now that they had had that conversation she would no doubt be more discreet in future, with no more shoes being thrown to the floor or audible laughter. Isabel rolled her eyes — how very Edinburgh I sound, how Jean Brodie. But then I *am* from Edinburgh and if people from Edinburgh cannot have just a touch of Jean Brodie in their attitudes, then who can?

They walked together to Bruntsfield, where Cat was behind the deli counter, serving a short queue of customers. Isabel decided to wait until the last customer had gone before she made the introductions. And once she did, she could tell from Cat's attitude that she approved of Antonia.

"Once Eddie comes in," said Isabel, "I'll leave Antonia here. I have work to do." There was a hint of reproach in the reference to work, but Cat appeared not to notice it.

"This is a fabulous place," said Antonia. "I love food."

Isabel caught her eye, and smiled. "Don't we all?"

Antonia gazed about her. "And look at all the salamis." She reeled off the names. "*Cacciatore. Finocchiona. Sbriciolona.* Oh, I feel so homesick now."

Cat was clearly enjoying this display of approval. "And our pastas too. Look over there."

230

Again, Antonia enthused. "This is like being at home," she said.

Cat indicated that she had to leave. Isabel had not asked her where she was going, and did not express any view on the length of her absence, which was to last the entire day. But when Cat drew her aside and whispered, "I haven't said anything about pay. I take it you're paying her?" she decided to hold her ground.

"You can't expect people to work for nothing, Cat. Be reasonable."

Cat looked at her reproachfully. "I don't expect people to work for nothing. I pay Eddie."

And me? thought Isabel.

"And anyway," Cat continued, "you're paying her, aren't you? She doesn't need to be paid twice."

Cat looked at her watch, a signal that the issue needed no further discussion. Isabel did not press the matter; Cat was exploitative by nature — and she was not going to change. Even if Isabel had wanted to argue the point, there would be no time: two customers had entered the shop and were waiting for service. Cat nodded in a friendly way to Antonia and left by the front door, turning briefly to wave to Isabel and Antonia once she was outside.

"She must be a very busy person," said Antonia.

Isabel handed her an apron. "Yes," she said. "She is. But now you should watch me for a little while. See what I do."

She sold cheese to the first customer — a small Saint-Félicien and a thirty-degree wedge of Parmesan — and to the second customer a dozen slices of prosciutto crudo. Antonia volunteered to cut this, and operated the machine quickly and expertly, while Isabel held her breath. How would she put it to the au pair agency if she had to report that Antonia had sliced off a finger? They would accuse her not only of endangerment but also, perhaps, of trafficking: au pairs were not meant to be employed in ordinary non-household jobs, especially if those jobs were unpaid. That took one into slavery territory.

Within less than an hour, Antonia had familiarised herself with the operation of the till, with the location of a wide range of stock items, and with the idiosyncratic habits of the espresso machine. When Eddie arrived, Antonia had already made friends with several customers and, through her explanation of the source and merits of various Italian products, persuaded them to buy rather more than they had intended.

Eddie was reserved at first, but soon came under her spell, and when Isabel announced that she would leave the two of them to get on with it, he was quick to agree. "We'll be fine," he said. "You can go home now, Isabel — don't worry about us."

Isabel hesitated. "Are you sure, Antonia? Are you happy to stay?"

"Very," she said. "My friend Eddie and I . . ." She glanced at him, exchanging a look for which Isabel could find only one word, *premature*; ". . . we'll be fine."

"I'll come back if you like," said Isabel. "I could come back and collect you."

Eddie now intervened. "I'll look after her, Isabel," he said. "Stop worrying."

But she continued to worry, all the way back to the house and into her study. There were worries about Antonia, whether she was going to be too much to handle, and about what her intentions were for Eddie; worries about Claire and what she was going to say to her about the Lettuce question — more complicated and ominous, Isabel suddenly thought, than the Schleswig-Holstein Question itself; worries about what Grace thought of both of them — Antonia and Claire; and worries about how when you think you are simplifying your life you might really be complicating it. At least life seemed to be going reasonably smoothly at present for Magnus and Charlie: for Magnus, the day was filled with small experiences and triumphs: expeditions with Grace to feed the ducks in the canal, extra apple pudding — he had a sweet tooth — and a bath-time in which he was turning into an inveterate and prodigious splasher. For Charlie, there was nursery and its low-level politics: the unchallenged possession of the sandpit, the grabbing of food at lunchtime, the securing of the attention of the popular teaching assistant — enough to keep any assertive four-year-old more than busy. At least their lives were simple and unassailed by doubt, as was Jamie's, it seemed to her — he did not agonise over what he had to do; he led a life in which the saliences were clear enough and could be spotted in good time: next week's concert, the following month's rehearsal sessions, the day-to-day task of teaching pupils at the Academy, although admittedly that involved the likes of Geoffrey Weir. Why could she not lead a life like Jamie's, in which everything seemed so cut and dried, so clear and unambiguous?

The Schleswig-Holstein Question . . . It was a long time since she had thought about that; not since schooldays, in fact, when as a sixteen-year-old she had listened to the history teacher, Miss Macleod Grant — she of the beige crinoline dresses, all the same, every day for however many years and generations of students — telling them about Palmerston's comment that only three men in Europe had understood it, one being Prince Albert, who was now dead, the second being a German professor who had become mad, and finally he himself, who had forgotten all about it. That was political wit of the sort that had all but faded from sight, although occasionally it appeared, a sudden shaft of sunlight in the gloom, as when Harold Macmillan, having been interrupted by Khrushchev banging the table with his shoe in a United Nations debate, had languidly asked for a translation . . . That cheered her up.

Claire was not due in that day — she would be coming tomorrow, *sans* Lettuce, Isabel hoped. This gave Isabel the opportunity to tackle a task that she had been putting off for some time: the shortening by two thousand words of a five-thousand-word review article by a particularly prickly professor of philosophy at a university in Nova Scotia. She had met this woman at a Hume conference in Edinburgh years earlier, and had been struck by her sense of self-importance. There had been no contact between them in the intervening years until Isabel had invited her, at the suggestion of another member of the editorial board, to write a review of a recent tome on the theory of sentiments in the Scottish Enlightenment. This invitation had brought forth five thousand words instead of the requested three, and Isabel's politely put suggestion that it be cut had been met with a blunt refusal. "I'm far too busy," the author wrote. "If you wish to edit it, that's up to you."

It was a rude rebuff, in its grandiosity worthy even of Professor Lettuce, but Isabel appreciated the quality of the review and did not want to lose it. That woman, she thought, can *think*. And so she had decided to precis it herself — a task that had been waiting until now to be tackled. It was not easy. The author was far from prolix, and when Isabel removed, or even just shortened one sentence, this seemed to unstitch at least five others. She worked through lunchtime, snatching from the kitchen, where Grace was administering lunch to Magnus, a home-made prawn sandwich that she took back into her study. The sandwich was a disaster: the prawns had given up, it seemed — were defeated — turning to soggy small strips of pink protein, and the supermarket bread was stale: Jamie had forgotten his promise to buy a country loaf from la Barantine. But she ate it nonetheless and continued with her editing until it was time for her to go to fetch Charlie from the nursery.

When she arrived, there was no sign of Patricia at the nursery gate — a relief for Isabel, as their last meeting had been an awkward one. She had decided that the way to handle the relationship was to be cordial rather than friendly. Earlier on she had sensed that Patricia was keen to involve her in her life, for whatever reason, and she had been made to feel uncomfortable by the immediate and rather overwhelming friendliness. She had thought about that, wondering whether it was simply a cultural difference: the Irish tended to be warm in their approach to others, with none of the natural reserve of the Scots. Patricia was perhaps simply being Irish, which was not something one could blame an Irish person for being. That might be the explanation — in which case she, Isabel, should reciprocate her friendliness. But she had been wary of embracing her as a close friend — not yet, at any rate — as she had enough work to do in maintaining her existing friendships and the claims that those friends made of her. She thought, for example, of Peter Stevenson; she had not seen him for weeks and at the back of her mind was a nagging awareness that she owed him a response to an email he had written her about something she could no longer recollect. If one could not remember what one's existing friends had said to one in their last email, then perhaps one's circle of friends and acquaintances should contract rather than expand . . . and quite apart from all that, her last meeting with Patricia had been awkward because the Irishwoman must have thought it odd that Isabel did not acknowledge her presence in the restaurant. And then there was the question of whether Patricia had spotted her in the street afterwards; that did not bear thinking about, and so she put it out of her mind and concentrated, instead, on examining a small arrangement of painted stones that the children had placed near the benches in the garden. It was a tiny version of Callanish, the mysterious circle of stones on the Hebridean island of Lewis. Isabel imagined that ants, making their way up the path, might have stopped and marvelled at the ingenuity and power of those who had placed such a mighty monument there. She played with the thought: being able to find the solution to any troublesome question could often depend on your perspective and your ability to look at things from above.

The children were late. Somebody had been sick in the sandbox and somebody else had put modelling clay in somebody else's hair and it had to be explained to the perpetrator, and to the class in general, that while the sandbox incident was nobody's fault, the hair incident most certainly was. Waiting outside while order was restored in the classroom, Isabel acknowledged the other parents whom she knew; there was still no sign of Patricia. A woman she had not seen at the nursery before came up to her and introduced herself.

"You're Charlie's mum, aren't you?"

Isabel looked at the woman addressing her. She was a bit younger than she was, dressed casually, but in a way that Isabel would have associated with an affluent suburban life: expensive shoes, a silk scarf, well-cut clothes.

The woman introduced herself as Carol, Patricia's cousin. "I'm looking after Basil today because Patricia's away playing in something or other. I knew who you were because I'd seen you in Bruntsfield with Charlie, and I'd met Charlie when he was round at Albert Terrace one day. Complicated, yes, but . . ."

The accent was Irish, but not pronounced.

"I knew of your existence," said Isabel. "Patricia mentioned you. Your husband works offshore, she said."

"That's right. North Sea. He spends a lot of time on the rigs, I'm afraid. He's an engineer."

There was an easy friendliness to Carol's manner, but it was not quite so insistent as Patricia's, and Isabel found herself warming to her.

"Charlie's quite the little man," said Carol. "He's good for Basil, I think."

"They're just at the stage where co-operative friendship gets going," said Isabel. "Prior to that, I'm not so sure."

"Oh, they can be little terrors, can't they?" agreed Carol. "We don't have a family ourselves, but . . . but I see a lot of Basil."

The regret was there in Carol's voice. Isabel held her gaze for a few moments, and then looked away. It was a private sadness that those with children often forgot about, but that could sometimes be acutely painful.

"Basil's great," said Isabel. Was he? She had not really paid much attention to what Basil was like as a little boy. Perhaps he was.

"He has his moments," said Carol.

The volume of voices drifting out from the classroom grew. "They'll be out any minute," said Carol.

"Yes."

Carol seemed to be studying her, and Isabel felt vaguely uneasy.

"Patricia said you had a very nice house. She said it's quite a place."

Isabel smiled. "We're lucky," she said. "It was my parents' house."

"And a lovely garden, I hear."

"I can take no credit for that," said Isabel. "I wish I could, but I can't."

"I had a garden when we lived in Cork," said Carol. "A rather nice garden. It's warmer down there, of course. We didn't have one in Dublin, though. We had a tiny patch and neither of us really bothered with it. Here in Edinburgh it's a bit better. We're out in Colinton, near that boys' school — you know the one?"

Isabel nodded. "Patricia mentioned being from Dublin. She said something about having a house there."

"That was her parents' place — it was in Donnybrook. They retired to Galway. He was an eye surgeon, you know. I knew their place in Dublin well, because we lived just down the road when I was young. Patricia and I were more or less brought up together. We were cousins, but we were more like sisters."

"Then it's nice for you that you're now both in Edinburgh," Isabel said.

"It's great," said Carol. "And when we were kids it was particularly good because we were both only children. I would have been lonely without her. No brothers and sisters."

Isabel's attention had been drifting; the door of the nursery was being opened from within. She turned sharply. "Only children?" She had not misheard it. "I thought Patricia had a brother."

Carol shook her head. "No. She's an only child."

Isabel wanted to say, "Are you sure?" but realised that such a question would sound absurd. She was silent.

"Here they are," said Carol. "Look, Charlie and Basil are holding hands. Now, doesn't that make you want to smile?"

Isabel was still silent.

"Two wee friends," said Carol.

"Yes," said Isabel, vaguely.

"Don't you love his freckles?"

"I do. I do."

Charlie saw Isabel and immediately dropped Basil's hand to run to his mother. Basil did the same, throwing himself into Carol's opened arms.

"Hello, Spotty!" said Carol, hugging the little boy to her.

Isabel was stunned. *Spotty*. It was a term of endearment, no doubt, but who would call a freckled child that, even in jest? It was about as bad as *Fatty* for a chubby child, or *Rickety* for one with bandy legs. She glanced at Basil. He did not seem to mind.

"Well, we must be off," said Carol. "I've enjoyed talking to you."

"Yes," said Isabel. "Me too."

She took Charlie's hand and began to walk down the path to the gate. She had a lot to think about.

240

"Basil smells," Charlie said.

Isabel looked down at him in astonishment. "No he doesn't, Charlie. That's a very unkind thing to say."

"But he does," said Charlie. "I told him. He said, 'I don't.' But he does."

Isabel looked over her shoulder. Carol and Basil were not within earshot. "Charlie," she said, "we don't say unkind things about our friends. We just don't."

She heard herself. *We don't say unkind things about our friends.* She thought: would that this were true. Then another thought occurred: if a friend *did* smell, should you tell him? Children operated at a lower level of moral sophistication than adults, but sometimes they got the answer right precisely because of their lack of sophistication and subtlety.

What you should say to people . . . That was her problem reduced to its essentials. Yet even when you reduced some problems to their essentials, they became no easier to answer.

CHAPTER
SIXTEEN

"Not simple," said Peter Stevenson.

"No."

Peter looked at Isabel across the table of his kitchen in the Grange. She had spent the last ten minutes telling her friend about the dilemma with which she was now faced. That dilemma had ruined her sleep the night before, and now, although it was only eleven o'clock in the morning, Isabel felt the heavy hand of fatigue.

Peter was wide-eyed. "You mean you actually *followed* them — as in . . ." He waved a hand airily. "As in some fanciful thriller? Followed?"

"Yes. Or rather, tried to follow. I'm not a very successful sleuth, I'm afraid."

Peter laughed. "I've never met anybody who has actually *followed* somebody. But I suppose it happens. We see it in films often enough. They follow people onto train platforms and then when the suspect — I suppose that's what you call the person being followed — gets onto the train, the person following does the same; and then the suspect gets off again just as the doors are closing." He paused. "I love that scene. It's used time and time again, but I still love it."

"I didn't even get that far," said Isabel. "As I said, I lost them immediately. But then . . ."

"Then you were accosted and ended up in the police station and saw a photograph of the freckled man." Peter relished the words. "*The freckled man*. That has a real ring to it, doesn't it? Isn't there something by Conan Doyle along those lines? Or is it the speckled band?"

"It's the speckled band. It's a snake. One of the best of the Holmes stories."

Peter looked at Isabel quizzically. "What do you want me to do?"

"I don't want you to do anything," she said. "I was rather hoping you might help me to decide what to do." She reached for the mug of coffee that Peter had poured for her. "That is, if you don't mind."

Peter was quick to assure her that he did not. "I suspect you already know what to do," he said. "Most people who ask for advice do, you know. The advice usually just helps to confirm their intentions."

"And what do you think my intentions are?"

Peter looked out of the window. "On past form," he began, "I'd say you're going to inform Basil Phelps — that is the organist Basil — that he's being taken advantage of. Then you're going to tell the Irishwoman . . ."

"Patricia."

"Yes, her — you're going to tell her the game's up."

"And what about the police photograph?"

Peter thought for a moment. "I think you're going to tell Patricia that you happened to see the photograph because . . ." he watched her reaction ". . . because if you don't, you will continue to wonder whether you should have done so, and you'll have no peace until you do."

Isabel took a sip of her coffee. "How can you be so sure?"

Peter smiled. "First, am I right?"

She reached the conclusion reluctantly, but she knew that he was. "Yes," she said.

"Well, there we are," said Peter.

She asked him what *he* would do. He answered without hesitation. "I'd find it very difficult to decide — just as you have. I can see the arguments either way: minding my own business — which is always a sensible thing to do — or helping to save somebody from being cheated, which is what is possibly happening here. I emphasise *possibly*. You don't really know." He paused. "I can't tell you what to do, you know. You want me to do that, I suspect, but should I?"

Isabel sighed. "You're right. It would be so much easier for me if you'd simply take this decision for me. That's what I've been hoping — but . . ."

"But I can't do that, can I?"

She shook her head. "No, you can't. And it's unfair of me to expect you to."

She looked into her coffee cup. "How do we decide on the limits, Peter? How do we decide what we can do about the world?"

Peter sighed. "I suspect there isn't a hard and fast rule. You have to do as much as you think is necessary for you and as much as you think you can realistically do. In other words, use common sense."

244

"I wish I could define common sense," said Isabel.

"Isn't common sense more or less a gut feeling as to what seems right?" said Peter. "You could have a more sophisticated definition, of course, but I think that's at least a start."

She thought of what lay ahead. "I'm going to go soon," she said. "Probably next week. I'm going to go and see Basil Phelps and tell him."

"And then?"

She was less certain as to how to answer that, but eventually she replied, "I think I'll warn Patricia."

"About the photograph?"

Isabel nodded.

Peter looked doubtful. "That's the bit I don't like."

"So I shouldn't?"

Peter sank his head in his hands. "We're back to square one. You want me to tell you what to do. So, all right, don't. That whole area is no business of yours — at least in my opinion. And although I'm not going to tell you what to do, I find myself saying: no, don't do that. Just don't." He paused. "So let's talk about something else. There must be something."

"I have another issue," said Isabel. "I wasn't going to mention it, but since you ask . . ."

She began to tell him about Antonia, but he stopped her before she had got very far.

"Isabel," he said, "other lives are other lives. Live yours. Leave it to others to live theirs."

She was silent as she thought about this. It was sound advice, in principle, but she thought it might be difficult to apply. "Lives aren't lived in isolation," she said. "Unless you cut yourself off from everybody."

"True."

She made a gesture of helplessness. "So we find ourselves caught up in the affairs of others."

"Also true."

"And by taking on an au pair, surely I'm responsible in some way for her. And she owes me something in return — she must make some concessions to my feelings."

He agreed with that. "You're entitled to state the house rules. Just be reasonable in what rules you make."

"Do you think I would ever be anything but reasonable?"

She asked the question with a smile, and he answered in the same spirit. "Yes," he said.

Again, they both laughed, and went on to discuss something altogether different. Peter's wife, Susie, who had been upstairs on a long telephone call to their daughter, came downstairs and joined them. Isabel did not burden Susie with her indecision, and their conversation flowed lightly around the themes that old friends in Edinburgh so enjoy: who had said what to whom; when they had said it; and what the implications were: not exactly gossip, but something so close to it that one might as well call it gossip. In the nicest sense of the word, of course.

On the way home, Isabel called in at the deli to buy eggs. She spoke to Eddie, who was busy cleaning the slicing machine; he abandoned this task when Isabel arrived and insisted on her sampling a consignment of olives that had just arrived. "There are peppers in the oil," he said. "And garlic. Taste this."

She took the proffered olive and popped it into her mouth. "Perfect."

Eddie was pleased. "You know that girl, that Antonia? The one who helped yesterday?"

"Yes, what about her?"

"She's coming back this afternoon. She's just phoned to tell us."

Isabel was slightly taken aback. She had seen Antonia briefly that morning and had discussed the ironing with her. Nothing had been said about how she would spend her afternoon.

"Cat's really pleased," said Eddie, nodding in the direction of the office. "And so am I."

Isabel reached out to help herself to another olive. "I need a dozen eggs, Eddie. The organic ones."

"Oh yes," said Eddie, "you must have seen what I read the other day. Organic eggs are really good for your eyes. They have something in their yolks that stops you getting macular . . . macular something or other."

"Macular degeneration."

"Yes."

She waited for him to fetch the eggs. She thought of what he had said: *Cat's really pleased. And so am I.* He whistled something — a few bars, tunelessly, but enough for Isabel to reach her conclusion. Eddie had fallen for Antonia. There was something about his manner that gave this away; Isabel had always felt that a person in love simply could not conceal it.

"Eddie," she said when he came back, "be careful."

He looked down at the box of eggs in his hand. "Of course I will."

"No," she whispered. "Not about the eggs. About Antonia."

He blushed, and looked directly into her eyes. She looked back at him. She had known this young man for some years now. She knew that he had been damaged, and she had helped him on his road to recovery; she had seen him flourish. There was a long history here; Eddie was not a stranger to her.

For a moment he hesitated, but then he put the eggs down and leaned forward to whisper in Isabel's ear. "Isabel, I've known you for ages, haven't I? And I really want to tell somebody about this, because I'm so . . . well, I'm so excited."

She placed her hand on his shoulder. "It's all right, Eddie," she whispered back. "I understand. It's just that I didn't want you to be hurt."

"Antonia and I are an item. We've . . . well, you know what I mean, we've . . ."

She felt herself reeling at the disclosure. Why was he telling her this? "When did this happen, Eddie?"

"Last night."

She wanted to laugh, although everything within her said this was not an occasion for laughter — anything but. He had met her that afternoon, and presumably that same evening . . .

Then she found herself asking, "Where?" Had this affair started in the deli office?

248

"In her room," said Eddie. "That's where we were last night. She said it was all right. She said you didn't mind."

Isabel thought: last night. That was Antonia's second night in Edinburgh. The first night had been the night when she had gone to Sandy Bell's and then come back to the house with the unidentified young man. That could not have been Eddie. Eddie was *last* night — after the conversation with Isabel about guests in rooms.

She drew back, making Eddie look at her with the sudden concern of one who thinks he has said too much.

"I shouldn't have told you," he said. "You shouldn't speak about sex. It's private — I know that — but I just wanted to tell you how happy I am. I wanted to be able to say that to somebody. And I think I know you better than anybody . . ."

She touched him gently on the forearm. "That's all right, Eddie. But just be careful. Remember that some people take these things more seriously than others. You don't want to go and fall in love with somebody who doesn't take them as seriously as you do. That's the way you get hurt." She struggled not to wince at her own words; Eddie was not a sixteen-year-old who needed warning about the power — and inconstancy — of human emotions. He was a young man in his twenties. And yet he was vulnerable; he was impulsive and had a puppy-dog enthusiasm for the world; having been hurt as a youngster, he could so easily be hurt again. It was all very well for her to limit the scope of her concern, to try to put into practice the advice that both Jamie and Peter consistently gave her — and that other friends did too — but Eddie was not on the margins of her moral circle, one might even say he was somewhere near its centre. She had no alternative, then, but to say what she was saying to him, trying to be as gentle as possible about it, avoiding being too much of a Dutch aunt. But perhaps that is what I am, she thought, a Dutch aunt: telling people off, advising them to do this, that or the other; sticking my nose into their business.

"Oh, I know that," he said. "But this is different, Isabel. She's in love with me. She told me that. Those were her exact words. She loves me, Isabel."

She saw Basil Phelps rather sooner than she had anticipated, and in circumstances that she had not planned. It was at a concert, two days after her conversation with Peter, and Eddie's disclosure — a concert at which, unusually, she and Jamie were both in the audience. Isabel was used to performances in which Jamie would be on stage, and it was a treat for her to be able to sit with him and enjoy the playing of others. This concert took place in the Queen's Hall, a converted church that made up in atmosphere for what it lacked in comfort; the church had been Presbyterian, and traditionally that meant hard seats at an upright angle, designed, it would seem, to ensure attention to sermons, and discouraging of anything but Protestant rectitude. Given over to the arts, the building had mellowed, but in its clean lines and unadorned surfaces still reminded the visitor of the culture from which it

250

had emerged. For Isabel and Jamie, though, it was a place of layered memory; here Jamie had first performed Mozart's Bassoon Concerto to a packed house; here Isabel had listened to him play a tortuous piece of Strindberg and had as a result developed a headache that lasted for eighteen hours; here they had both heard an orchestra of children from a town near Stirling play to an audience largely composed of their parents. Isabel had found herself weeping at that concert, not from watching the children with their half-sized violins and their missed cues, but from seeing the expressions of pride on their parents' faces. One of the fathers had caught her eye — a bruiser of a man with a broken nose — and he had smiled in recognition of her engagement with the performance, making a thumbs-up sign of triumph.

Now she was sitting with Jamie halfway down the main body of the hall, waiting for the concert to start. They were early, which gave them time to inspect the programme notes for the concert of Jacobean songs from the court of James VI, both before he left Scotland for England, and after he had taken up the glittering heritage conferred on him by the English. The English had chopped off his mother's head — and would, in time, chop off his son's — but in spite of that, James, who had been a late convert to music, came to be an enthusiast for all that England had to offer in terms of the music and the arts the religious zealots back in Scotland had so enthusiastically repressed.

A few minutes before the concert was about to begin, Jamie nudged Isabel gently. She looked up from the programme notes.

"The French manner," she muttered. "They liked the French musical style."

"Over there," whispered Jamie. "See? The third row from the front."

Isabel followed his gaze. "Who?" Her mind was on Orlando Gibbons. "They're going to sing 'Trust not, fair youth, in thy feature'. A madrigal by Gibbons. Isn't that a wonderful line? Does 'feature' mean 'features', do you think? If it does, then what salutary advice for any fair youth . . ."

"There," said Jamie. "Basil Phelps. Sitting next to that woman in red."

This ended thoughts of Gibbons as she stared at the back of Basil Phelps's neck. But then, when he turned round, she recognised the organist. "Yes, it's him," she said.

Jamie tapped her lightly on the sleeve. "Not here," he said, his voice lowered.

"Of course not," she said. And then added, in reproach, "Do you really imagine I'd . . ."

She did not finish. The singers were coming onto the open stage and the audience was applauding. The accompanist was a lutenist, and he was taking his seat near the front of the stage, the five singers standing immediately behind him. Isabel saw Jamie's expression of rapt interest and she reached out and touched his arm; she knew what this music meant to him. He

252

placed his hand lightly upon hers in a gesture of shared anticipation.

The programme followed a chronological course, starting with the music with which James would have been familiar in his youth in Scotland before moving on to the music of the London court. Isabel followed the words printed in the programme. The theme, she thought, intentional or otherwise, was loss. Love and loss — two things that went together, it seemed, with a poignant inevitability; we loved, knowing that we would lose, but loved nonetheless because . . . She stopped. Yes, because we did not *choose* to love; we loved because we had to. Love was something that happened to us; it was never planned, even if we knew that some day, at some moment, it might alight upon us and — we hoped — change everything.

"This next one," whispered Jamie, pointing to the programme. "I know this song. It's Scottish. I really love it."

One of the singers, a tenor, moved to the front of the stage. He nodded to the lutenist, and the song began. Isabel read the title: "Remember me, my deir". The old spelling added to the charm. My *deir*. The song went on to refer to *my deir hart*. She glanced at Jamie, and thought, *my deir*. And then, curiously, the question crossed her mind: was it possible for thoughts to have idiosyncratic spellings?

The song finished. Engrossed in her reflections on the expression of thought in language, Isabel had hardly listened — nor had she read the words in the programme. Nor did her concentration improve as the evening went on. Now she found herself thinking of Antonia and Claire, of what she should say to them — if anything — and of whether it had been a bad idea to disturb the delicate ecology of the house by bringing in strangers. Antonia obviously had an eye for young men and risked hurting Eddie, of whom Isabel was very fond. He was bound to be hurt, she thought; she was playing with him, and he, poor boy, believed her. The thought distressed her, especially since she felt responsible for creating the situation in the first place. Then there was Claire: she would have to speak to her about Professor Lettuce and that would not be easy. If her intuitions were correct and the two of them were having an affair, then Claire would not take kindly to any criticism of Lettuce, and even less to any request that she not invite him into the office. These were difficult matters, and they kept intruding in Isabel's mind, a nagging overlay to the Jacobean songs.

At the end of the concert, Jamie suggested that they call in at the bar, a large room at the back of the hall and a popular place for concert-goers to catch up with friends. It was usually a place where Isabel would recognise at least a few friends, while for Jamie there would be even more acquaintances, it being a favourite haunt of musicians. And that evening, even before they ordered drinks, Jamie was waylaid and taken off to the green room to meet the lutenist. Isabel said that she would order him a drink and keep it for him until he came back.

She took the two glasses of wine she had ordered to a free table she had spotted. As she approached the table, she had to negotiate her way round a small knot of people huddled around somebody recounting some apparently compelling anecdote. One of them turned round, and she saw it was Basil Phelps. He smiled at her.

"It's Isabel Dalhousie, isn't it?"

Her surprise must have shown, because he smiled again, clearly thinking that she was unable to remember his name.

"Basil Phelps," he said.

"Of course. Sorry." She had a glass in each hand and she nodded in that direction. "These aren't both for me. I'm not being greedy."

He reached out. "Let me help you. I can put one of them down for you."

He took the glass from her and placed it carefully on the empty table. "You're a friend of the Museum, aren't you? I think we met there — at the Friends' Dinner."

"Yes, I remember that," said Isabel. "And then at a concert, I think — a few weeks ago."

Basil asked her if she had enjoyed the Jacobean songs. She had, she said, although her mind had been active and she had been a bit distracted. As it was now — with thoughts of whether she should do what she felt she had to do, or whether she could take the easy option and simply continue with small talk until Jamie returned from the green room. *I have to,* she told herself. *I have to. If I don't do it now, I'll put it off indefinitely. I have to.*

She had not prepared herself for this encounter and now that it was occurring she found that she had no idea of how to broach the subject. She took a sip from her glass of wine. It tasted unfamiliar; it was too sweet for her palate.

"Your son and my son," she said, "are friends."

The unplanned words spilled out. They sounded stilted, and she immediately regretted them.

Basil Phelps looked at her impassively. For a few moments she thought he was not going to react at all, but then she saw the knuckles in his right hand tighten against the stem of the glass he was holding. So might a skilled interrogator, accustomed to detecting the slightest chink in a suspect's demeanour, spot the tell-tale sign of vulnerability.

"I don't have the opportunity to see him," he said. "It's the way of things, I'm afraid."

"I'm sorry to hear that."

He looked away. She noticed that his right hand was shaking, making a small splash of wine fall against the fabric of his jacket. He brushed at it with his other hand, but only succeeded in spilling more.

"I know the background," she said. "I've heard about what happened."

He brought his gaze back to her. His expression was pained.

"I suppose everybody knows," he said quietly. "Edinburgh's that sort of place. People talk."

She wondered whether there was reproach in this. *People talk.*

"I can't help wondering," she said, "whether there might be a mistake. There must be cases where a person is made to pay for the upkeep of a child who isn't really his."

He tensed. "I'm not with you, I'm afraid."

She had gone too far. Now there was no going back.

"I don't know if I should tell you this, but I saw Patricia with a man who looked . . . well, he looked so like Basil. Freckles, you see. I thought —"

He cut her short. "Excuse me," he said. "I know very little about you. You come up to me here — in public — and you start talking about . . . about my private business. What makes you think you can do that?"

Flustered, she tried to explain. "I felt I had to say something. I didn't want to. I felt . . ."

He interrupted again. "May I suggest you mind your own business?"

She looked down at the floor. "I'm sorry."

He had begun to turn away, but he seemed suddenly to have second thoughts. "I've been rude," he said. "Please forgive me for that. But it really is nothing to do with you, is it?"

"I'm the one who's been rude," said Isabel quickly.

He seemed to be weighing her apology. Then he said, "All right. Let's forget it. I'd better get back to my friends."

Jamie returned from the green room a few minutes later. He saw from Isabel's demeanour that something had happened. Looking around the room, he saw Basil Phelps with his friends. Basil turned briefly and looked in their direction, and Jamie knew immediately.

Jamie looked unbelieving. "You didn't, did you?" he groaned. "Surely not here."

Isabel shrugged. "I had to."

Jamie rolled his eyes. "What happened?"

"He told me to mind my own business."

Jamie sighed. "I'm not going to say it."

She knew what it was that he was not going to say, and she thought: he's said what he's not going to say before — many times. He did not need to say it. He did not need to say what he was not going to say.

"I told you so?" she said.

"Words to that effect," said Jamie.

Isabel steeled herself for further criticism, but none came. Rather, Jamie reached for his glass of wine and raised it to hers. "To my *deir hart*," he said. "Obstinate, interventionist, nosy, yet . . . yet one who does the right thing — where lesser mortals . . ." and here he pointed at himself, "where lesser mortals fear to tread."

She replied, "*My deir hart*." He was; that was what he was, and she dwelled on the thought of her good fortune — so complete, so undeserved, so hard to believe.

CHAPTER
SEVENTEEN

Cat's telephone call came the next morning while Isabel and Jamie were having breakfast with the boys. It was a Saturday, a day on which Jamie often had playing commitments, although that day he was unexpectedly free. He watched Isabel as she took the call and when she rang off he guessed correctly what Isabel would say.

"Crisis?"

Isabel, switching off her mobile, nodded. "Yes, crisis."

Jamie, who was feeding Magnus with his favourite soldiers — strips of toast dipped in soft-boiled egg — sighed. "Requiring your presence?"

Again Isabel nodded. "Yes, requiring my presence."

Jamie's frustration showed. "Can't Antonia do it? She's been spending a lot of time there. Can't Cat just leave you alone for once?" His voice rose. "Just for once, for heaven's sake."

Isabel's answer took him by surprise. "The crisis is to do with Antonia, apparently. And Eddie." She had told Jamie about her conversation with Eddie, and he had expressed concern but had told her to stay out of it.

"Did she say what?"

Isabel shook her head. "She just said that it was to do with my au pair. That's how she referred to her — as *my* au pair."

"Suggesting that it was somehow your fault." There was now an unmistakable note of anger in his voice. This was unusual for him; Jamie was rarely anything other than calm. "You know something, Isabel? With Cat it's always about her, isn't it? Always."

Isabel was loyal to her niece, but she could not disagree. Cat was selfish, and always had been. The giveaway test, in Isabel's mind, was whether somebody ever asked about *you*. She never did. Whenever she saw Cat, there were never any questions asked as to what she had been doing or how she felt about things.

"Perhaps she'll learn one day," said Isabel. "People change."

Jamie looked sceptical. "Do you really think so?"

"Everybody does — to a greater or lesser extent. As you get older, you become more . . ."

"Crabbit?" suggested Jamie. *Crabbit* was one of those Scots words that captured certain qualities in a way that ordinary English words could not. *Crabbit* meant cantankerous and difficult.

"Sometimes," said Isabel. "But sometimes you become more tolerant. Less bound up in yourself." She paused. "I've changed, I think. I don't know about you, but I think I have."

Jamie looked at her quizzically. "How?"

"How have I changed?"

"Yes."

She thought for a moment. "I hope that I've become a little bit less disapproving. I used to disapprove of things — and people — I didn't like. Then one day a friend said to me, 'Can't you be a bit more charitable?' And I felt so ashamed of myself."

"But you are charitable," said Jamie. "You're one of the most charitable people I know."

"I doubt it."

"No," he said. "You are. You'll go to any lengths to help people. You'd give most of your money away if you had the chance. You're kind about people."

Isabel blushed. "No more than anybody else," she said.

"Except Cat."

"Let's not talk about poor Cat — she's stressed. She has too much on her plate."

Jamie felt that Isabel had just proved his point. "There you go," he said. "You're making allowances for her again."

Isabel raised her eyes towards upstairs. "Is Antonia in?" she asked. "Have you seen her?"

"Not since yesterday morning," replied Jamie. "Didn't you tell her she could have the weekend off?"

"Yes," said Isabel. "I was just wondering. Did she say anything about her plans?"

Jamie shook his head. "I haven't spoken to her very much. She seems shy when I'm around. I don't know why."

Charlie had been listening. Now he surprised them. "Antonia's going to bite you, Daddy. I heard her. Talking on her phone."

"Really?" asked Isabel.

Charlie continued. "She said she could eat Daddy up. She said that. You must be careful, Daddy." He looked beseechingly at Isabel. "Don't let Antonia eat Daddy, Mummy."

Isabel and Jamie looked at one another. Then Jamie laughed. "Her grasp of English might be imperfect," he said.

"True," said Isabel. "But it gives one pause for thought." And to Charlie, she said, "I won't let that happen, darling."

"Good," said Charlie.

Cat greeted her with a nod when Isabel arrived at the deli. There were two customers at the counter, but Isabel saw that Cat was not single-handed — standing behind her, wrapping sliced meat in greaseproof paper, was Leo. Isabel did not disturb them, but made her way directly to the office where clean aprons were hung up on a line of pegs. Choosing her favourite, a red-striped one, she slipped it on. Then she washed her hands in the basin in the corner of the office; she was scrupulous about that, although Eddie, and sometimes even Cat, seemed not to bother. "You can't get rid of every single germ," Eddie had observed. "You'd spend all day washing your hands and you'd have no skin left. Then what? You'd end up giving people your own germs from your blood and from all the bits of skin. No thanks."

Her customer attended to, Cat came into the office, followed a few moments later by Leo, wiping his hands on the front of his apron. That was another thing you

262

were not meant to do, thought Isabel: aprons were fertile breeding grounds for germs — whole colonies, whole dynasties of microbes lived on aprons. Leo gave Isabel a non-committal glance — not a smile, but neither was it a scowl.

"Thanks for coming so quickly," said Cat.

It was a grudging thanks, Isabel thought, but she nonetheless replied, "You did say it was a crisis."

Cat perched on the edge of her desk. "It is. It's a serious crisis."

"Well, I'm here to help," said Isabel. "Tell me what's happened."

Leo, who had sat himself down on the spare chair, answered. "That boy's gone."

Isabel looked to Cat for confirmation. "Eddie?"

Cat nodded. "He left a message on my phone last night. He said he was taking a few days off and wouldn't be back until Thursday morning."

"Just like that?" asked Isabel. "He hadn't arranged anything?"

Leo chipped in again. "Just like that."

"He's never done this before," said Cat. "So I called him back first thing this morning and he was on a bus — on the way to Skye. He said that he and that au pair of yours were going up there for a few days. He said that she's always wanted to see it, and he was going to show her. He has a tent, he said."

Isabel struggled to take this in. "Antonia? She's gone with him?"

"Yes," said Cat. "She's put him up to this. I noticed her making a play for him."

"She's a nympho," said Leo. "The real thing. I've seen her when she's been in here — eyeing up any likely-looking guy who came in. Undressing them with her eyes. You know what I mean. A nympho."

Isabel turned to look at Leo. "I'm not sure many people use that word these days," she said.

Leo seemed unabashed. "Don't they? So what word do they use?"

Isabel thought for a moment. *Nymphomaniac* was a degrading word, often used in the past to condemn women who were merely highly sexed. The male equivalent — the condition of satyriasis — was rarely used because there were double standards at work here: women were not expected to have as active a sex life as men. She looked at Leo: he would not be interested in any of this.

"That's neither here nor there," interjected Cat. "The point is that she's seduced Eddie. She's turned his head and put him up to going off to Skye. In a tent, I ask you."

"I can just see it," said Leo, bursting into laughter. "Not much room in a tent, though."

Cat looked at Isabel accusingly. "You didn't know she was going away?"

Isabel shook her head. "I had no idea. This morning I assumed she was up in her room. I haven't seen her since . . ." She searched her memory. "Since yesterday lunchtime, I think. She wasn't in for dinner last night."

"So she never told you?" asked Cat.

"No. As I said, I had no idea."

264

"Where did you get her?" Leo asked. "What did her references say?"

"I got her from an agency," answered Isabel. "And they didn't give me any references. They said that she'd be a good worker. That's about all."

Cat looked annoyed. "You should have asked for references. I'm surprised you didn't. Letting somebody into your house like that without getting a reference is asking for trouble."

"I wouldn't do it," Leo said.

Isabel threw him what she hoped was a dismissive glance. *Where are your references?* she thought.

She felt the back of her neck becoming warm. She had been right in her feeling that they were in some way blaming her for all this. They had no right to do that, she decided, and she should defend herself. "What do you think a referee would have written?" she asked.

" 'A hard worker, but a nympho in her spare time,' " said Leo. "That would about sum it up."

Cat snapped at him. "Don't joke about this, Leo. What are we going to do? I have to be in Glasgow on Monday afternoon, and then there's Tuesday and Wednesday and presumably most of Thursday morning before Eddie condescends to show up. Unless he's too love-sick . . ."

". . . or exhausted," added Leo, smirking.

There was a long silence, eventually broken by Cat saying, "I wish you hadn't brought that girl here, Isabel. If you hadn't done that, then we wouldn't be in this mess."

"So it's my fault?" Isabel challenged.

Cat nodded. "If you say so."

"I wasn't saying so. Definitely not."

Cat shrugged. "Well, whatever. I don't know what we're going to do. You can't help, I take it."

Isabel drew in her breath. She was thinking of what Jamie would say when he heard of this blatant manipulation, but her mind was already made up. "I'll help," she said.

Cat jumped at the offer. "Thank you. I knew you would."

Of course you did, thought Isabel. "I'll have to phone Jamie and tell him."

"Help yourself," said Cat, gesturing towards the telephone on her desk.

When Jamie answered, Isabel heard Charlie crying in the background. "Don't worry," said Jamie. "It's not real tears. He's cross because Magnus threw a spoon at him. It wasn't intentional — just a sort of infantile tossing away — but he was pretty incensed."

She told Jamie that she would have to stay and lend a hand in the deli. He replied that he thought that would be the case, and asked her what had happened. "I'll tell you later," she answered. "But just go up and take a look in Antonia's room, would you? Check up on it and call me back if you find anything."

"Like what?"

"Anything," she said. "Just take a look."

He asked her if she knew where Antonia was. "I think she's on Skye."

For a few moments Jamie was silent and then he said that he would call her back if necessary. And he did —

266

five minutes later — to tell her that he had found a note on her table. It was addressed to Isabel, but he had opened it and read it to her. "I need to take a few days off," Jamie read. "I've always wanted to visit Skye and I have the chance now. It's been a last-minute decision, and so I didn't want to wake you up and tell you. Love, Antonia."

Isabel could not think of what to say, other than "I see". Jamie then said, "I assume that's the end of her."

"It looks like it," said Isabel. "We can't really —"

Jamie interrupted her. "Of course we can't. She's shown herself to be thoroughly unreliable. You can't have somebody like that looking after children."

"No," said Isabel. "You can't."

"Fire her by text message," said Jamie. "That's virtually what she's done herself."

Isabel was tempted to agree, but said instead that she would talk to her when she came back. "We'll pay her fare back to Italy," she said.

Cat had overheard this conversation — or one side of it — and was nodding her head in vigorous agreement. "I could scratch her eyes out," she muttered.

"That's a bit extreme," said Isabel. "Although I know it's a metaphor."

Leo smiled. "I love seeing women fight," he said. "Scratching, pulling each other's hair. It's very funny."

Cat ignored this, but Isabel looked at him sideways. Her earlier impression had been right, she decided: he's crude. What sort of man likes watching women fight? She asked herself this question, but had no answer to it. So many men were voyeurs of one sort or another, she reminded herself — and their tastes were sometimes hard to understand, if you were a woman. There were men who liked watching women wrestling in mud. It was hard to believe, but there were. And yet, she suddenly remembered, there were women who loved going to wrestling matches to watch beefy men throwing one another round. The women in those wrestling audiences were always the most vocal, the loudest in their howls of encouragement. Then there were the *tricoteuses*. So perhaps women were as bad as men after all.

Cat looked at her. "You have to go, don't you, Leo?"

He nodded. "Sorry. I have to."

Cat reassured him that she would cope now that Isabel was there. "I'll see you this evening," she said. "Remember that Tommy and Ann are coming round."

He leaned forward to kiss her on the cheek. Isabel watched, fascinated, as his lion's mane fell forward around Cat's face. What would it feel like to kiss a lion? Rather like that, she thought, although she had read somewhere that lions had a powerful smell, like tom-cats, and that would presumably be overwhelming. Somewhere, in the back of her mind, she had a memory of reading an early explorer's account of being attacked by a lion in Africa. He described the experience as almost euphoric: discovering that this ultimately horrifying event — being eaten by a lion — was not as bad as expected; the nervous system shut down in the face of such pain, it seemed, and so it did not hurt all that much. Of course such an account would have to come from one whose experience stopped short of completion, and it was possible that such euphoric acceptance was replaced by a less equable state of mind. Regret, she thought. To be eaten by anything must seem such a waste to the victim — and a humiliation as well: to become no more than part of the food chain.

Since it was a Saturday, and a busy one at that, they worked hard, with very little let-up. At four o'clock Isabel realised that she had not taken time off for lunch and she made herself a quick ham sandwich to placate her growing hunger. Cat urged her to sit down and have a cup of coffee, but Isabel declined. "I'll survive," she said.

Cat looked at her appreciatively. "You know, I think I should apologise to you."

Isabel asked her why.

"Things I said this morning. I blamed you for this business with Eddie."

Isabel assured her that no offence had been taken. "You were understandably upset," she said.

"Yes, maybe. But that's no excuse to get at somebody who . . ." she hesitated before continuing, "somebody who's always helping you. Me, I mean. Helping me."

"That's all right," said Isabel. "Don't worry."

Cat was staring at her. "Do you like Leo?" she suddenly asked.

Isabel found it difficult to lie. "He's your boyfriend, not mine."

"That's no answer," Cat said.

"But it is," said Isabel. "What it means is that how I feel is neither here nor there. What determines my view is the question: are you happy? Does he make you happy?"

Cat looked thoughtful. "But you'll still have your views."

"Of course."

"Well what are they?"

Isabel decided that she could not sidestep the question. "He's not really my type." She did not wait for a reaction before adding, "But then I shouldn't imagine that will surprise you."

Cat looked away. "Not your type? Why? Because he's not interested in the things you're interested in?"

This provided Isabel with the opportunity she felt she needed. "Exactly. And that doesn't mean that he shouldn't be your type. As I've already said, that's the important question here." She paused. "Anyway, I don't think we should discuss this any longer. Give me time to get used to him — I'm sure I'll like him better the more I get to know him." Her words were badly chosen, and for a few moments she thought that Cat would treat this as an admission of Isabel's dislike of Leo, but this seemed not to happen. Cat turned to make a cup of coffee for both of them, while Isabel busied herself with cleaning the chopping boards. Nothing more was said on the subject for the rest of the afternoon.

At six o'clock Cat locked up and they said goodbye to one another. Isabel promised that she would be there shortly after nine on Monday; that would not give her time to see Claire briefly when she reported for work at nine-thirty. Jamie would be taking Charlie to nursery school and could cover the afternoon, while Grace would be only too pleased to be in charge of Magnus for the entire day.

She walked slowly back towards the old post office at Boroughmuirhead and the start of the winding crescent that led to her own street. Students from the nearby Napier University were making their way back from the library, and she heard snippets of conversation from a couple of these — two young men — who were walking directly in front of her.

"I don't know what her problem is," said one of them. "She thinks she's too good for me. Can you believe it? Her?"

"Unbelievable."

"Yeah. And you know what she said? She said she wouldn't go on a date with me if I were the last guy alive. She actually said that. I said: are you *serious*?"

Isabel suppressed an urge to laugh. The student turned round, and seeing Isabel behind him stepped aside to allow her to pass him on the pavement. He made eye contact with her, but he looked away quickly. Isabel smiled.

"Sorry," he muttered. She was not sure whether it was an apology for blocking the pavement, or for any embarrassment caused by his remarks.

"Thank you," said Isabel, and continued on her way. That's what it's like to be nineteen, or whatever it is they are, she said to herself. That's when you have strong views and strong uncertainties; when you can't believe that others may not see you as you see yourself, or love you as you love them. It was a wonderful age in so many respects, and yet so horrible in others. You thought of yourself as more or less immortal, with all the time in front of you that near-immortality conferred — forty, fifty years, even sixty — and yes, you would achieve most of your ambitions. And yet you worried so much about what people thought of you, about your looks, about the clothes you wore, and you could hardly believe that the world was so slow to listen to your opinions.

She continued walking, with these thoughts going through her mind, and after a few minutes turned into her own street. This was a broad road, with large trees dominating the front gardens of the houses. A few cars were parked further down the street, but otherwise it was empty. The early-evening sun, still high in the sky at this time of year, painted the treetops with gold. Above the trees, above the roofs of the houses, was a largely empty sky, the blue broken only here and there with sweeps of feathery cirrus. Ice crystals, thought Isabel; that's what those high clouds are — falling veils of ice crystals, even now in high summer.

She thought of Eddie, on the Isle of Skye with Antonia, infatuated, unaware of the likely brevity of the affair into which he had thrown himself. She rehearsed what she would say to Antonia on her return, but it all sounded too preachy, and she knew that she would say none of it. She would simply say that the arrangement had not worked out as she had hoped and that they would pay for her flight back to Italy; there would be only indirect reproach about Eddie and about insensitivity to the needs of others. And to Eddie himself she would say nothing, and she would ask Cat not to bring up the subject of the unauthorised holiday. Every young man should be allowed his bad decisions and personal disasters; for most of these there would be the excuse of youth and inexperience — excuses based on the impulsivity and sheer bad judgement that were a concomitant of being under thirty, or thereabouts. Twenty-eight was the cut-off point, Isabel had heard; after that there was full responsibility. As for Antonia, she, being a woman, might be held to a higher standard: the female brain was wired differently, which was why young women did fewer reckless and dangerous things than their male coevals. People might wish to deny that, might pursue their androgynous agenda with intimidating ruthlessness, but the scientific evidence was there for all to see — men and women were different, and women, in general, were *safer*. What was to be gained by denying the obvious?

She was approaching her house when she noticed the car. It was parked on her side of the street, almost level with her gate, and she could tell that there was somebody sitting in it. She wondered whether this was somebody who had come to see her — had she forgotten something in her diary? There had been an occasion a few weeks ago when she had failed to remember an appointment with an insurance agent and had arrived to find him sitting patiently in his car, having been there for at least three-quarters of an hour.

She slowed down as she approached the stationary car. The driver was at the wheel, and when she drew level with the car he turned round and faced her. He

273

had been observing her in his rear-view mirror as she came down the road, and now he was staring at her directly. The shock brought her to a halt, and for a time their eyes met, locked in a moment of shared recognition. It was the freckled man — the man that Patricia had claimed so coolly and so mendaciously was her brother.

Isabel was only a few feet away from the open window of the car. She could have reached out and touched him, and he her, but every instinct in her told her to back away. As she did this, the man's lips broke into a thin, icy smile. At the same time, he reached up with his right hand and, fingers separated in a V, pointed to his eyes and then at Isabel. It was the *I'm watching you* sign, and its meaning was as clear as it possibly could be. This was intentional intimidation.

Isabel took a few steps back, and then stopped herself. She would not be threatened outside her own house; she would not.

She stepped forward. "What do you want?" she challenged, her voice quivering.

The man did not get out of the car, but addressed her from where he was.

"What do *I* want? I could ask you the same thing: what do *you* want?"

She caught her breath. There was something in the tone of his voice, in its slightly nasal quality, in its coldness, that made her heart pound.

"I'll call the police," Isabel said.

The man laughed. "This is a public road, if I'm not mistaken. I can park here if I like."

274

"But not threaten or intimidate people."

The man sneered. "We'll see about that. Anyway, I just wanted to give you a message. Keep out of things that don't concern you. Got that? *Comprende?*"

His warning delivered, he leaned forward to start the engine. Crashing the car into gear, he shot off down the road, the car's brake lights glowing red as he approached the junction at the bottom. Isabel remained in the street for a few moments longer, and then walked quickly up her drive to the safety of her front door. As she fumbled with her key, she felt a sudden moment of panic; she felt eyes upon her, she felt that somebody — possibly the freckled man — was in the garden now, watching her. She knew that this was impossible, but the feeling was strong enough to make her experience momentary terror.

The door opened even before she managed to turn the key — and that was a further shock.

"You frightened me," she said, her heart racing.

Jamie smiled. "I heard you at the door — I thought I'd welcome you home." He looked at her with concern. "Is there something wrong?" He put his arm about her. She was shaking. "Isabel? Are you all right?"

She sat down on the chair in the hall. Her voice was every bit as unsteady as she felt. "There was a man outside in the street. He threatened me."

Jamie gasped. "What man?"

"In a car. That man with freckles. The one we saw with Patricia."

Jamie went to the front door and looked out. "Was it a blue car?"

Isabel nodded.

"I noticed it earlier on," said Jamie. "It's gone now."

He crouched down to be beside her.

"He did a horrible thing," she said. "He made that sign that means somebody's watching you; you know, fingers to the eyes — that sign."

"Oh, God."

She tried to pull herself together. "I need to tell the police."

"Of course."

But then she asked herself what proof she had. She knew his name — the woman down in Leith had told her that — and she knew that he was somebody the police were watching for other reasons. But of the incident itself there were no witnesses other than her, and she knew that the police would be unable to do anything about it unless there was an actual complaint to be made. People were entitled to park in public streets, and even if they were not entitled to make threatening gestures, it would be very hard to do anything about it unless there was some form of corroborative evidence.

She stood up. "No," she said. "I'll ignore it this time. If he does anything else, then we can think again."

"But surely you should —"

"No, Jamie. What does that man want? He wants to frighten me, to bully me. How do you deal with bullies? You ignore them, which is one way of standing up to them. You don't give them the satisfaction of thinking they've frightened you."

276

"But you are frightened," Jamie pointed out. "And the police can stop him."

"Yes, once he does something that they can pin on him. He hasn't done that yet."

Charlie walked into the hall, and rushed up to Isabel. She lifted him up and hugged him.

"I saw Brother Fox today," said Charlie.

Isabel's manner had changed. She remembered something: *cover hatred and fear with love and delight, and with innocent things. With love and delight, and with innocent things.* The trouble was that people were cynical about innocent things, or too embarrassed to celebrate them. The proponents of confrontation, violence, the acerbic comment, laughed at innocent things, thought them naïve, considered them beneath them. How easy it was to destroy the civilised structures of the world; how easy to poison the wells.

She kissed Charlie on his cheek; once, twice. "Oh, did you?" she said. "And what was he doing, my darling?"

"He was playing a trumpet," said Charlie.

"Really? Does Brother Fox play the trumpet? He's a clever fox, isn't he?"

"Fooled you!" cried Charlie.

Jamie still looked concerned. "Are you sure?" he asked. "About what we've just been discussing?"

Isabel nodded. "Absolutely," she said. "Normal life resumes." And then to Charlie, she said, "Did Daddy give you your dinner?"

"Spaghetti," answered Charlie. "Lots of spaghetti."

Isabel put on a thoughtful expression. "I wonder if there's room for some chocolate cake?"

Charlie squirmed with delight and slipped out of her arms, to run headlong into the kitchen and the high-carbohydrate treat. Isabel turned to Jamie. "Another major ethical dilemma: how many carbohydrates to give our children when we know what carbohydrates — or the wrong sorts of carbohydrates — can do."

Jamie shrugged. "You can't have life without chocolate cake."

"I know," said Isabel. "A modern paraphrase of St Augustine . . ."

"O Lord, give me the willpower to resist carbohydrates — but not just yet . . ."

"Precisely," said Isabel, following Charlie into the kitchen. Perhaps there were low-carbohydrate saints, she thought, who would be examples to all those struggling with the temptations of gastronomy — thin, ascetic saints who believed in the mortification of the flesh and the denial of appetite. What banquets must have awaited those saints in Paradise — groaning tables laden with bowls of sweetmeats, creamy confections, succulent roasts; a time when all restraint and self-denial might be cast off and forgotten, like sins atoned for and forgiven.

Charlie was looking at her expectantly.

"Mummy's thinking," said Jamie. "That's what she does, you see. I'll get the chocolate cake."

That evening, Isabel wrote a message to Claire, who was due to come into work again on Monday morning.

She composed it carefully, weighing each word before she read it for a final time and pressed that most irrevocable of all keys — the *send* button. "Dear Claire, I was looking forward to seeing you on Monday but I'm afraid I shall have to be helping my niece run her deli — unexpected staff problems. [She thought, but did not write: *Her young assistant, a rather nice but vulnerable boy called Eddie, has been seduced by our new au pair, whom you've met. Who would have thought that she would have such an appetite for men? I didn't. Perhaps your radar for such things is more acute.*] So I shall be out of the house all day, I'm afraid. I've left a pile of submissions on your desk — some look all right, others are not going to take up much of your time. [She did not write: *One of them is from a certifiable lunatic; I wonder if you'll spot which one that is.*] I've also left some proofs for you to read. [She did not write: *I can't stand that job — anything to avoid it.*] There's another thing I wanted to discuss with you but have not had the opportunity to do so. [She did not write: *Or the courage . . .*] Professor Lettuce mentioned that he would drop in from time to time to help. I would prefer it if he did not, for entirely private reasons. [She did not write: *Extreme, visceral distaste for somebody should always be kept private.*] So please would you explain to him that his coming into the office is not a good idea? [She did not write: *Because you're his lover, aren't you, and presumably can get the message across.*] Thank you. Isabel.

CHAPTER
EIGHTEEN

When Grace arrived on Monday morning, Isabel explained to her about Antonia. Grace listened wide-eyed, and said nothing until Isabel had finished. Then, after a good minute of silence, she shook her head and said, "I'm not surprised. Not in the least. Not in the least."

"Well, I must admit that I was," said Isabel. "I was very surprised."

Grace's smile had a superior look to it. "You're too charitable, you know. I'm not criticising you, of course, but you're always too ready to see the good side of people. You never seem to see the bad side."

Isabel had heard Grace on this subject before. "I see."

"Yes. That girl, the moment I saw her — the very first moment — I said to myself, *She's interested in only one thing.* I could tell — I could tell straight away. Anybody in trousers had better watch out when she's around — sorry to be so direct, but that's exactly what I thought. You can always tell. Always."

Isabel raised an eyebrow. "But how can you tell? Is this some sort of special intuition?"

"I don't know about intuition," said Grace. "It's the way she looked at Jamie. You saw it in her eyes. She was thinking about . . . well, you can imagine what she was thinking about. Sorry, but she was. It was every bit as clear as if she had a big flashing neon sign above her head, spelling it out."

"Really?"

"Yes, really. And then there was the way she walked. Did you notice that? It's a dead giveaway. Girls like that walk in a special way — it's extremely hard to imitate, but when you see the real thing there's no doubt about it. That's the way they walk." She gave Isabel an eloquent look, conveying so much about things that could not be spelled out, but that were perfectly understandable to those who understood. "And now she's got her talons into that poor boy, Eddie. That nice Scottish boy is being led astray by that Italian *besom*." Grace used the Scots word, *besom*, in its original sense, which meant an immoral woman or temptress. An Italian besom, in her view, would clearly be more immoral, more tempting than a Scottish besom — who could possibly disagree with that?

Not Isabel, although if she thought about it . . . "Well, there we are," she said.

"She'll drop him after a few days."

Isabel said that this was very much what she feared would happen. "I'll be sending her home," she said. "We'll buy her a ticket back to Italy."

Grace beamed with pleasure. "I'll go and pack her stuff. We can leave it in the hall so that she doesn't have to come in."

"That's a bit harsh," said Isabel.

"It's for the best," said Grace.

Isabel's view was different. "No, we'll treat her with more consideration than she's treated us."

"Pity," said Grace.

That morning, Isabel did not have time to think about anything other than serving the steady stream of customers who came into the deli. Although she was busy, she was not single-handed: Cat was there in the morning and Leo would arrive at midday to help in the afternoon.

"I have to go to Glasgow this afternoon," she said. "A friend is getting married in the register office there and I'm one of the witnesses." She added that the friend was a childhood pal — for anyone else she would have cancelled the trip. "I know how awkward all this is for you, Isabel."

"I don't mind," said Isabel. "It will give me the chance to get to know Leo a bit better."

A shadow crossed Cat's face. "Give him a chance," she muttered.

"Of course I will."

"It's just that sometimes you . . ." Cat left the sentence unfinished; the first customer had arrived and was asking for anchovies.

Leo arrived just before the lunchtime rush began. They exchanged perfunctory greetings; Isabel thought him aloof, but that was his manner, she discovered, with customers as well as with her. He was quick and efficient, and she saw that he had a good manner with female customers, who clearly liked him.

Shortly after two, in the first lull of what was proving to be an unusually busy day, Leo offered to make a sandwich for both of them. Isabel accepted; she was tired, her feet hurt, and all she wanted to do was to sit down. Leo set to the task and within minutes had produced a tasty club sandwich, laced with the products of the fresh food counter — dill pickles, hummus, and an exotic cheese that Isabel had never tasted before and that Leo could not identify. "We'll call it expensive cheese," he said. "Expensive cheese from somewhere exclusive."

In the absence of customers, they sat down at one of the tables.

"You look shattered," said Leo. "Are you all right?"

Isabel would normally have given a stock, reassuring answer to that question, but on this occasion something prompted her to reply differently. "No," she said. "Not really. I had a difficult weekend." She hesitated; she wanted to talk. "In fact, something rather shocking happened on Saturday."

Leo encouraged her to tell him, and without considering why she should tell this near-stranger about what had happened, she gave him the whole story from her first meeting with Patricia through that bizarre evening in Leith, to the appearance of the freckled man outside the house. He listened attentively, only breaking off for five minutes or so, to attend to a customer, and then returning.

At the end he shook his head in wonderment. "How do you get caught up in something like that?" he asked.

"It just seems to happen," said Isabel. "I know I shouldn't — my husband is always telling me not to — but you know how it is."

"I do," said Leo. "And you know something? I agree with you. I can't stand not being able to do something about things that I think need to be sorted."

Isabel was warming to him. "You must have a strong sense of justice," she said.

"Too true." He looked at her. *The colour of his eyes,* she thought; *lion's eyes.*

He ran his hands through his mane of hair. She wanted to touch it, to discover its texture. What would happen, she said to herself, if I leaned forward and did just that? That, of course, was a dare to herself of the sort that we often tantalise ourselves with: the doing of something that we know we shall never do.

"You know," he continued, "when I was a kid I used to get really upset by unfairness. If I saw somebody get away with something they shouldn't, then I used to sit there and boil with anger. I really did."

"Young children have a vivid notion of fairness," said Isabel. "It tends to pale a bit as they get older."

"Bullying is one thing I can't stand," said Leo. "It makes me see red."

"It's horrid," said Isabel.

"Horrid?" Leo snorted. "Sure it's horrid. It's completely out of line."

"Zero tolerance," said Isabel.

"Yes, sure. Zero tolerance."

284

Leo looked thoughtful. "This guy — this freckled guy — what was his beef?"

Isabel was not quite sure how to answer that. The most likely explanation, she thought, was that Basil Phelps had spoken to Patricia. Although he had summarily rejected her approach, it was possible that he had been sufficiently piqued by her suggestion to raise it with Patricia. Presumably she would have denied the allegation, but could have mentioned to Archie McGuigan — if that was who the freckled man was — that Isabel had spoken to him. The idea of intimidating Isabel might be his, or Patricia's, although Isabel imagined that it was more likely to be his. His manner in the car, crude and threatening, showed what sort of person he was — and his presence in a police rogues' gallery of photographs pointed in much the same direction.

"It's complicated," she said to Leo.

"Try me."

She told him, and he nodded as she spoke. "Yes," he said. "Yes. This all makes sense."

Perhaps it made sense to him, she thought, but to her it seemed utterly improbable. People did not threaten one another on the streets of Edinburgh, in broad daylight . . . She stopped herself. Of course they did. People did such things to one another everywhere, at all times of the day and night; and they did far worse. People used violence, people stole, tricked, lied, killed. People were ruthless, and if it seemed to her that none of this happened in her world, that was because her world was something of a parallel universe to that occupied by most of humanity. Most of humanity did not live in the circumstances in which she lived, insulated by good fortune from the economic realities that made life a struggle; most of humanity did not earn its living by editing the philosophical observations of others; much of humanity did not have the happiness and contentment of a marriage such as hers. So, yes, it was perfectly feasible that when she strayed into the murky business of others, then she would risk being subjected to this sort of thing.

She felt herself blushing at the thought: the naïve, privileged wilting at the first experience of gritty reality. When she had described bullying as *horrid*, she had seen Leo begin to smile — he must have been thinking just that: *You're out of your depth.*

Their break was over. A couple of customers had wandered into the deli and one of them was looking pointedly — and impatiently — in their direction.

"Don't worry," said Leo under his breath as he rose from his chair. "Don't be frightened."

"But I am," she said.

"Just don't. Understand? Just don't."

Which was all very well, Isabel thought, when your name was Leo, you looked like a lion, and you were built as he was. Built, she thought; some people are just thrown together, but others are built. There was a difference. She found herself staring at his shoulders, and then, quite accidentally, but with a certain inevitability, her gaze slipped down across his chest and to the buckle of his belt, a pitted brass affair, larger than necessary for its purpose, not an ornament, she thought, but a brazen statement of physicality. He saw this, and she looked away sharply. He reached out and put a hand on her shoulder, very briefly, but in that moment something seemed to pass between them. She stepped away, confused and embarrassed, regretting the fact that having strayed into one murky world she now found herself on the perilous, seductive edge of another. Confusion and embarrassment became shame.

Later on in the afternoon, shortly before they were due to close and lock up, Leo said to her, "That story you told me this morning — amazing, really amazing." He paused. "Actually, it's shocking. And it happens, you know. Women think they can do that to men — make them pay for another guy's child."

"I'm not sure if it happens that often," said Isabel. "And I think we need to bear in mind that there are many, many men who don't pay up for their children — the ones they really are responsible for."

"Oh sure," said Leo. "There are some men like that, but it's easy, isn't it, for a woman to pick some random guy to come up with the cash for her kid? What's to lose?"

Isabel thought that it was probably not all that easy, and said so. There were DNA tests, too, that could resolve the matter beyond a shadow of doubt, and could do so quickly and easily. Genetic tests worked both ways: to refute just as much as to confirm paternity. She had wondered why Basil Phelps had not asked for a test to be carried out. It was possible it had not occurred to him that Patricia had another lover during the currency of their affair. Or there might have been a gentlemanly reticence that prevented his confronting her; that was possible, of course.

Leo was still thinking of female perfidy. "They shouldn't get away with it," he said.

Isabel shrugged. "I'm with you on that, but . . ." She made a helpless gesture with her hands. "Something I'm learning is that you can't set everything right in this life. You have to let things happen."

Leo simply said, "Negative."

She wanted to laugh. Who said *negative* and *affirmative* like that? Army officers? Astronauts? People who had lost all their day-to-day words — the words that ordinary people used when conversing; words that were simple and direct and that had the patina of the ages about them; words like *yes* and *no*.

When she arrived home, Jamie was bathing the boys. For Charlie, the evening bath was a high point of the day — an opportunity for rumbustious aquatic play, a pretext to soak his parents and enjoy their reaction to the inundation, a chance to make Magnus cry by splashing him in the face — all of these things added anticipation to bath-time. Isabel stood in the bathroom doorway unseen, and watched for a short while before announcing her presence.

"Mummy!" shouted Charlie. "Magnus is drinking the bath water."

Half turning round, Jamie said, "Not on my watch." And to Charlie, he said, "That's a fib, Charlie, and we don't tell fibs, do we."

"I won't interfere," said Isabel. "I'll do a story for Charlie if you get Magnus to bed."

Jamie agreed, and then remembered something. "Major drama here," he said. "Claire."

Isabel froze. "Oh?"

"Resigned," said Jamie.

Isabel's face fell. She did not have to enquire as to the reason: her letter had forced Claire to choose between carrying on in her post — and offending her lover — or declining to say anything that risked her relationship with Lettuce. She had obviously chosen the latter option — and who could blame her for that?

They waited until the boys had both been settled before they sat down in the kitchen and discussed the day's events.

"Claire arrived shortly after you'd gone to Cat's," began Jamie. "She said she was sorry to have missed you and I said that she could call you there if she liked, but she seemed unwilling to do that. Then she became quite weepy — just like that — out of the blue. I asked her what was wrong, and she said that she had had a really hurtful message from you. I said, 'Can I read it?' but she was dead set against that. She said you'd put her in an impossible position."

"That's a bit of an overstatement," Isabel said. "I merely asked her —"

"To tell Lettuce that he wasn't welcome?"

"More or less."

The gesture that Jamie made seemed to say: what can one expect? Isabel swallowed. Everything was going wrong. "I know," she said. "I know. I know."

He looked at her sympathetically. "You could have a word with her, you know. Patch it up."

Isabel hesitated. If she had offended Claire, then she should at least make an apology. That might have the effect of getting Claire to change her mind, but she thought that was unlikely. And perhaps she should not be surprised at that: people stuck by their lovers, for the most part, and Claire was obviously enthralled with Robert Lettuce. No, she would leave things as they were, an option that was rapidly becoming more attractive. She had admitted two new people — Antonia and Claire — to her life, and now they were dropping out of it. They had both been, in their different ways, a mistake.

She turned to Jamie. "I don't think I'll do anything," she said quietly. "I want to get my life back."

He waited for her to say more.

"You do see what I mean?" she asked.

"I'm not sure that I do."

She spelled it out. "I thought that taking on Antonia and Claire would make my life easier," she said. "In fact it hasn't. There was nothing wrong with the way things were before."

He protested that she had been too busy. "You needed help," he said. "You couldn't go on as you were."

"I could," she said. "I had been doing it for years."

"But . . ."

"No, I had. Granted, there were things that were wrong — I had a bit too much to do, I suppose, but then I made the mistake of thinking that there was an easy fix. Well, there wasn't — and there often isn't. We think that we can fix our lives by taking some simple step, but it's not like that. Most problems need lots of little sticking plasters. They need coaxing and massaging and looking at from all sorts of different angles."

He did not argue. "So now we're back to square one?"

"Square one," she said. "The view from square one." Isabel now smiled. "That would be a good title for a book: *The View from Square One*. The autobiography of one who has tried, but not made much progress . . ."

"Or a song?" suggested Jamie.

"If you say so."

Jamie's eyes lit up. "I do." He tapped the table metronomically. "*I've been thinking of moving forwards*," he sang, "*But somehow I've moved right back/I've been thinking of things I wanted/But now it's of things that I lack/From Square One the view is familiar . . .*" He did not finish it. "What rhymes with familiar?" he asked.

"No idea," replied Isabel. "Not much, I suspect."

"Samovar?"

But she was thinking of Square One as a house name. One might bestow it on the house in which one expected to finish one's life — a house occupied in later retirement when one had done all the exciting things one was likely to do. Square One would be a sort of Mon Repos, an address with a note of acceptance to it. Somebody who lived at Square One would be one who knew that much of our achievement is temporary, if not even illusory, and that ultimately we all return to the place we started from, if not geographically, then at least metaphorically. We were born with nothing, and left this life with nothing, whatever glories and conceits we created for ourselves.

They looked at each other. What did it matter? thought Isabel. If she was to be back at Square One, then there was nobody with whom she would prefer to be than Jamie. And she knew — not just assumed, but *knew* — that he felt the same about her.

Antonia returned late on Wednesday afternoon. She did not announce herself but, still having her key, let herself in through the front door and went straight up to her room. Grace heard her arrive, and knocked quietly on the door of Isabel's study with an urgent, half-whispered message.

"She's back! She's gone upstairs. Directly. No *I'm home*, of course. Just straight upstairs."

Isabel put down the book she was reading. She was working her way through a pile of books submitted for review by publishers. Each came with a letter, tucked neatly into the advance reader's copy, stating just how excited the publisher was by this new offering and suggesting review. Publishers, it seemed to Isabel, must spend much of their time in a state of febrile excitement — if one were to believe these letters.

She sighed. She was not sure what she could do for the book she had been flicking through. It did not excite her, and she feared it would not impress any reviewer she might pick. But that was not what made her decision difficult. This book, for all its leaden prose, was written by a philosopher who clearly harboured immense admiration for Professor Lettuce. One chapter, indeed, entitled "The Lettuce View", set out in some detail and with hagiographic enthusiasm, the opinions expressed by Lettuce in his last book. There was warning of that in the introduction, where the author mentioned the debt he owed to Lettuce's works. These, he said, "were the cornerstone on which my own views of the subject have been built".

The problem for Isabel was this: if she did not publish a review of the book, then the Lettuce camp — as she thought of Lettuce's supporters — would draw the inference that she had chosen not to do so because of her suspected views on their leader. If she did arrange for a review — and there was a real risk it would be a disparaging one — then she would be accused of allowing personal feeling to enter into a professional matter. Then again, if she asked a reviewer to be as gentle as possible, that would be compromising the dispassionate stand that an editor should adopt.

Grace was only too ready to misinterpret the sigh. She thought Isabel could not face a confrontation with Antonia; well, Grace could, and would relish it.

"Don't worry," she said. "I'll tell her. I'll give her her notice."

Isabel rose to her feet. "No, I must do that."

"I'll help with her bags," Grace said. This was something, at least, even if she would be denied the satisfaction of delivering the *coup de grâce*.

Isabel went up alone. She found Antonia's door open and the au pair sitting on her bed, in the middle of an animated telephone conversation in Italian. Looking up, Antonia beckoned to Isabel to come in. She pointed silently at a chair, and Isabel, now feeling like a supplicant in her own house, sat down.

The conversation, voluble and largely one-sided — in Antonia's favour — lasted a further five minutes. Isabel knew some Italian, but this was dialect, as far as she could make out, and mostly uttered in combative outbursts. Eventually, though, the call came to an end and Antonia tossed her telephone down on her bed in a show of evident disgust.

Antonia looked across the room at Isabel. "You've been very kind to me," she said. "Very kind."

Isabel was not prepared for this; she did not know what to say. Had she been kind? She had tried. But why the mention of this now? Was it intended to disarm her in the matter of the unapproved absence?

"And that makes it even harder for me to do this," Antonia continued.

"Do what?" asked Isabel lamely.

"Go home. I have to go home, you see." She pointed at the mobile phone. "That was my fiancé, you see. He is being very difficult."

Isabel's mouth opened. There were no words.

"He's a very sweet boy," said Antonia. "But he gets very envious of me being away like this. He's blue with envy."

"Green," Isabel said. "Green with envy."

294

"Yes, of course. That's very good that you correct my English like that. Green with envy. I'll remember that now. When I see him tonight I'll say, 'You must not be green with envy.'"

"So you're leaving that soon," said Isabel.

"Yes, I'm sorry it's so quick. But I don't think you will miss me too much — you have that other lady, that Grace woman. She will be happy to see me go."

"Oh, I don't know," said Isabel vaguely. Of course she knew.

But now what she had heard was sinking in — in all its enormity. "My fiancé"! She was aware that she was staring at Antonia, and that her stare must have been transparently one of disbelief, if not shock.

"I didn't know you were engaged," Isabel said. "I didn't think . . ." She glanced at Antonia's left hand; a small diamond ring caught the light. She had not noticed that before, or perhaps it had not been there in the first place and had only now been put back on.

Antonia appeared to be preoccupied with her fingernails. "Yes," she said, in a matter-of-fact tone. "Massimo is a student too. We have known one another since we were six. His father has a big factory that makes ceramic tiles. He is very rich and has many important friends. He knows Mr Berlusconi."

"Very impressive."

Antonia nodded. "And his father is also the nephew of the Pope — not this pope, of course, but one of the previous, proper Italian ones."

So, thought Isabel: the Poles, the Germans, the Argentinians *were* viewed as interlopers. "A pope," exclaimed Isabel. She looked thoughtfully at Antonia. What went on in that head? What gulf lay between them — what impossibility of understanding? And she thought of the fiancé, of this Massimo, with his ceramic prospects and his papal connections, and his jealousy — what sort of wife would Antonia make for him, if they ever got that far? What would happen if Massimo were to find out that she had apparently spent her time in Scotland picking up men? Would there be a great tempestuous scene, followed by a storming out, and then reconciliation? Having turned blue with envy, would he turn ochre with rage?

CHAPTER
NINETEEN

Grace rallied round.

"I know things are difficult for you at the moment," she said. "What with that girl going . . ." And here she fixed Isabel with a look that was a combination of reproach and sympathy. "What with her letting you down like that and then all that business at the deli; I know it's hard for you."

Isabel accepted the rebuke. Grace had seen through Antonia, as had Jamie; everybody had, it seemed, except Eddie and her. She had made the wrong decision in getting an au pair; she had made the wrong decision in employing Claire; she had made the wrong decision in getting involved in Patricia's affairs. She had bungled everything.

"So," continued Grace, "why don't I move in here for the next few days. It'll be easier that way. I'll be able to look after the boys more easily."

Isabel thanked her. "It would be a help," she said. "I'm going to help at the deli today in case Eddie . . ."

Grace's eyes narrowed. "That poor boy! Taken off to Skye like that. Whisked away. Abducted. Shocking."

"I think he was a willing party," said Isabel mildly. "And he's over twenty-one."

"Pah," said Grace. "He's just a wee boy."

Isabel had yet to see Eddie after his return, and was not sure what the situation would be. She wondered whether Antonia had told him about her return to Italy, or whether she had simply disappeared. If she had not told him about having a fiancé, then it was perfectly possible that she would not have bothered to tell him about her departure. Eddie would not take it well, Isabel imagined; he had been under the fond misapprehension that Antonia had been as much in love with him as he had been with her, and he would be unprepared for this rapid dismissal. She was not sure what she would be able to say to comfort him; very little, she thought.

Half an hour later, when she arrived at the deli, she found Cat at the counter, serving a woman who looked vaguely familiar. A surreptitious glance confirmed Isabel's suspicion: this was the woman with whom she had sparred earlier on over the subject of the thinness of ham. Cat was, in fact, wrapping ham for her, suitably thinly sliced.

Cat caught Isabel's eye and nodded in the direction of the office. "He's in there," she mouthed.

Isabel made her way into Cat's office, to find Eddie sitting in a chair beside Cat's desk, scrolling through the address book on his mobile. He looked up as Isabel entered and gave her a broad smile.

"I didn't know you were coming in today," he said. "She didn't say."

Isabel put her bag down on Cat's desk. "I thought I'd come in just in case . . ." She did not finish. She had intended to say "because of you".

Eddie looked defensive. "I told her when I was coming back. I'm only a little bit late."

Isabel decided to make light of this. She had decided that Eddie did not know of Antonia's departure and that he should be handled gently.

"The important thing is that you're here," she said, adding, "Did you enjoy Skye?"

Eddie nodded — not very enthusiastically, she thought.

"You were camping?" Isabel asked. "Did it rain?"

"No. No rain."

There was a momentary silence. Eddie looked down at his mobile, as if waiting for a message. Antonia, thought Isabel.

"Did Antonia like Skye?" she asked.

Eddie's response surprised her. He shrugged. "She's more of a city person, I think."

"Ah."

There was a further silence.

"What did you do?" asked Isabel. It was an innocent question, but no sooner had she asked it than she thought that it might not be the most tactful thing to ask.

Eddie was staring at her. His expression had changed; he was frowning now, and Isabel thought that this must be because an expected message from Antonia had not arrived.

"What did we do?" said Eddie. "Well, we went to Skye. We had this tent, see, and we pitched it near a burn, and . . ." He stopped. Isabel saw him blush, and she tried to change the subject.

"Skye's so beautiful in the summer," she said quickly. "Jamie and I have been thinking of going up there some time soon."

"Isabel," stuttered Eddie. "I feel really awkward about this. I know you really well, you see, and I wondered if I could speak to you about something."

She sat down in Cat's chair, facing Eddie across the desk. "Eddie, you can talk to me about anything. Any time. Anything. You know that."

He reddened further. "This is something I'd never normally mention."

She shook her head. "Anything. I mean it. Anything. And it'll go no further; I promise you."

He was looking down at the floor now, intently, avoiding her gaze. "You see," he began, almost under his breath, "she seems to want to do only one thing. All the time."

He looked up to see the effect of his words. Isabel struggled. This was completely unexpected, and yet the warnings had been there. Leo, at least, had spelled it out, even if crudely.

"Oh dear," said Isabel. And then she added, "How tiresome."

She was aware of how ridiculous she sounded; just like Georgie Pillson in the Benson novels, who found things tiresome, or *tarsome*, as he put it. This was tarsome.

"Yes," said Eddie. "I was tired out."

Isabel made a non-committal sound.

"Isabel," Eddie continued, "I don't know how to put this, but are men meant to go on forever?"

She had to laugh; she could not control herself. "Of course not."

Eddie looked relieved. "I told her that, but she wouldn't listen."

"Oh dear," said Isabel, who could think of nothing else to say. But then she saw that this was her chance, and she continued, "It's a good thing she's going back to Italy."

Eddie looked up sharply. "Going back?"

"Gone back, actually," said Isabel. "She left yesterday. I'm sorry, Eddie . . ."

Her sympathy was clearly unnecessary.

"Great," said Eddie. He shook his head in relieved disbelief. "I was going to ask you another question: how do you get rid of somebody you don't like all that much?"

She thought for a moment. "You do it as gently as possible. You talk. You explain yourself. If needs be, you say sorry." She scrutinised his expression. He was listening; and learning, she thought. She wanted to embrace him; she wanted to say, "Don't worry, Eddie. We all make mistakes. It gets better." And then she wanted to add, "And you must remember — we all love you. Cat, me, Jamie: all of us — we love you a lot."

With Eddie back at work, Isabel did not need to stay at the deli. She had a brief discussion with Cat, though, while Eddie was attending to a customer, and she was able to reassure her that everything was all right.

"What did he say?" asked Cat discreetly. "What happened?"

"I can't really say," said Isabel. "I promised him I wouldn't. But suffice to say he's come out of it unharmed, as far as I can make out."

"Poor boy," mused Cat. "I feel responsible for him, you know."

Isabel nodded. She was pleased that Cat had said this. We are all responsible for Eddie, she thought, just as we are all responsible for those who are easily hurt, or who need us, or who are anxious about who they are or what they should do. Of course we are, and those who say we're not are simply wrong. Just wrong.

On impulse, Isabel said, "Are you and Leo free tonight?"

Cat looked surprised. "Both of us?"

"Yes," said Isabel. "Both of you. I wondered if you'd like to come and have dinner with us. In the kitchen. Jamie was going to cook something, but I'll let him know so that he can get a bit more."

Cat hesitated. "Are you sure?"

"Of course I'm sure."

"Then, yes, we'd love to."

They agreed a time, and Isabel left, receiving, as she did so, a wave and a smile from Eddie that she judged to be relieved — if somewhat tired.

When she got back to the house, Graham, the postman, was on the garden path, at the point of walking up to her front door.

"Save me the journey," he said, handing her a small packet of letters.

302

Isabel stood on the path, shuffling through the mail. There were two bills, a copy of the National Museum of Scotland's *Bulletin*, an auction catalogue from Lyon & Turnbull, and two ordinary envelopes. She opened the first of these, and extracted a card. *Richard and Caroline — At Home — Drummond Place.* She read the note below from her friend, Richard Neville Towle: *We both hope you and Jamie can make this. We're going to have some Bach on the harpsichord. And some curry. I know, I know . . . Bach doesn't go with curry, but there has to be a first.*

The second envelope bore the typed address: Ms Dalhousie, The Review of Applied Ethics, Merchiston, Edinburgh. She opened it.

The Lettuce Institute. She read the heading on the paper again, just to confirm what she thought she had seen. *The Lettuce Institute.*

She read on. "Dear Ms Dalhousie, I shall come right to the point. I am very surprised at the way you have treated my research assistant. I consented to her taking a part-time post with you on the grounds that this would provide her with useful experience and you would be a considerate employer. I can see that I was wrong. I suppose that times change, and with them general mores. One should not be surprised, they tell me, if one encounters discourtesy and selfishness as one travels through life. Even so, when it is demonstrated by those with whom one has professional dealings, then it is always a bit of a shock. I trust that this letter finds you well. Yours sincerely, Robert Lettuce."

Isabel stared at the letter and then re-read it. Somewhere above her head, a thrush chortled in the branches of the large yew tree next to the path. She looked up, and smiled at the bird she could not see. Then she tucked the letter back in its envelope and made her way into the house.

Grace was in the hall, struggling to get Magnus into a small red jacket. She looked up at Isabel. She was used to Isabel smiling at some private thought. "Something amusing you?" she asked.

"Yes," came the reply. "A wonderful letter. So full of unintended humour." And there was something additionally funny, she thought, when people behaved exactly as you expected them to behave.

"Oh, yes?" said Grace, untwisting a small red sleeve yet to be filled by a small resisting arm.

"From Professor Lettuce," Isabel explained. "I think I've told you about him."

"Oh, him," said Grace.

"He now has something called the Lettuce Institute."

"Ridiculous," said Grace.

"Yes," agreed Isabel. "My thoughts exactly."

"Pay no attention," said Grace, at last succeeding in enclosing Magnus within his coat. "Ridiculous people usually go away if you pay no attention."

"I shall ignore him," said Isabel. She wondered whether good manners required her to write to somebody to inform them that you are ignoring them. No, she said to herself, some things were a *reductio ad absurdum*, and one of the skills one had to develop in life was the ability to distinguish true absurdity from reality, which was not as easy as one might think. The Lettuce Institute was an absurdity, but it was real. Professor Lettuce himself was real, engaged in real plots, a real affair with a real young woman, and writing real letters like this. Isabel sighed. And her sigh was a real one too.

That evening, as she helped Jamie in the kitchen, Isabel could tell that he was tense.

"Just relax," she said. "It'll go swimmingly."

He made a face. "It's just that . . ."

"Cat?" she prompted.

"Yes. Her. You know how she is."

Isabel did. Cat had forgiven Isabel for becoming involved with Jamie, but it was not clear whether she had extended this forgiveness to him — or at least it was not clear whether such forgiveness as she had summoned was complete.

"She can still be a bit prickly," Jamie continued. "And then there's this Leo character: he sounds a bit odd from what you tell me."

"Not so much odd," said Isabel, "as rough." She paused. "Do I mean that? Nope, probably not. He's not exactly *rough*, he's more . . . more *animal*. No, that's wrong. He exudes something that I can't quite put my finger on."

"Sexual allure?" suggested Jamie. "She goes for men like that, doesn't she?"

"Yes, to an extent. He's certainly the sort who ends up modelling men's undies. You know the type? You see them in the magazines — standing against a desert background in their designer pants."

Jamie laughed. "One wonders what they're doing in the desert . . ."

". . . in their underpants? Yes, it does seem ridiculous. Mind you, models always look ridiculous in my eyes. I can't take them seriously."

Jamie stirred the sauce he was preparing. "I'll do my best," he said.

"Thank you," said Isabel. "It's important. She's making an effort these days, I think. I think we really do need to make this move. We need to show her that we accept him. He might be the one, after all."

Jamie looked dubious. "There have been so many contenders."

"Yes I know, but I have a feeling about Leo. He's such a lion — and perhaps that's what she's been looking for all this time. A lion."

Jamie laughed. "And they'll form a little pride, and have cubs."

Isabel closed her eyes, and smiled. In her mind's eye she saw a picture of Leo, dressed in a tawny suit, with Cat beside him . . . and then the thought struck her. "Nominal determinism," she muttered.

Jamie was puzzled. "What's that got to do with it?" And then it dawned on him. "Oh, of course: Leo."

"No," said Isabel, "I was thinking of her."

The dinner went far better than Isabel had imagined possible. Cat was in a good mood, and showed no signs of resentment — or of anything negative. Leo was attentive and seemed to get on well with Jamie, showing interest in his life as a musician. They talked briefly about Eddie; Leo disclosed that he was teaching him golf — a kindness, thought Isabel, notching up a further good point to Leo's account. At one point in the evening, though, when Isabel and Cat were attending to the dishes — Jamie, as cook, had been excused washing-up duties — she witnessed an intense exchange between the two men. Their voices were lowered and she could not make out what was being said; she was worried that there was some sort of argument developing. As she watched, though, she decided that the expression on Jamie's face was not so much disputatious as astonished. He looked at her from across the room, as if to say, *You'll never guess what I've just been told*; then he resumed his conversation with Leo.

Isabel became aware that Cat was addressing her.

"Sorry. What was that?"

Cat pointed to one of the plates. "I like your plates," she said. "These ones. They're beautiful."

"Haddon Hall," said Isabel. "Minton made them, but not any longer. I use a lost china service to find replacements."

"They're understated," said Cat.

Isabel looked at the plate. "Yes, I see what you mean." She shot a glance in Jamie's direction. He was still looking surprised.

They had coffee after the meal, but Cat and Leo did not stay long. Leo was going to Aberdeen first thing the following morning, Cat explained, and would have to get up at five. "That's what I used to do in the bush," Leo said. "Up at five. The best part of the day."

Cat looked at him longingly, Isabel noticed, and she knew. This was what was transforming her. Cat was in love — it was as simple as that: the simplest of transformational magic was love. But was Leo in love with her? Isabel looked at him. She saw his eyes. She kept looking at his eyes — she could not help herself. There was a light within them — a light redolent of somewhere other than Scotland, and it bathed Cat, and gave Isabel her answer.

The door closed behind the guests and Isabel and Jamie were alone. They stood in the hall, and looked at one another. Jamie was shaking his head in disbelief.

"You won't believe this," he said. "You won't."

"No, I'll believe anything." She was thinking of the eyes.

Jamie shook his head again. "Leo's been talking to people. He spoke to Patricia, but he also spoke to her friend."

Isabel gasped.

"He told me," Jamie went on, "that you'd have no further trouble with that man — you know, the man with the freckles. That Archie somebody."

"McGuigan."

"Yes, him. He said he'd sorted things out with him."

Isabel blinked. "Sorted?"

"Had a word with him," said Jamie.

Isabel gave a start. "About . . ."

Jamie nodded. "About his intimidation. And it's been effective, it seems, because . . ." He hesitated. "Because he used violence. He said, 'People like that only understand one thing.'"

Isabel said nothing.

Jamie continued. "Apparently, he found him down in Leith — you must have given him that information." He looked at Isabel enquiringly, and she inclined her head. "So he went to see him and told him . . . Well, I don't know exactly what he told him, but it must have been to lay off, and if not . . . Then he said he made his point — got him up against the wall, he said — and this guy just folded up once he began on him. That was it."

Isabel was open-mouthed. "Hit him?"

Jamie shrugged. "Something like that. He said, 'I rearranged his nose a bit' — and then he laughed."

"Do people do that sort of thing?"

"It seems that they do — or some of them do."

She closed her eyes.

He was concerned. "Are you all right?"

She answered automatically; yes, she was all right, but she was not — not really, because what he had told her shocked her so much. Of course she knew that violence occurred, but she had never thought of it as happening in her immediate circle. Leo was Cat's boyfriend, and it looked as if their relationship was becoming more serious. Yet he was, by his own admission, a man who used violence to achieve his ends. How could she accept somebody like that into her family?

They had been talking in the outer hall, in the half-light. Now they went back inside. Jamie looked at his watch and yawned. He turned to Isabel, his expression one of amusement. "Not quite the evening I'd imagined."

She was still thinking of what he had told her. It was slow to sink in.

"I had no idea any of that would happen," she said. "Leo . . . Why should he take it on himself?"

Jamie was smiling broadly now. "Don't you see?"

"See what?"

"Leo is *you*, Isabel. He's behaved exactly as you behave."

She did not see what he meant. "Do I get people up against the wall?"

"No, I didn't mean that. What I meant is: he did something about somebody else's issue — yours, as a matter of fact. He *intervened*. Intervened. That's what you do. That's what I've always warned you about. You stumble across these odd little problems in people's lives — stuff that most of us stay well away from — and you think it's your duty to do something about them. You've done it time and time again." He paused. His tone was gentle; he knew that this was sensitive territory.

"So here," Jamie went on, "is somebody who thinks just like you. All right, he's called Leo and he looks like a lion and there's lots of testosterone floating about. All right, he's not exactly sophisticated and he doesn't talk about circles of moral proximity and all the things you

310

talk about before you put your oar in, but it amounts to the same thing, you know."

He looked at his watch again. "I'm really tired. Let's turn in."

She shook her head. "I'm too . . ." She shrugged. "I need to think."

"Should you?"

"I'm not in the mood to sleep. Too much has happened."

Jamie made his way to the stairs. Turning round, he addressed an afterthought to Isabel. "I liked him, by the way."

Isabel did not think about her response. "So did I," she said. *But how can I like him now?* she asked herself. *How can I like somebody who uses violence?*

"You see?" said Jamie. "You two have more in common than you think."

Isabel went into her study. She looked at the rows of books on the shelves. She looked at her desk; papers piled up on each side. The printed word, thousands upon thousands of printed words, occupied this room, kept it safe — she had always imagined — from the enemies of reason. She had thought of these words as having power, because they described for us the limits of what might be done, but did they really do that? What weight had the considered, rational statement against crude force? Leo had a short answer to that, it seemed.

She sat down at her desk. It's my fault, she told herself I created this situation. I interfered in something that was not my business at all and in doing so I have been responsible for threats and violence. She felt ashamed. She looked at her hands, as if they were the agents of what had happened in that tawdry scene in Leith. I pulled the trigger, she muttered, I pulled the trigger.

She wondered why Leo should have taken it upon himself to deal with the freckled man. Was it some sort of crude loyalty to her on the strength of her relationship with Cat — a relationship that entitled her to his protection? Or was it simply a result of the distaste that he felt for bullying? If that were so, then perhaps Jamie was right: she and Leo had a lot in common. She took up the cause of those with whom she was in a relationship of moral proximity; perhaps he did exactly the same, although in his case he used physical means.

She looked for justification. Was it self-defence? Leo's victim had made threats; he was dangerous. Reasoning with people like that tended not to work, but they did understand physical force. That was what Jamie had reported Leo as saying. Leo was not a thinker — he acted. And there were some circumstances in which you had to act, because if you did not, then the world would never be as you would want it to be. If you believed in something, then you had to act on its behalf, or its antithesis would prevail. That was an ancient, incontrovertible truth, demonstrated time and time again when good had prevailed. The Second World War, that titanic struggle against pure evil, had ended the way it had because there had been people like Leo who had acted; not talked or agonised about what to do, but acted. Violence was not always bad; wielded righteously, it could be a disinfectant, like incense in a thurible.

Her gaze moved across her desk. The pile of books for review was topped by one with a light orange cover. *Buddhist Ethics: Doing Right in a Fractured World.* The title momentarily reproached her. Compassion; non-violence; gentleness. And what had she just thought about violence? She was part of that vicious cycle that perpetuated it.

But what if Churchill had been a Buddhist? His speeches would have been very different. *We shall meditate on the beaches, we shall meditate on the landing grounds* . . . She stopped herself, embarrassed at the levity that mocked the moral seriousness of Buddhism. And she was not sure that she should parody Churchill either. She closed her eyes and sighed. She was lost. She, the philosopher, was adrift and confused.

On impulse, she reached for *Buddhist Ethics* and opened it at random. It was printed on cheap paper, and the type in places was slightly indistinct. But the message was not. She saw a paragraph heading, spidery in its italics: *Love and compassion are the only balm.* She reached for a pencil and underlined the words. Then underlined them again. When had she last done this in a book? At school probably, when it had been her practice to underline subjunctives in her French grammar. It had become a habit and then a superstition. If you did not underline your subjunctives you would fail the French exam — better to be safe.

She arose from her desk and made her way into the kitchen. She did not turn on the light, but relied on the bulb in the refrigerator when she opened the door. There was a half-finished roast chicken on a plate — Grace had cooked it for the boys earlier that day. She picked up the carcass gingerly, the unwelcome grease cloying on her fingers. She opened the kitchen door and stepped outside into the darkness of the garden.

There was a small patch of lawn outside the kitchen and beyond that, riotous and undisciplined, the growth of rhododendrons. She placed the chicken on the ground, close to the place where there was a low gap in the vegetation. He would come that way, Brother Fox, on his nightly prowling, and would find the chicken. It would be unexpected — manna from whatever god foxes believed in; the moon, perhaps.

Compassion for all life: it was too late for the chicken, but not for the fox. And the insight came to her, in a moment of comfort: in an imperfect world, we make the best of what has already been done; that is what we do.

She made a deliberate effort to keep the following day low-key and routine. She would try to lead her life as she had led it before she tried to improve it with an au pair and an assistant. She would apply the balm of love and compassion in the very ordinary things of life. She would pay attention to her own metaphorical garden rather than to the metaphorical garden of others.

That was her intention, and it would have led to an uneventful day had it not been for the fact that the unexpected occurs irrespective of our intentions. The first surprise was a conversation with the nursery school teacher when she went to collect Charlie.

"He's been a bit unsettled today," said the teacher.

"Perhaps there's a bug brewing," suggested Isabel. Children of that age were walking reservoirs of infection, she felt, with microbes of every description passing like wildfire through schools and nurseries.

The teacher looked doubtful. "No, I don't think it's that. It's more likely to be his friend's departure."

Isabel frowned. "Basil?"

"Yes. His mother's taken him out. I don't know what her plans are, but she's withdrawn him. Somebody said that she's moving back to Ireland. She had a partner here but . . ."

A child's scream distracted the teacher; one of the boys had pulled a girl's hair and the teacher was needed to deal with the resulting fracas. "Excuse me," she said hurriedly. "Peace-keeping duties."

Light was to be thrown on that surprise by the second surprise. This was an email that Isabel opened on her computer later that afternoon. The screen revealed the sender as Basil Phelps, and Isabel stared at it for some time before opening the message. She wondered whether it would be further reproach — another rap over the knuckles for unwanted interference. But it was not that.

"I'm not sure if this is the right address," Basil Phelps wrote. "I got it from a friend who knows you, but she said it could be out of date. Anyway, I'll send this as a proper letter later on — I just wanted to get it off my chest right away. I have behaved badly — appallingly, really. When we spoke after the concert, my immediate reaction was to reject what you had to say. But then I gave the matter further thought, and I decided to face up to something I should have faced up to a long time ago. You were just the messenger — and like all foolish people I lashed out at the bearer of unwanted news. So please forgive me for that. You were right, you see, and I have acted accordingly. The issue is now settled — thanks to you. I wish I could have discussed this with you face to face, but I find these things difficult in the flesh, and so I hope you will not mind my writing to you about it. After all, sorry means sorry whether the words are uttered or written down on paper. Yours, Basil Phelps."

At the bottom of the message was the usual request to consider the environment and not print out the email. It was advice that Isabel tried to heed, but now, applied ethicist though she was, she made an exception to her normal rule and printed it out so she could show it to Jamie later on. He was at a long rehearsal and would not be back, he said, until seven at the earliest. She would cook. She would prepare something special for him. They would sit and talk in the kitchen, then they would gravitate to Jamie's music room and he would play something on the piano. She would listen. She would think *How lucky I am, how fortunate.* Her day would close on that note — the best possible note for a day to close upon.

And yet there were doubts still to be addressed, self-reproaches still to be made. *The issue is now settled*, wrote Basil Phelps. Presumably that meant Patricia's scheme had been exposed and Basil had extricated himself from the financial trap in which she had ensnared him. It was right that he should be able to do that, but there was still a small boy in all of this — an innocent small boy with freckles and a grin and all the hopes and plans that small boys had. Would Patricia be able to provide for him at the same level as she had been in a position to do with the support — admittedly ill-gotten — of Basil Phelps? Would the freckle-faced man step into the breach, or was he . . . Isabel stopped. She had not thought it through. The teacher had said, "She had a partner here but . . ." and then the affronted girl had screamed and the teacher had been unable to finish the sentence. Isabel herself had then been distracted by Charlie and his demands, and she had not remembered the teacher's unfinished words until now. She imagined what the end of the sentence was: ". . . but that's over" or "but they've split up". Of course . . . of course. Leo had spoken to Patricia as well as to the freckle-faced man. Jamie had told her that, but she had paid no attention to that detail. Now what had happened became clear to her. Leo knew about the police photographs — she had told him all about her discovery. He had then mentioned them to Patricia, who was probably unaware of the unsavoury activities of her lover. That could well have ended the affair because few women, even those intoxicated with a man, would ignore the fact that he was a sexual predator. Some did, of course, but Isabel had a feeling that Patricia was not one of them.

So Patricia and young Basil would find themselves back in Ireland. She would be free of that troublesome man and have time to reflect on her dishonesty. Would she? Isabel tried to have faith in humanity, but she knew that there were people who did not behave as they should, and relatively few of those who were capable of serious wrong had the ability to see it for what it was and to regret it. Patricia might, she just might. Isabel remembered the conversation the two of them had had on their first meeting, when Patricia had expressed reservations about her country's past conduct. She had disapproved of Mr de Valera. That was something. The Irishwoman had a moral sense, and perhaps it would reassert itself.

Her thoughts moved to young Basil. He had been Charlie's friend, and she had wrecked that. She had meant to do it, but her actions had resulted in Basil's disappearance from Charlie's life. It was another example, she thought, of how our actions have unexpected consequences: a big matter resolved, and a small matter ruined — if a child's friendships were ever small. No, they were not; a child's friendship was a subject for grand opera, with full orchestra, scored for passionate performance. Parents should venture into that territory with caution, and preferably not at all.

Now, in the music room, their dinner over, Jamie said to Isabel, "What a relief."

She said, "Yes."

"It's good of him to thank you," said Jamie.

"Yes, it is."

Jamie looked thoughtful. "And Patricia might too."

Isabel could not imagine why that might happen. "I doubt it."

"But can't you see?" said Jamie. "You've probably saved her from him. I think she's moved. Gone somewhere else because she split up with him — with Archie whatshisname."

"McGuigan."

"Yes, him."

Isabel did not see it, but as Jamie explained it to her, she realised he could be right. "I did tell you, didn't I, that Leo spoke to her as well as to that man? Well, did you tell Leo about the police photograph?"

She frowned. She had told him. And she had shown Leo the photograph taken in the restaurant; the photograph of the mirror.

"Then," said Jamie, "there's every chance that Leo passed on to her the fact that her lover had attracted the attention of the police. She probably felt that she had to do some rapid re-evaluating of her relationships."

"Yes," said Isabel. She had already reached the same conclusion.

"Perfect, isn't it?" said Jamie. "Everything you thought needed to be put right, has been put right. Complete success."

She was still doubtful. "I don't know."

"We never know absolutely everything," said Jamie. "But does it matter? When you get where you want to get, does it matter how you got there?"

"Sometimes it does," said Isabel. "Sometimes it matters a great deal."

Jamie grinned playfully. "You say that because you're a philosopher."

"No, you don't have to be a philosopher to think that," Isabel countered.

Jamie changed the subject. "Cat and Leo," he said. "Shall we call them the Felines? An affectionate nickname?"

"We could."

"Do you think they'll stay together?"

Isabel thought for a short while before answering. "Her past performance doesn't exactly fill one with confidence, but in this instance I think so. She has to settle down some time." There was something else. "I think she's happy. At last."

Jamie agreed. "And as for Leo — will you thank him for . . . how did he put it? For sorting things out?"

Isabel felt uncomfortable. There were too many question marks over what he had done for her to feel unqualified gratitude. Yet, he had done his best for her.

"I should, I suppose."

Jamie looked relieved. "If the Felines are going to stay together, it would be best for you to be on good terms with him, I think."

"I'll thank him," said Isabel. "Tomorrow."

"Good," said Jamie. "Now, how about some music?"

He sat down at the piano and warmed up briefly before he turned to Isabel and said, "I want to play you that song we heard at the Queen's Hall. The Jacobean one. 'Remember me, my deir'."

320

She sat down as he selected a sheet of music from a small pile on top of the piano.

"Are you going to sing?" she asked.

"Yes, of course. The whole point of this song is the words." He paused. "And they need to be sung very quietly — passionately, but quietly. Because . . ." He met Isabel's gaze. "Because real passion is usually quiet. People think it will be loud, will proclaim itself, but it often doesn't."

"No," she said. "It doesn't."

He began, and Isabel closed her eyes as she listened. Music tended to evoke images in her mind's eye; now she saw a wooded hillside, a gentle slope. Deer grazed, and one looked up and stared in her direction, as deer will do. The sky was light. The land was Scotland.

Remember me my deir,
I humbly you requier,
For my request that loves you best,
With faithfull hart inteir.
My hart shall rest
Within your breast,
Remember me, my deir.

Remember me, deir hart
That of pains he's my part,
Your word unkind
Sinks in my mind
And does increase my smart,
Yet shall ye find me true and kind,
Remember me, deir hart.

He finished, and the notes of the piano died away. He stood up, turned to her, and embraced her. They held one another gently, as we should all hold those whom we love, as we should all hold the world.

TO THE LAND OF LONG LOST FRIENDS

Alexander McCall Smith

At a wedding, Precious Ramotswe bumps into a long-lost friend, Calviniah, who confesses that her only daughter Nametso has inexplicably turned away from her. Not only that, but an old acquaintance has simultaneously lost all her money and found solace in a charismatic ex-mechanic turned reverend, who has seemingly cast a spell over several ladies in the region. With little work on at the agency, Precious and Mma Makutsi decide to investigate. Meanwhile, part-time detective Charlie is anxious. He has few prospects and little money, so how can he convince his beloved Queenie-Queenie's father to approve of their marriage? As Precious and Mma Makutsi dig deeper into the stories of Nametso and the mysterious reverend, it will take all their ingenuity and moral good sense to get to the heart of the matter.

A DISTANT VIEW OF EVERYTHING

Alexander McCall Smith

Recently distracted by the arrival of her and Jamie's second son, Magnus, Isabel Dalhousie, editor of the *Review of Applied Ethics*, has a lot to worry about, including the delayed next issue. It is with some relief, therefore, that she returns to helping out at her niece Cat's delicatessen, where surely the most taxing duty is the preparation of sandwiches. But it's not long before she's drawn into customers' problems, specifically that of ambitious self-proclaimed matchmaker Bea Shandon. Bea has staged a potentially dangerous liaison involving enigmatic plastic surgeon Tony MacUspaig, who may not be quite what he claims. Intrigued, Isabel dives into the mystery. And when the truth finally reveals itself, she must conclude that no one, including herself, is immune to misunderstandings, or the neurotic fantasies that arise from keeping secrets . . .